ISBN: 978-1-7348599-9-7

DV BERKOM

A LEINE BASSO THRILLER

FINAL ENCOUNTER

1
———

Remy Corrigan checked the time as he clicked the hand counter and dropped the money in the cash box. They were getting close to a full house and it was only half past nine. Already, club-going wannabes lined the block to try their luck at getting inside to see the most popular revue in Seattle.

He stopped the young woman who was next in line as he waited for the crowd in the entrance to clear. The Kardashian-wannabe's coat looked like it cost ten times what Remy made in a week. She rolled her eyes at her plus-one, obviously impatient at the delay.

"You'd think they'd have this down by now," she scoffed. "It's not like this is the hottest club in town or anything." She shook her long hair back off her shoulders and flicked her perfectly manicured nails at Remy as she tried to brush past.

Remy stepped in front of her, barring the way.

"What are you doing? Let me by." The woman's botoxed forehead refused to frown, but her eyes told him she wasn't used to being held accountable by the help.

Remy leveled his gaze at her and she froze. She broke first and looked away. "*Please* let us go inside?"

Remy glanced over her head at the remaining crowd. "You get in when I say you get in."

Just then, the logjam blocking the entrance broke free. From inside the club, Laura gave him the nod and Remy unhooked the velvet rope. "Looks like it's your lucky day," he said, allowing the woman and her friend to go inside. She scurried past him, avoiding his eyes.

Most of the time the eager customers coming to Luck Be a Lady Revue were polite and patient, although there were always one or two assholes who'd had too much to drink. Remy's theory was that it was their first time at a drag show and they were frightened of being turned on by men dressed as women, so they got a shot of liquid courage beforehand. Remy had a sixth sense about assholes.

At least he was putting his training to good use.

Pablo sidled up to him with a shit-eating grin, and play-walked his fingers up Remy's sports coat. "Ready for a break, handsome?"

Remy smirked and handed the counter to his fellow bouncer. "All yours, sweetheart." Well over six feet with beefy shoulders, dark hair, and a perpetual five o'clock shadow, Remy dwarfed the wiry Pablo by a mile. Still, the smaller man had a black belt in karate and could hold his own in a bar fight.

He looked pretty good in Vera Wang, too.

Remy had the velvet rope in hand and was about to enter the club when Laura walked over. He bent down so he could hear her over the din.

"Have you seen Brett?"

Remy shook his head. "Didn't he show?" Brett was the most popular performer at the venue—one of the greats, according to aficionados. His Lady Gaga impersonation was transcendent, especially combined with the new virtual reality system the club's owner had installed.

"No, and Ethan's not here, either."

Ethan was Brett's manager and long-time partner, as well as a sometime-performer. Laura's expression clouded over. The deeply etched lines around her eyes mapped every one of her forty-seven years. The club's bookkeeper and floor manager, Laura acted as a strong and steady hand, a confessor and therapist to many of the performers. Remy had caught her sobbing her heart out a couple of times, and he'd asked her why she put herself through the hurt. She'd replied that she thought of them all as family and wanted to help in any way she could.

Remy checked the time again and frowned. The word late wasn't in Brett's vocabulary. A consummate professional, the performer was normally there early, making sure his costumes and makeup were good to go and tweaking his act to perfection.

Remy shrugged. "Probably just got held up in traffic. He'll be here."

"God, I hope so." She scanned the line of customers waiting to get inside. "We'll have a riot on our hands if not."

Remy turned to walk inside the club, when a bloodcurdling scream erupted from the alley. Remy and Laura exchanged looks before Remy sprinted down the concrete steps toward the scream.

He slowed when he reached the corner of the building and reached for the concealed SIG Sauer 9mm in his shoulder holster. Holding the pistol in a two-handed grip, he rounded the corner. Several yards away, swathed in moonlight, a dark figure writhed on the rough pavement.

Remy raced over and knelt next to the man, grimacing at the bruised and bloodied face. The acrid scent of urine hit Remy like a wall, and he choked back his reaction. He wrapped his arm around the man's shoulders and lifted him to a sitting position. A security light on a building nearby lit his features and Remy froze.

"Ethan?" Though covered in blood, Ethan's distinctive beak of a nose and thick shock of ice-white hair were unmistakable.

Remy felt for a pulse. Thin and reedy. Blood saturated his abdomen. Remy tore his cell phone from his pocket and called 9-1-1 as he ripped off his jacket, bunched it up, and pressed it hard against Ethan's stomach.

"Who did this?" Remy asked, unsure if Ethan would still be alive when the EMTs showed up.

Ethan moaned again and tried to speak. Remy lowered his head to hear him.

"You, you—"

"Me? What?" Remy asked, trying to parse his words.

Ethan barely shook his head. He took a shaky breath. "You, es—"

"What?" The blood from Ethan's wound had soaked through the jacket. The injury appeared to be the result of a stabbing, but it was dark so Remy couldn't be sure.

There was a lot of blood.

"Brett..." Ethan's voice was weak.

"Stay with me, Ethan." Remy pressed hard on the wound. Blood seeped through his fingers. Whoever had attacked him had known where to stab.

Ethan's head lolled back on Remy's arm. *Dammit. I'm losing him.* "Hold on, Ethan. Help's coming." A crowd of onlookers had formed at the end of the alley. Shocked voices echoed toward him. Someone sobbed.

He's coding. Right here in my arms. Memories from years before surfaced, so similar it felt like a punch to the gut. *Shit. Shit. Shit.* "Don't die on me, motherfucker. Don't. You. Die."

Remy clamped down harder on the wound, but it was no use. Ethan's lips parted in a gasp for breath. His body shuddered and went slack. Remy squeezed his eyes closed and bowed his head.

In the distance, a siren wailed.

2

————

Remy gave his statement to the police, then walked inside the club. Pablo passed him on his way to give his statement. Their eyes met and Pablo shook his head—neither of them had seen anything to suggest who might have killed Ethan, or why. A few remaining customers were being herded out the front entrance, as two performers dressed in full regalia handed out tokens to either receive a refund online or attend another show.

Desi, the club's owner, stood near the bar, talking with Laura. Her face was streaked with tears. Ethan's murder had hit her hard.

Remy pulled Desi aside.

"Have you heard from Brett?"

Normally calm and in control, his boss radiated stress. "Not yet, no."

"I think I need to pay him a visit."

"Laura called him, but he didn't pick up, so I don't know how much good it'll do."

"We need to find him before the cops do." Desi knew his

history with Seattle's finest, so Remy didn't need to remind his boss of his distrust of certain detectives.

Desi glanced at him. "You think something happened?"

"I don't know, but I got a bad feeling."

He rubbed his hand through his hair, and nodded at Remy. "Yeah. Okay. Go for it. Check in if you find anything."

Remy slipped out the side door, avoiding the press and the investigators working the alley.

He arrived at Brett's houseboat on Lake Union less than thirty minutes later. Traffic had been light and he'd made good time. He parked a block away in case the police showed up while he was inside and had to bug out, then pulled a pair of booties and nitrile gloves from the console.

Remy slipped through the shadows along the dock, a ballcap pulled low to keep any doorbell cameras from getting a good look at him. If his bad feeling about Brett proved true, he didn't want the cops crawling up his ass, thinking he was a suspect.

He reached Brett's home and moved to the front door. The windows were dark, and the motion-sensor porch light didn't blink on. Remy listened for a moment, trying to discern if anyone was inside, but heard nothing. He knocked softly and rang the doorbell. Still nothing. The door appeared intact, with no evidence of forced entry.

Remy put on the booties and nitrile gloves and hopped the low wall surrounding the outdoor deck. The two-story house-boat juddered slightly under his weight. The faint scent of diesel and mildew was evident in the air as he slid his lock picks from his back pocket. He moved to the slider, which was better concealed from prying eyes, and went to work. Seconds later, the lock clicked open and he let himself in.

He flicked the beam of his mini-Maglite around the room, checking to make sure the blinds were drawn on what windows he could see. He relocked the door behind him, pulled the blackout curtain closed, and used the light to scan the interior.

Furnished in Danish modern with blond wood and light, natural colors, the comfortable floating home smelled of cinnamon and orange and oil-rubbed wood. Remy remained still and listened. The only sound was the low hum of the refrigerator and the faint slap of water against the hull.

The kitchen took up most of the far wall, with an eat-in island separating the room. He moved through the space checking for anything unusual. The sparkling clean, empty counters reflected Brett's well-known fastidiousness. Finding nothing of interest, Remy made his way down a short hall past a spiral staircase to the first bedroom.

Set up as a home office, the small room contained a closet, a two-drawer file cabinet, and a large desk with a chair. He checked inside the closet, but didn't find anything. Then he checked the powder room down the hall, but found more of the same.

Nothing.

He moved into the second bedroom. Slightly larger than the first, the room was obviously the master with an *en suite* near the back. Large windows boasted charcoal-gray shades pulled low against Seattle skies and nosy neighbors. Snow-white carpeting covered the floor. Two upholstered chairs were to his left, with a decorative Moroccan-style coffee table between them. A huge mirror leaned against the right wall, reflecting the king-size bed.

And a pair of legs.

Remy skirted the bed and froze.

Lying on his back, dressed in a pair of sweatpants emblazoned with the logo for the local hockey team, Brett stared at the ceiling, eyes and mouth open in a startled expression. A dark stain haloed the carpet beneath his head. There was no sign of a bullet wound or trauma to his face, leaving his features intact.

Remy rolled him onto his side. The back of his skull had been crushed. A gruesome mass of blood and clumps of brain marred the pristine white carpeting.

Bile riding his throat, Remy stared for a moment as he attempted to get his bearings.

Work fast. Get out.

Galvanized into action, Remy returned the body to its original position, searched Brett's pockets, then the room and the bath. The lack of a computer or phone was worrisome. Brett didn't go anywhere without his mobile. No sign of a break-in suggested he might have known his killer. Remy scanned the room, noticing a reflection in the heater vent near the ceiling. He pulled the chair over and checked inside. A small camera was affixed to the grill. He pulled a plastic baggie from his pocket and dropped the device inside the bag.

Remy checked the time. He'd been inside seven minutes.

Two minutes too long.

He retraced his steps to the living area and conducted a more thorough search. Finding nothing of interest, he climbed the spiral staircase to the second floor. Here, the blinds had been pulled halfway up to capture the view and the twinkling lights of the crowded harbor and the city beyond. An overstuffed sectional, two chairs, and a tufted ottoman took up a majority of the space and were positioned to take advantage of both the view and a full-sized screen that covered a far wall. A second slider opened onto a small balcony with two lawn chairs.

Training his flashlight low to the floor so that someone outside wouldn't see its glow, Remy searched the room. Behind a row of novels in a narrow cabinet, a slim, portable hard drive rested inside a false book. He placed it inside the plastic bag with the camera. Mindful of the time, he moved quickly but methodically through the rest of the space.

Not finding anything, he did a quick check under the chairs

and the sectional before moving to the ottoman. Remy tugged at the cushion and the hinged top came free, revealing a storage compartment with some DVDs and several sex toys. A quick perusal of the DVDs revealed they were commercial porn and not something to be worried about. He sealed the plastic bag containing the hard drive and camera and lowered the ottoman lid, then turned to leave. Something on the floor near the ottoman caught his eye.

He shoved the tufted footstool aside to check underneath. What looked like a plastic piece from a board game lay on the floor. Remy picked it up and studied the half-inch by half-inch square. He pulled and a section came free, revealing the end of a flash drive.

The houseboat shuddered. Remy crossed to the window and peered out, expecting to see the disappearing lights of a cruiser going by. Instead, two men dressed in black huddled near the downstairs slider. Moonlight illuminated a pistol in the second guy's hand.

Shit. Remy crossed the room to the slider and quietly lifted the lock. He stepped onto the balcony and closed the door behind him.

Inky black water glittered below him. Waves lapped at the sides as the boat thudded against the quayside. Remy wasn't much for water, but desperate times called for desperate measures. He slung his leg over the rail as the two men gained access downstairs and the sound of footsteps echoed through the lower level. No words were exchanged.

Police wouldn't break into a house unless they had a no-knock warrant or suspected exigent circumstances, and there hadn't been enough time for that. Plus, there wasn't any justification for either. Remy pulled off one of his nitrile gloves, dropped the flash drive inside, and tied it off before stuffing it into his pocket. Then he slid the plastic bag containing the hard drive and camera under his shirt.

The sound of the two men rummaging through the lower floor told him they'd be coming his way soon. He swung his other leg over, slid onto his stomach, and gripped the railing. Footsteps banged up the circular staircase. He lowered himself until he was holding on by his fingertips, then let go and dropped into the lake with a *splash*. His breath caught at the shock of the ice-cold water.

The sliding door slammed open and one of the intruders ran to the edge of the lower deck. At the same time, suppressed rounds from the second-floor balcony pierced the surface near Remy, the hiss of hot metal cut short as they hit water.

Remy dove, tensing for the white-hot round that should have come. Bullets carved through the water past him as he breast-stroked away from the houseboat, kicking his shoes off as he did.

He didn't surface until he reached the far side of the neighboring boat, lucky to be alive.

It was still dark when Remy reached his Capitol Hill apartment. He unlocked the door and went inside, then closed and locked it behind him.

He stood in the entry, too exhausted from the adrenaline crash and the long night to remove his sodden clothes. He dropped his car keys into the Space Needle ashtray on his hall table and emptied his coat pockets. The nitrile glove had kept his swim in Lake Union from dampening the flash drive, and it appeared that the plastic bag had done a good job of keeping the hard drive and camera dry. Remy palmed the flash drive and deposited the glove in the ashtray. Thankfully, he'd left his phone inside his car in his quest to toss Brett's place. The same couldn't be said of his car keys. The key barely worked now that lake water had fried the electronics. He'd have to replace the fob.

With a sigh that barely registered, he crossed the room, socks squelching with each step, grabbed a bottle of whiskey from the bar cart, and slumped onto the couch, too tired to turn on the light.

At least it isn't winter, he thought as he swigged whiskey straight from the bottle. Lake Union would have been a hell of a lot colder. He'd waited next to a neighbor's houseboat until he heard car doors slam then raced to see the two men drive away in a dark-colored sedan. Remy wanted to follow them, but they were too quick. By the time he made it back to his car, they'd disappeared.

The whiskey burned its way down his throat as he stared at both drives. He took another swig and slid his computer closer, typed in his password, and connected the hard drive.

Brett hadn't used a password to protect the drive. Several files, all videos, populated the screen. He chose one at random and double-clicked it open. The camera panned over the image of the king-size bed in the master bedroom, pausing at one point and focusing on the lamp on the bedside table. A hand appeared on the left side of the screen and waved. The camera remained static. The hand disappeared. Then it reappeared, but this time instead of waving, it gave the middle finger. A chuckle could be heard in the background. The camera panned left, revealing Ethan, nude and lying on his back on the bed, masturbating.

Not interested in seeing the rest, Remy clicked out of the video and opened the next file. This one depicted Ethan and two other men engaged in a threesome on the same bed. He fast-forwarded through the sex tape for anything that might be detrimental to Desi or the club.

There was nothing.

He skimmed through several more home movies but didn't find anything of concern. The last two recordings were shows from the club that featured Brett, which he likely used to critique his own performance.

Remy took another drink. Had the camera in the bedroom been set to automatically record? And, if so, where were the results saved? Probably either on Brett's missing computer or somewhere in the cloud. He disconnected the hard drive and plugged in the USB drive. A dialog box requesting a password popped up on the screen.

Remy took another healthy swig from the bottle. There was no use trying to guess Brett's password. That was best left to a professional.

He disconnected the USB, then leaned his head back and closed his eyes. The old anxieties that normally plagued him had taken a backseat tonight. Action and focus helped tamp down what the Veterans Administration had labeled PTSD— post traumatic stress disorder. Now that he was home for the evening, the familiar knot in his stomach returned and his heart raced, signaling the onset of an anxiety attack.

He opened the drawer of the side table next to him to retrieve the paper bag he'd stashed next to his pistol. Slowly breathing into and out of the bag, it only took a few minutes before the hyperventilation ceased to be a problem, although the anxiety remained.

Remy unbuttoned his shirt and slid his hand along the still-damp, satiny fabric underneath. As his fingers caressed the familiar piping, his heart rate slowed and the knot in his stomach began to loosen.

"Seriously?"

The unexpected voice jolted him from his reverie and sent his pulse skyrocketing. Remy went for the pistol and opened his eyes. A slender, dark-haired woman of about thirty stood in front of him, hands on her hips, wearing a fierce expression. Her hair was swept up in a loose bun, with dark tendrils framing her delicate features.

"You going to shoot me?" She crossed the room to the couch and straddled him.

"I thought you promised not to come in through the window."

"I hate stairs." She gave him a disapproving look as she studied the camisole he wore. His cheeks burned from embarrassment at being caught in his self-soothing ritual.

In one swift movement, she removed her shirt and let it fall to the floor, then pulled his face to hers.

"It better not be one of mine," she whispered, before she covered his mouth with hers.

3
———

Leine Basso finished the last set on the bench and grabbed her water bottle from the floor. She took a sip, studying the dozen other people in the gym as they grunted and gasped, working toward ever-increasing weights. The people around her were younger, owing to the age group of the SHEN academy, although there were a couple instructors. Several students competed with each other, vying for dominance. Leine wasn't interested in a competition—only in maintaining her strength.

She walked over to a mat and rolled onto her back to work her core. Later that afternoon, she was scheduled to teach a class on self-defense. Jinn, the young girl—now young woman—Leine had rescued from the streets of Tripoli in Libya a few years before, would be assisting her as part of her internship. The academy, created to train cohorts of skilled field operatives in an effort to bring down human trafficking networks, had successfully embedded several graduates with police departments and other task forces worldwide.

After class, she was going to meet Santa for dinner. Currently working a triple murder case that required all his concentration, the LAPD detective normally ate at his desk or on the road. Even so, she'd talked him into meeting her for a quick bite.

He'd always had a hard time refusing her.

Ever since she'd made the decision to move back to Los Angeles, she'd busied herself with activities so she wouldn't think about what she'd left behind in Italy.

A wistful sigh escaped her at the thought of the bookstore and the friends she'd made in the small coastal town of Scivoloso. She missed how the light painted the walls of her tiny back room after a winter storm. How a cup of tea felt in her hand as she perused the bookshelves at the front of the store. The unmistakable scent of roasted garlic combined with the sea air when she walked from her building past a local restaurant on her way to the seaside park. The way her friend, Manny, would always make sure he had a glass of her favorite wine ready for her at his café.

She shook herself from her reverie. *Stop thinking about it, Leine. You had to leave.*

Her past had collided with her future when an old enemy tracked her down, vowing to kill her and everyone she held dear. With the help of old friends and new the town had survived, but the cost had been high. Innocent people lost their lives.

Because of her.

That wouldn't happen again. Not if she could help it.

The theme from *The Godfather* erupted from her satchel, which hung on a hook nearby. Leine dug out her phone and answered. "Leine Basso."

"My God. You sound exactly like you did fifteen years ago."

The caller sounded familiar, but Leine couldn't place the voice. "And this is?"

"You don't remember my voice? I'm crushed." The caller paused for a moment. "It's Desi Manning."

That was a blast from the past. "She-Rah? How the hell are you?" Desi Manning, also known as the Unconquerable She-Rah, Egyptian Queen of the High Sandy, had been a popular female impersonator at a club in the Tenderloin, a neighborhood in San Francisco where her first love, Carlos, lived. After Carlos' death, Leine moved on, ultimately losing touch with most of the players from her past life as an assassin. With a few exceptions.

"I've been better."

"What's going on?" Leine asked.

Desi had been close to Leine's daughter, April. In addition to occasionally taking care of her when Leine was out of town, he gave April tips on makeup and clothes—two subjects in which Leine had absolutely no interest, other than the odd times when she had to seduce a target. Leine owed him.

"I hate to call you out of the blue, especially since Carlos... you know."

Leine remained silent. There wasn't anything left to say. It had been a long time since he'd died, and frankly, she was talked out.

Desi cleared his throat. "Anyway, I've got a situation."

"You still in The City?" Most locals referred to San Francisco as The City, not the old-fashioned "Frisco" prevalent in the rest of the country.

"No. I moved the club to Seattle."

"How did you get my number?" Leine checked the time. It was getting late. She grabbed her bag and started for the front door.

"I did some research on the internet. You'd be surprised how much a person can find out about you on there."

That wasn't great. She'd have to see if Lou could scrub the information.

"And you're calling because..."

"Like I said, I've got a situation." He took a deep breath and let it go. "Someone's murdering my performers."

"What happened?"

Desi proceeded to describe the murders. "I put my guy, Remy, on it, but he's got history with the detectives and it looks like they're going to slow-walk the case. I say it's a hate crime, but Seattle's finest don't agree."

"Any idea who'd want to kill them?" Leine pushed through the front door and headed for the parking lot.

"Not really. Brett and Ethan were well known and well liked in the community. Nobody wanted them dead.

"There was a third murder—another employee named Scott. He wasn't exactly *loved* by everyone, but he did a great Mae West."

"Who found the bodies?"

"Remy found Brett at his house on Lake Union, and was with Ethan in the alley behind the club when he died. A neighbor found Scott."

"And you're sure Remy's not involved?" In Leine's experience, most murders ended up being crimes of passion or opportunity —very few rose to the level demanded of premeditation. Plus, Remy had been both places, and possibly the third.

"Remy's not the killer. He was working the door when Ethan was stabbed. He thinks Ethan might have been a witness to Brett's murder and ran. When he came to the club, whoever it was got to him before he could tell anyone. Some guys showed up at Brett's when Remy was there. Remy got away, but not before they used him for target practice."

"What do you need, Desi?"

"That's the Leine I remember. No fucking around."

"I didn't think you were calling to catch up."

"Sorry. It's been a long night. With the cops and the freaked-out employees, I haven't been to bed yet." He sighed. "That's three murders in our community in just a few days. I've got a bad feeling there's going to be more."

"So, tell the police you'd like protection at your club." She rounded the building, headed for her vehicle. Two guys somewhere in their twenties dressed in T-shirts and baggy jeans were standing next to her car. The taller one watched the entrance to the parking lot, while the smaller one faced her car. As she neared them, the one facing her car hit the window with a tire iron. The glass shattered.

"Hey!" Leine yelled, reaching for the Beretta inside her bag.

"Leine? What's happening?" Desi's voice barely registered in her earbuds.

The lookout swiveled his head toward her. The guy who broke her window reached inside the car to open the door. Lookout Guy pulled a pistol from behind his back and waved it at her. He narrowed his eyes, trying to look threatening.

"Best stay back, bitch, know what's good for you."

Leine wrapped her fingers around the Beretta and pulled it free, letting the bag fall to the ground as she took aim.

Lookout's eyes saucered and he yelped at the other guy. "Bitch is *packing.*"

The other guy swiveled to see what he was talking about, registered her gun, and dove behind the front of the car. Lookout Guy raised his gun in a side grip, but his hand trembled. He hadn't expected to have to shoot anyone.

Leine sighted on his head and walked toward him. She didn't say anything. She didn't need to.

"What the hell is happening? Leine?" Desi's voice floated through her earbuds. She didn't respond.

"Back off, bitch." Lookout Guy wagged the gun at her, still trying to look threatening. Leine continued toward him.

"Get away from my car, now," she warned, her voice calm, "and you live."

Lookout sneered. "Fuck you." He raised the gun. Leine shot him in the right shoulder. He screamed. His arm went slack, and he dropped the gun. It hit the ground and bounced twice. Not the best place for a gunshot wound, but at least he wasn't dead.

Then the idiot dove for his gun. Leine shot him again, this time in the left quadricep. He cried out and gripped his thigh as a bloodstain bloomed beneath his one good hand. She walked over and kicked his gun out of reach.

His partner rabbited from his hiding place near the engine, running low and fast, zigzagging between cars until he made the lot entrance. He turned his head to see if she was following him, and didn't realize he was in the street until it was too late. The tires of a fast-moving Cadillac Escalade squealed as the driver slammed his brakes, but it was too late. Leine winced as man and SUV collided with a bang. The guy's body flew up and over the hood and cracked the windshield.

That had to hurt.

The kid groaned and rolled off the hood onto the street.

By the way his leg canted out at an angle, he wasn't going anywhere.

"Was that a gunshot? Leine? Are you still there?" Desi's voice was an octave higher than normal.

"All good, Desi." Leine walked back to her car, giving a wide berth to the asshole who pointed his gun at her. He was on the ground, leaning against another car, breathing heavily as he applied pressure to his leg to stop the bleeding. It wasn't working very well. Leine reached into her bag and tossed him a tourniquet. Sirens could be heard in the distance.

"I need a doctor." His face was the color of overcooked oatmeal. Beads of sweat formed on his forehead. He rocked back and forth and stared at his blood-soaked thigh. "I could die, man."

"Maybe you should have thought about that before trying to steal my car."

The sirens were close. She'd have to stay and give a report. There went her afternoon.

"You still there, Desi?" She moved away from the thief so she could hear.

"I'm afraid to ask what happened."

"Someone just broke into my car." She'd have to make an appointment at the glass place.

"Oh, my God. That's terrible. Are you all right?"

"I'm fine."

"Okay. Good."

"So, what were you saying before we were interrupted?"

"You sure?" Desi didn't sound convinced.

"Absolutely. I believe my last suggestion was that you should request police protection."

"Remy says the detectives assigned to the case are part of the mayor's new "Family Values" task force. I don't think I can trust them to protect folks living alternative lifestyles, if you catch my drift."

"Then hire security."

"Already done."

Leine sighed. "C'mon, Desi, spit it out. What do you want from me?" First responders were close. She glanced inside her car. She hadn't left anything on the front seat that might entice a thief, which meant they were looking to boost the '66 Chevelle Super Sport—a loaner from Santa. He was going to be pissed.

"I need you to find out who killed Brett and Ethan." His meaning was clear. *And I want you to do something about it.*

Leine closed her eyes. Back in the day, Desi used to tease her and Carlos about their occupations, making wild guesses that grew more and more outrageous over time. Funny thing was, he'd gotten a lot of it right. She'd neither confirmed nor denied his assumptions.

"Look, Desi. I'm happy to help you with whatever you need. But I don't do detective." Well, that was only partially true. She most certainly "did" Detective Santiago Jensen of the LAPD, but that wasn't what he'd meant.

"I wouldn't ask, but could you at least fly up here and talk to Remy? Obviously, I'll pay whatever. I'm worried this might be beyond him."

"What exactly does this Remy do?"

"He's one of my bouncers. But he's got certain...abilities."

"A fixer, then."

"You could call him that."

"What's his background?"

"He used to be a cop. A detective, to be exact."

"Let me guess. He used to work the same division as the detectives on the case?"

"You must be psychic."

"What happened? Why isn't he a cop anymore?"

Desi hesitated. "The why's a little unclear, but he got booted for conduct unbecoming or some bullshit."

Great. Desi wanted her to work with some schmuck who hid behind the badge to do bad things. Conduct unbecoming was a serious charge. She'd met cops who were let go for the same reason. Most were assholes who didn't become cops because they wanted to serve and protect.

"Please, Leine? For old times' sake?"

"That doesn't work with me, Desi." Leine considered her options. It would probably be a quick trip. She hadn't been to Seattle since she'd moved back to LA. Years before, she sublet her apartment in Belltown when she took a job as security on a reality television show, and never looked back. Truth be told, she needed something to distract her from the guilt she felt about what happened in Scivoloso. At least the weather would be all right. Summer in Seattle could be a crapshoot, but it was normally a warm, pretty crapshoot.

"All right. Get me on a flight tomorrow afternoon. I have some things to take care of first. And Desi?"

"Anything."

"I'm going to need you to keep my identity quiet."

"What should I call you, then?"

"Leine is fine, but don't use Basso. Use Gardner." An identity that still had an active legend due to her old handler and partner at SHEN, Lou Stokes.

"Consider it done. Thank you, Leine."

"Don't thank me yet." Leine ended the call and turned as the police cruiser pulled alongside her.

"Hey, Leine." The patrolman nodded at the felon rocking back and forth on the ground. "Looks like you been busy."

Leine smiled. The responding officer was an old pal of Santa's. This might go faster than she thought.

4

———————

Leine walked out of Sea-Tac Airport onto the sidewalk to wait for Desi. The scent of car exhaust and cigarettes marred what had turned out to be a warm summer day. A few minutes later her ride pulled to the curb—a dark green Subaru Forester. She tossed her bag in the backseat, climbed in the passenger side, and gave Desi a sidelong look.

"Since when did you drive a family car?"

Desi waved the comment away. "We got older." He studied Leine. "Well, some of us did. Besides, it's all-wheel drive. Good to have in the north."

Desi hadn't changed much, other than a few extra pounds around his midsection. Upon closer inspection, the reason why became clear: it was subtle, but the telltale signs of a full facelift were there. Too-taut skin, laugh lines that didn't relax, an almond shape to the eyes that wasn't there before. With a mental shrug, Leine leaned her head back and watched the traffic and scenery flow past them. Whatever floated his boat. "You drive like my grandmother."

Desi faked offense. "Well, aren't we judgy? It's not like I'm in my twenties anymore."

"Don't remind me."

"Oh, please. You haven't aged a day in fifteen years. Have a painting in a closet somewhere?"

Leine rolled her eyes at the reference to the Oscar Wilde story.

They caught up with each other's lives, giving Leine an odd feeling of déjà vu that brought bittersweet memories of carefree times with Carlos and April, and all the characters from the old neighborhood. Leine gave broad brushstrokes of her own life and Desi did the same, as though neither wanted to get too specific for fear of breaking the spell.

They drove north on I-5 to Ballard, once a blue-collar city within spitting distance of downtown, now gentrified with upscale condos, restaurants, and shops lining the main street.

"Things sure have changed since I left."

"When did you leave?"

"Something like ten years ago."

"That's about the time I arrived. If I'd have known you were here, I would have looked you up. Why did you go?"

Leine shrugged. "A job."

"Not a man?"

"That would be the reason I stayed."

He pulled into the parking garage of a newer high-rise condo complex and parked on the lower level.

Leine glanced at Desi. "You live here?" A condo didn't seem his style, but it had been a long time since her gig in San Francisco—things changed. Back in the day, Desi had been adamant about living in the most exclusive neighborhood he could find, no matter the cost.

"I know, right? It's just easier." He shrugged. "I'm not interested in showing off anymore. Too busy."

"You have gotten older."

Desi gave her a look.

Leine opened the back door and unzipped her bag. "You sure it's all right for me to stay?" She'd taken the extra step of checking her luggage so that she could have her gun as soon as she landed. Thankfully, no one had bothered to go through her things, as there wasn't the dreaded tape on the bag indicating a weapon inside. Often when that happened, some less-than-upright baggage handler would help themselves to the hardware. She snapped a magazine into her 9mm and slid it into her shoulder holster.

"I've got plenty of room and I'm hardly ever here, so yeah. It's perfect."

"Great."

Desi hesitated. Leine arched an eyebrow at him. "What?"

"What happened with the car break-in yesterday?"

Leine zipped her bag closed. "It's taken care of."

"Weren't shots fired? Don't the cops want you to stick around?"

"Self-defense. And I know a guy."

He shook his head. "Must be nice."

"It is."

As they walked toward the elevator, Leine studied the garage layout and took note of the different vehicles parked there. Three partially concealed cameras watched their every move, their steady green lights telling her they were actively recording.

"Have you had problems in the past?" She nodded toward the camera over the elevator doors.

"Some punk kids found a way in and prowled a couple cars. Tagged the wall over there."

Leine glanced at the concrete wall. Vestiges of red and black spray paint were still visible on its surface. "Sure they were punk kids and not gangbangers?"

Desi shrugged. "If they were, not much we can do other than

what we've done. We're just crossing our fingers they don't come back."

"The cameras are new?"

"Yeah. They're decoys, though."

"Seriously? Why not real cameras? They're hella cheap these days."

"None of the residents wanted to pay for monitoring."

"You guys have security guards?"

"Homeowners association voted it down."

"Huh. I guess crossing fingers works better than spending coin on, you know, experts."

Desi ignored the sarcasm as he swiped his access card and pressed the elevator button. The door slid open.

They rode to the fifth floor and stepped into a minimalist-inspired hallway. A brushed concrete floor led to 5C. Leine couldn't tell where the other condos were situated.

"Exclusive."

Desi cracked a smile. "Okay. So, I haven't changed *that* much. Baby steps."

He opened the door and stepped aside to let her walk in first. The substantial entryway continued the stark minimalist décor. Brushed concrete and acid-washed metal walls gave it an industrial feel, although the metal's coating lent a slight patina. A spot-lit single white rose graced a slender vase in front of an oval mirror. Other than that, there was little else to draw the eye.

"Kind of reminds me of you." Leine nodded at the towering entry.

"You mean regal and impressive?"

"Empty and lacking in warmth."

Desi snorted. "Ouch. Come on in and see the rest of the prison camp."

They walked into the living area, which featured floor-to-ceiling windows with a view of the bay, and a white baby grand sporting yet another single rose in a narrow vase—this one blood-red. The furniture was spartan but looked comfortable. A low table in the center of the room held a single magazine, *Architectural Digest,* artfully displayed on the surface. Leine didn't have to look—it would be the latest issue. The kitchen was to their right. A long, concrete counter with five metal stools matched the stainless and gray kitchen. Three red pendants hung over the counter, the only nod to color.

"Such personality." Leine watched a sailboat glide across the bay. She turned to Desi. "Interior designer?"

"Of course. You don't think I'd risk my own taste?"

Desi showed her to her suite, where she stashed her bag, and they returned to the kitchen. Leine sat on one of the stools as Desi produced a bottle of Don Julio 1942 and filled two shot glasses. He slid one toward Leine and picked up the other. "To old friends."

Leine raised her glass. "Old friends." They threw back the shots. The sipping tequila went down just the way she liked it— easy, with a hint of vanilla. Desi offered another, but Leine shook her head. "Tell me about Remy."

Desi poured himself another drink, downed it, and set his glass on the counter. He checked his phone. "Ask him yourself. He should be here any minute."

"Well, that's efficient."

At that moment, his mobile buzzed. "Yes?" he answered. He listened for a moment before he said, "Entrée," and punched a button. He set the phone down and poured himself another shot. "Speak of the devil."

5

———

A short time later the front door opened and closed, and a swarthy, dark-haired man who looked to be in his early forties appeared around the corner. Leine studied him as he walked to the kitchen, noting his fluid movements and large, pugilist-worthy hands. He was attractive in an alpha-male kind of way; tall, with broad shoulders, narrow hips, and a muscular build. His nose had been broken more than once, she'd bet her life on it, and a scar sliced across his stubble-filled chin—whether a childhood injury or something else, she couldn't tell.

A man who wasn't afraid to get his hands dirty.

He pulled out the stool next to Leine and sat. Desi brought out another glass and poured a shot.

"Leine, Remy. Remy, Leine."

Remy raised the tequila and gave Leine a nod. "Your health," he said, and threw it back. He placed the glass on the counter and shook his head when Desi offered another.

"What can you tell me about your discharge from the force?" Leine's abrupt question was designed to throw him off guard, see how he reacted. Besides, she hated small talk.

Remy studied her, his dark eyes steady in their assessment. "Conduct unbecoming."

"And?"

"And nothing." He shrugged. "It is what it is."

"Jesus." Leine rolled her eyes. "I hate that saying. What happened?"

"Why do you need to know?" By his tone, she'd put him on the defensive.

"Because if I'm going to work with you, I'd like to know what kind of person I'm dealing with."

"You don't have to worry." The defensiveness had now morphed into belligerence.

"And I'm supposed to take your word for it, is that right?" Leine's patience was MIA. By the look Desi shot Remy, he wasn't happy, either.

Desi poured Remy another drink and slid the glass in front of him. "Leine's here as a favor to me. There's no reason to wind her up like that. Just answer the damn question."

Remy ignored the drink and continued to study Leine. His gaze drifted to the gun in her holster, then back to her face. "I'll answer the question." He rested his elbow on the counter and leaned in close. "As soon as you tell me *your* story." He leaned back and turned to Desi. "I don't work with criminals."

Leine swallowed the sarcastic remark struggling to break free and stood. "Good to see you, Desi." She walked back to the bedroom, picked up her bag, and checked her watch as she headed for the door. She'd be back in LA in time for dinner.

Desi intercepted her as she grasped the door handle. "Leine. Stop. He didn't mean it."

Leine waited, looked at Desi. "Didn't mean what?"

"He didn't mean to be an *asshole*." He raised his voice on the last word so Remy would hear him.

"It just comes to him naturally, then?"

Desi put his hand on her arm. "Please? Stay?"

"I don't need this shit, Desi. When you want an adult to take over, let me know. Until then," she nodded toward the kitchen. "Good luck."

"Wait. Wait. Let me talk to him, explain things." The pleading in Desi's eyes gave Leine pause. "Just wait here. All right?"

She nodded. "Two minutes."

Desi raced back to the kitchen. The men could be heard arguing, but Leine was unable to make out the exact words. Just the tone. After what she figured was long enough, she opened the door.

Desi came around the corner. "Stop. Don't leave. I think I have a solution. Please?"

Leine took a deep breath and closed the door. She dropped her bag on the floor and followed Desi back into the kitchen.

Remy watched her approach with narrowed eyes, like a cop sizing up a dope dealer. Desi led her to the counter and stood between them.

"Remy, tell Leine why you were let go from the force."

"Not that it's any of your business, but I was framed."

Leine crossed her arms. "Yeah. Never heard that one before. By every convict, ever."

Remy scowled. "Fuck you. I was gathering evidence on a couple dirty detectives, but somebody tipped them off and lo and behold, a key of pure-grade heroin conveniently shows up in my car."

"Video?"

"Turned off."

"*Tres* convenient." Leine glanced at Desi, then at Remy. "Why should I believe you?"

"Answer me this. Why should I work with *you*? I got a sixth sense for bad actors, and my inner warning system is going off like the fireworks on the Fourth of July. You're a killer, plain and simple. Tell me I'm wrong."

Now it was Leine's turn to study Remy. So that was the problem. She'd run up against other law enforcement types who had a sense of who she was, or might once have been. Not every cop or operator she ran across had the instincts—just a few. Like Santa. He'd had a feeling her past ran deeper than it appeared.

He was right.

"Okay. I can work with that. You should probably know I'm not on the side you think. Never was. But my past activities could be construed by the uninitiated as such, so I'll give your assholery a pass."

"Said everybody who ever did anything illegal," Remy deadpanned.

"Yes!" Desi fist-pumped the air. "I knew it."

Leine gave him a look. He adopted a wounded expression.

"What? I always thought you and Carlos were professionals. You just never confirmed my suspicions. I'm glad I was right."

"You were what, CIA? DIA?" Remy twirled his shot glass in his fingers. "Or one of those private assholes?"

Ignoring the question, Leine pulled out the stool and sat. "Let's talk about the men who framed you. They're the detectives assigned to the murder case?"

"One and the same."

"What's your theory?"

Remy and Desi exchanged looks. Desi cleared his throat.

"What?"

"We think this is more than a hate crime."

"Because of the third victim?"

"That, and because Remy found a couple of interesting items when he searched Brett's place."

"Such as?"

Remy answered. "A hard drive and a USB stick."

"What's on them?"

"The hard drive has a recording of two of the virtual-reality performances at the club, as well as some... home movies."

"And these home movies are not for public consumption?"

"Correct."

"Are there people on them who shouldn't be? Politicians? Celebrities?"

"Mainly Brett and his partner, Ethan, and a couple other randos," Desi replied. "But it's what's missing that's concerning."

Remy leaned forward. "There was a concealed camera in the bedroom. From the angle of the videos, that's where most of the recording was done."

"You said you found Brett in the bedroom, right? Where did you find the hard drive?"

"That's just it. The hard drive was in a hollowed-out book upstairs behind some other books, so Brett wanted to keep it hidden."

"Did you find his phone? A laptop, or a tablet?"

Remy shook his head. "Both his phone and computer were missing. He could have been saving the footage to the cloud. But if the killer took his phone or computer and were able to access the apps, that evidence could be long gone."

"Any way to find out?"

"The camera's one of those cheap Chinese models that's not connected to a specific service. You basically set it to auto-upload to a personal cloud server and then forget it. There are a ton of possibilities for storage."

"It's somewhere to start. What's on the USB drive?"

"Password protected," Remy said.

"You got a way to hack into it?"

"I gave it to a friend to try." Remy glanced at Desi, who nodded encouragingly. "She's working on access as we speak."

Leine said, "And this friend of yours, she knows a lot about hacking?"

"She works at an AI startup, so, yeah, a bit."

"You're worried whatever's on the USB drive might have gotten Brett and his partner killed?"

Desi shrugged. "We just don't know. Until we do, we need to be careful."

"I'm meeting her later tonight," Remy said. "I should get more answers then."

"Got a motive why someone would want to kill the victims?"

Desi shook his head. "I'm not sure about Scott—he mainly kept to himself. But Brett was a top performer, so maybe jealousy? Though that wouldn't explain Ethan. Everybody loved them both."

"Obviously not everybody," Remy said.

"You mentioned the hard drive had a couple of performances on it?" Leine asked. Desi nodded. "Can I see them?"

"Sure. I saved them to my laptop." Desi disappeared into the back of the condo and reappeared with his computer. He typed something on the keyboard, then turned the screen toward Leine.

The camera panned over a large crowd as the emcee built up excitement for the performance.

"Everyone, please reach under your seats, where you will find a box. Slide out the box and remove the gear you find there."

Heads bent as the audience did as instructed.

"The larger item that looks like a futuristic helmet is your entrée into the virtual reality that is the brainchild of Brett Wilcox and Luck Be a Lady Revue. Please put the headset on and Velcro the strap beneath your chin. The gloves are self-explanatory. If you need assistance, just flag one of the attendants."

Several of the staff roamed the room, helping some of the attendees put on the items correctly. The video then zoomed closer to the stage and the room lights darkened to an ethereal purple and pink.

The emcee's voice boomed over the loudspeakers. "Ladies and gentlemen, get ready to explore, examine, and explode your mind…"

The theme from *2001: A Space Odyssey* played as a disco ball slowly lowered from the ceiling and began to spin, showering the audience with sparkling light. At the crescendo of the piece, the curtains *whooshed* open to reveal several performers dressed in what appeared to be alien costumes straight out of *Star Wars*. The audience went wild.

Leine looked at Desi. "What are they seeing?"

"Everything. The headsets are wired with surround-sound and 3D imaging, so they feel like they're actually on stage with the performers."

"But it's more than that," Remy added. "The presets put the dancers and the audience on the surface of an alien planet." He shook his head. "I've never seen anything like it."

Leine raised an eyebrow. "Really? So, it feels and looks that real?"

Remy nodded. "Mind-blowing." He pointed to one of the performers on screen. "That's Brett."

They watched the performance a while longer. A murmur swept through the crowd and a couple attendees removed their headsets.

"What happened there?" Leine asked.

Desi rolled his eyes. "That must be the performance where the show glitched. One of the files was corrupted. We had to upload a whole new program after that. What a nightmare."

"Does that happen often?"

"Never," Desi said. "At least, not until that point."

Leine sat back on her stool.

"I think I've seen enough. Do you have many other performances that use the program?"

"A few, but none as advanced as Brett's. He was working on creating more when he was…killed."

"How did Brett and Ethan die?"

"Brett's head was bashed in," Remy answered. "Somebody stabbed Ethan multiple times."

Desi grimaced. "There was a lot of blood."

"There usually is. CCTV?"

Desi shook his head. "Not in that alley."

"The houseboat?"

"I've got a call in to a buddy on the force, see if any doorbell cameras caught anything, or if there are street cameras in the area." Remy narrowed his eyes. "The men who showed up that night weren't what I'd call your garden-variety criminals."

"Why do you say that?"

"Not many make that much noise breaking in, or dream of driving a sedan."

"What do your cop buddies think happened?" Leine asked.

"A robbery gone bad. Same with Scott."

"And Ethan's murder?"

"They're going with the witness angle. The official line is the thieves came after him to shut him up."

"Was anything else stolen from Brett's place?"

"Other than the missing phone and computer, nothing that I could see." Remy said. "Although I've only been to the house a couple of times."

"Where did you get the equipment for the performances? It's got to be pretty expensive, right?" Leine nodded at Desi. "Is the club making that much coin?"

Desi shrugged. "The place was barely holding on, at least until we started the virtual reality shows. We were lucky enough to be chosen to try out the system, help the inventor work out the bugs."

"Don't be modest, Desi." Remy snorted. "He's besties with Sebastian Fellowes."

"The tech billionaire?" She looked a question at Desi, who nodded.

"He came to see one of our shows a couple years back. We hit it off, so when the time came to try out his new program, I jumped at the chance."

"Sounds like it would be a lucrative invention," Leine said. "Is it possible that whoever killed Brett and Ethan might have been looking to steal trade secrets? Corporate espionage gone bad?"

Desi shrugged. "That's a possibility, except Brett didn't have a copy."

"And that doesn't explain the other vic," Remy added.

"The third murder?" Leine had been wondering about that. "How did he die again?"

"Strangulation. In his own home." Desi shuddered. "What if it's a serial killer going after female impersonators?"

"Could be," Remy mused. "The way things are going in the world today, I wouldn't be surprised. We should get the word out for folks to be careful."

Desi shook his head. "I can't believe that's true. Not here in Seattle."

Leine glanced at Desi. "Underestimating an opponent is generally unwise."

"That's experience talking." Remy studied Leine, then tapped the shot glass. Desi poured him another.

She returned Remy's gaze. "You have something to say?"

Remy raised an eyebrow. "Nope. Just an observation."

"Experience is everything, Remy. Everything."

"Agreed."

Desi set the bottle of tequila on the bar. "Now that you two have finished your pissing contest, can we deal with the issue at hand?"

"Looks like we start with Remy's cop buddies." Leine watched Remy for a reaction. She got one. His pupils dilated and the tips of his ears grew pink.

"Let me handle that." Remy threw back the shot.

Leine nodded. Obviously, the police were hands-off for her. For now. "Great. Desi, can you get me a list of staff who were at the club that night? And if you have information on any audience members, that would be helpful."

"Done. The audience signs waivers before the show. I can access them online."

"Good. What time does the club open?" Leine asked Desi.

"Staff shows up between four and five for prep. Club opens at eight, but it's a ghost town until at least ten."

"Mind if I use the club for interviews?"

"Sure."

Leine rose from the stool. "How many bouncers?"

"Five part-timers and Remy, who's full-time. Pablo was working with Remy that night."

"Performers?"

"Six regulars on rotation—each has a minimum of five shifts a week."

"Except for Brett," Remy interjected.

Desi nodded. "Except for Brett. He writes—wrote—his own schedule." He sighed and closed his eyes. "I gotta find another headliner with his kind of star power, or the club's toast."

"That bad?"

"We've got some rising stars, for sure, but none with Brett's ability to work a crowd. Especially with the VR stuff."

She turned to Remy. "Let me know when you find out more about what's on the USB drive?"

"Will do."

Leine pulled out her phone to text Santa. Looked like she was going to be in Seattle for the duration.

6

─────────

Remy picked up his espresso from the barista and turned back toward his table. The fingernails-on-a-blackboard scream from the foaming attachment hitting the bottom of the metal milk pitcher pierced his inner ear like a rocket-propelled grenade. Mercifully it subsided quickly, only to be replaced with the mildly annoying strains of the mellow hipster background music. He set his cup and saucer down, pulled out a chair, and sat across from his old friend, Noah.

Like Remy, Noah was in his early forties and could be considered handsome, depending on the person doing the considering. Unlike Remy, the lines on his face showed every arrest, every altercation, every fight for the innocent against the underworld, a visage unique to big-city cops. Noah had been on the force since his twenties, had risen up through the ranks, and was now the coordinator of the Bias Crimes Unit, or BCU, part of the Seattle PD Violent Crimes Department.

"So, you're telling me that Carter and Benson froze you out of the investigation?" Remy leaned back heavily in his chair. "Those fucks are protecting somebody. I can feel it."

"Winters, maybe? Dude does not want publicity—especially not the kind these murders represent."

Winters was the newly elected mayor of Seattle, a relatively unknown politician running on "family values" who had stunned many Seattle residents with an unexpected win.

Noah blew on his coffee before he took a sip. "I don't see shit for cases anymore since that dickwad got into office. I'm telling you, Remy." Noah leaned forward, cutting his eyes to the side to make sure no one was listening. "It's like night and day since you left. All the new recruits are being told they're a target and they should shoot first, ask questions later."

"Forgiveness instead of permission."

Noah nodded. "It's a different force. The hard-liners are taking over and nobody's doing shit about it." He shook his head and leaned back. "At least Broadmoor listened." Former Mayor Jane Broadmoor had championed an extreme agenda of her own in her short term in office and was widely accused of being the reason for the backlash at the ballot box, but she'd at least supported the police and tried to fix things, however badly. To Remy's mind, extreme politicians from any side were rarely a good choice.

Remy drained his espresso and set his cup down. "You mean talking about bustin' Antifa heads and shit like that? They did that when I was there."

"No, man. It's way worse. Antifa-bashing's the least of my concerns." He leaned closer. "It's out in the open now. No one even pretends anymore. I've seriously been afraid for my life on a couple of occasions."

Remy's mood darkened. He and Noah had sought each other out during Remy's tenure on the force. Both men found they had a similar view of policing—one that included getting to know the community they served and attempting to work things out before employing more drastic methods. Through the years there'd been a few slurs used within earshot of Noah, who was Black and Pacific Islander.

"You talk to Dunfield?" Jim Dunfield was Noah's commanding officer. He'd been a straight shooter and fair enough during Remy's time.

Noah shook his head. "Nah. The mayor's got him massaging the numbers so they make him look good."

"If I were Dunfield, I'd do my damnedest to make Winter's life difficult."

Noah cracked a smile. The first one Remy had seen since meeting his friend at the coffee shop.

"Of course you would. But you'd be out of a job right quick. Dunfield's a political animal. He's been through how many mayors? He's not going anywhere. This too shall pass."

Noah was right. The tightness in Remy's chest caused by thoughts of his old job loosened its hold slightly. He didn't miss the politics and Machiavellian maneuvering for power. What he missed was the job itself. And a few of the people he worked with.

"Sounds like it might be time for a transfer, eh?"

Noah shrugged. "I like where I landed. If I keep my head down, I can do some good."

"Yeah, but what if something gets buried you know isn't right? Like the murders that just happened?"

"Carter and Benson are pretty tight-fisted about the case."

"And?"

"And I saw their report. Honestly, you could read it either way. There wasn't any video of a break-in. Sorry. The mayor wants fewer hate crimes in our fair city, so robbery-gone-bad it is."

"What about the third vic? The other performer who was strangled two nights before?"

"Another robbery. A safe in a closet had been forced open.

According to the insurance company, the vic had a couple of expensive watches and some gold jewelry."

"Yeah, it still stinks. Three female impersonators? What're the odds?"

"You think a serial killer's targeting them?"

"Like that's a stretch?'

Noah shook his head. "There'd be similarities. One got his head bashed in, the other was stabbed. Strangulation makes three completely different methods. Takes a different kind of killer."

"Oh, so now you're an expert in profiling?"

"C'mon, Remy. Don't make waves, all right?"

Remy leaned forward and lowered his voice. "I think they're covering up something."

"Yeah?" Noah leaned closer. "Like what?"

"I don't have any proof yet, but my gut says so."

"Your gut ain't good enough. You know that. Find some proof. The sooner we can get rid of those assholes, the better."

"Not until I find out who did Brett and Ethan."

Noah narrowed his eyes. "I know that look. You think you can bring 'em all down." He shook his head. "Haven't you suffered enough with their bullshit? Why you want to stir up more trouble?"

"Since when do you take their side? You know what they did to me."

Noah waved his words away. "I know somebody planted drugs in your car. I don't know for a fact it was those two. The camera in the property room was turned off, remember?"

A knot formed in Remy's gut. "They got to you, too?"

"What? No." Noah stared at his cup. "I just think you're too hard on them. There wasn't any direct evidence linking them to the stash, or to Julia's death. You gotta admit you were pretty paranoid at the end."

"Paranoid because I was a target. And Julia paid the price."

Noah looked down, avoiding Remy's eyes. "You don't know that."

Remy stared at Noah, not wanting to accept that his old friend was now in the enemy's camp. He wouldn't be much help, not if he doubted Remy's version of events. Remy reached in his pocket for some bills and dropped them on the table.

"It was good to see you, Noah." He got up to leave.

"Aw, come on. Don't be like that." Noah gestured to the chair Remy had vacated. "Just because I keep an open mind about Carter and Benson doesn't mean we can't be friends."

"An open mind? You just called me a liar." Remy shrugged. "Maybe it's better this way. Make a clean break."

"You always were a stubborn fuck." Noah shook his head, then looked Remy in the eyes. "When are you gonna learn life isn't all or nothing?"

"When you learn what loyalty means."

REMY HEADED BACK TO HIS APARTMENT AND WENT STRAIGHT FOR the whiskey. The two-tiered bar cart made of glass and brass was a hand-me-down from his folks who had enjoyed all things Mid-Century Modern. Remy's mother had died young from a particularly aggressive form of lung cancer and his father took it hard, turning into an abusive alcoholic. Remy'd gone out on his own as soon as he could manage, working menial jobs while attending night school and couch surfing with friends. He'd graduated from the local community college and applied for a position with the Seattle PD. When his father was too drunk to come to his swearing-in ceremony, Remy cut him out of his life.

He sat heavily on the couch and set the bottle on the coffee table. He was about to pour himself a drink when he heard something in the kitchen.

Remy set the bottle down and slid his pistol from the side table. Gun raised, he crossed the room in three strides, sliding up next to the wall in the dining room. His heart beat like the lid on a boiling pot, and he swallowed back the adrenaline spike. Remy took a deep breath and ducked low as he rounded the corner, gun first.

"I wondered when you were coming home."

"Jesus, Alice!" Remy lowered his gun and scowled at the figure standing next to the partially open window. His heart rate came off the apex and ran downhill as it slowed. "How many times have I told you to use the freaking door? You're gonna give me a heart attack sneaking in like that."

"Sorry. Hazard of the job." Alice smiled, transforming her beautiful, pixyish face. Her slender form, perfect teeth, pale skin, and glossy black hair wouldn't have looked out of place on the cover of Vogue. But Alice was a different kind of animal. She didn't like trading on her looks—hated it, in fact. She preferred to drift through life without making waves.

Making waves tended to put a spotlight on her activities, which didn't go over well with the local police. She may have been legit working by day for one of the ubiquitous startups racing to invent the next best iteration of artificial intelligence—but it was her nocturnal activities that could get her in hot water.

They moved to the living room and sat on the couch. Remy set the gun on the table and handed her the glass of whiskey. She took a sip and handed it back.

"Were you able to hack into the flash drive?"

She nodded. "Getting in was relatively easy. Whoever thought up the password wasn't all that clever."

"What's on it?"

"Some kind of executable file."

"You mean like instructions for a program?" Alice nodded. "Any idea what it's for?"

"I've isolated some of what it can do, but I'm not finished with it yet."

"Any hints for a non-techie?"

She shook her head, her glossy hair falling around her shoulders. "Not yet. But soon. I promise."

Remy studied the diamond necklace she wore. "Something new?" When she nodded, he added, "A successful night, I see."

She grinned. "Not like I'd ever get anything like this from you." She snuggled beneath his arm and sighed contentedly.

Remy craned his neck to look at her. "That's okay, right? We're still good?"

"If we weren't, I wouldn't be here. You couldn't afford me. I know what you make, Cupcake." She traced the stubble on his chin and smiled. "My mother taught me to do for myself. 'Why wait for a man to give you things, Miss Plum?' she'd say. 'You're better off getting it yourself. At least then you'll appreciate the gift.'"

"Your mother is a supremely wise woman."

"And my father is a supreme piece of shit."

Remy brushed her hair from her face. "And I am a supremely lucky man."

"I came by earlier, but you weren't here."

"Had a date with an old friend who's not anymore."

"Old or a friend?"

"The second one."

"Sorry. So how did the meeting with Desi's guard dog go?"

Remy thought for a moment before answering. "She's tough, I'll give her that. And she has a murky past that she refuses to talk about. I wouldn't be surprised if she'd been a contract killer."

Alice sat up. "Seriously? That's so cool."

"What do you mean, cool? That she killed people for money?"

"Well, yeah. You gotta admit—that stuff's usually done by a dude. Having a woman in the position is righteous."

Remy shook his head. Times like these reminded him of their age difference. Usually, they got along well. He'd marveled at their similarities: neither of them liked crowds, both were content to stay in and watch television rather than go clubbing, they both loved Greek food and pulp fiction. But their differences were sometimes stark. She drank to party, he to forget. She loved TikTok and being on social media, he'd rather hack off his arm.

And he'd been a cop—would always be one, whether he was on the force or not.

In addition to being a computer programmer, she was a professional thief.

Darkness and light. Yin and yang, she'd said. He supposed she was right.

"So, is that what Desi wants her to do? Find out who murdered Ethan and Brett and kill them?"

Remy took a sip of his drink and studied the glass. "Not in so many words."

"Then what? Why call in the exterminator if you're not going to get rid of the rats?"

"You been listening to your uncle too much." Alice's Uncle Chen, a bookie who worked the International District, was well known by the old school Chinese bosses still active in the city. The old guard's influence was waning, though, as younger, more aggressive criminals took over the protection, drug, and gun-running rackets. Some were expert hackers who made their money stealing industry secrets, then selling them on the deep web.

Alice waved his comment away. "Uncle Chen knows how to work the system."

"Somebody oughta tell him that system's DOA."

"Stop changing the subject. Tell me what she's like."

"Like I said. She's tough, doesn't back down. I doubt she's easy to work with."

Alice gave him a sly smile. "You like her."

Remy rolled his eyes. "Why? Because she's tough?"

"Well, yeah." She traced the tip of his nose to his lips with her finger. "Like me, right?"

A warm sensation ignited low in Remy's groin and curled its way up his spine, unleashing the desire he could never fight when Alice was near. He grabbed her wrist and pulled her onto his lap.

"You need me, don't you?" she whispered. "Say it."

Remy shook his head and pulled her to him, but she resisted.

"Say it." Her words demanded capitulation, but he refused. She threaded her fingers through his hair and pulled his head back, making him wince. "Say it," she hissed. Her breath smelled of mint tea and whiskey.

Still, he didn't acquiesce, and started to unbutton her shirt. She pushed his hands away and ground her hips into his pelvis, slowly at first, then increasing the rhythm until there was only the two of them, joined in an age-old dance, proving that he did need her.

Alice smiled in victory as she unbuttoned his shirt.

Leine checked the time—she'd been interviewing club staff for three hours and still hadn't gotten anything useful. Brett and Ethan were universally liked by everyone, but the most-loved was Brett. By all accounts he treated everyone well, even going so far as remembering birthdays and anniversaries. The third victim, Scott McKenzie, not so much.

She glanced at the list. One more employee to go.

The club's bookkeeper, Laura, walked into Brett's office and had a seat in one of the two chairs across the desk from Leine. She appeared nervous, clasping and unclasping her hands, one moment smiling, the next serious.

"Hi, Laura. I'm Leine, an old friend of Desi's."

Laura smiled briefly and nodded. "He mentioned something about San Francisco?"

"So many years ago. He took my daughter under his wing a few times when I was away for work. I owe him. She turned out great, I believe in large part because of your boss's care for her."

"He's a great boss."

"I've been looking forward to talking with you." Leine closed the personnel file she'd been reading. "I'm told you're like a den mother to the employees here. That you're always available if someone needs a shoulder to cry on or needs a little money to get by until the next paycheck."

Laura shrugged. "Everybody needs someone in their corner."

"Who's in yours?"

"I'm sorry?"

"Who's in your corner?"

The confusion cleared, and Laura smiled. "Like I said, Desi's a great boss."

"But isn't it a little hard to divulge everything to your boss? You must have someone else who fulfills that role."

Laura paused. Her eyes glistened with tears. "Brett and Ethan. People called us the Three Musketeers."

"I'm sorry for your loss. It must have been a terrible shock."

"It was."

"Do you mind if I ask you a couple of questions about Brett and Ethan?"

"Sure. I've told the police everything I remember, though."

Leine nodded. "Sometimes going over events again can bring fresh memories to the surface. Often people don't know what they know."

"I'll do what I can."

"Tell me a little about your relationship with Brett. You two were close?"

"Yes. Well, as close as two people can be without being intimate."

"Desi said you helped him and Ethan put together the virtual reality show—gave him suggestions?"

Laura's cheeks grew pink. "I only helped a little. Brett was the genius behind the show. I was just there for moral support."

"You're being too modest. Several employees said you were the brains behind the costumes."

"It was really a collaboration between Brett and Ethan and me. Brett had an amazing sense of what would and wouldn't work." Her eyes welled up again. She dug in her pocket for a tissue and wiped her nose.

"I'm sorry. I can imagine it's difficult to talk about him—them. It must bring up painful memories."

She shook her head. "Not painful. Just really sad. They were so vital and full of plans..."

"And you knew the other performer who was murdered?" Leine checked her notes. "Scott McKenzie?"

Laura closed her eyes and nodded. A couple of tears escaped. "I knew him, yes."

"Were you close?"

She shrugged as she dabbed at her eyes. "Not particularly."

"But friendly?"

"More like acquaintances."

Not wanting to distress her further, Leine switched tactics. "Did you see anything suspicious leading up to the night of the murders?"

Laura shook her head. "I've been wracking my brain, trying to remember, but everything seemed normal."

"What happened when you and the staff learned of Scott's murder?"

"There was a general sense of shock, but no one thought past that."

"Meaning no one thought there might be someone targeting performers in the community?"

"Heavens no. We were all shocked. Brett and Ethan were beloved by most everyone around here."

"Are you telling me that Scott McKenzie was not?"

Laura cleared her throat. "I don't mean that, exactly. But he wasn't Brett."

"How so?"

"I don't want to speak unkindly, but Scott was known to be ambitious. The kind of person that would go to extremes to be on top. Don't get me wrong. Brett was competitive, but he was open to everyone's input and didn't mind when someone else outshined him. Scott didn't give a lot of credit to the people who helped him succeed."

"So, he might have stepped on toes on his way up?"

"I'm certain he did."

"Which could give us a motive for his murder. But why Brett and Ethan?"

Laura didn't respond right away. By the look on her face, she had a theory.

"You have some thoughts?"

"Maybe?"

"I'm listening."

"Desi told you about Sebastian Fellowes?"

"He mentioned that he donated the equipment and program for the virtual reality shows."

"Donated?" Laura grimaced. "That's an interesting take."

"What would you call it?"

"Technically the equipment and source code were 'free.'" She used air quotes. "But Sebastian got to use the audience's emotive feedback for the AI's machine-learning phase."

Leine perked up. "How do you mean?"

"The headsets measured all kinds of things. The program monitored and analyzed biometric data like heart rate, facial expressions, pupil retractions, temperature, and speech in real time, recording audience reactions to the holographic interface. That's what made the show so good—generative AI filled in the blanks, personalizing the performance for each audience member."

"So, if an attendee became excited by a part of the show, as evidenced by a higher heart rate or perspiration, the AI would give them more of that?"

"Exactly."

A generative emotion detector. That could come in handy in an interrogation. If the results were correct. "The audience was okay with that?"

"They signed a waiver before each performance."

"Ah, but did they read what they were signing?"

"Rarely. The show became so popular that I doubt anyone would have objected if someone told them what was happening."

"What about false positives? If the program decided something was one way, but really, the attendee felt the opposite? Did that ever happen?"

"Oh, yeah. Several times. Thankfully, everyone else was into their own show and didn't pay attention to the outliers."

"What happened?"

"One woman freaked out—the AI misinterpreted her excitement for a positive experience, when it was really her having a panic attack. According to that woman, the images became even more disturbing. She couldn't get the headset and gloves off fast enough."

"Like being caught in your own private nightmare."

Laura nodded. "Another man threatened to sue when he believed he was inside a hovercraft, and fell off the stage trying to get out of it. He cracked a rib and fractured his leg."

"Yikes. I assume the waiver took care of the club's liability."

"It seems to have. Sebastian's attorneys made sure of that."

"I'm curious. What are your feelings about the show? Did you support Desi and Sebastian's efforts?"

"I did, at first. It was new and exciting, you know? And it certainly put the club on the map."

"What changed?"

"Sebastian's people started hanging out more. They tried to control the production. Brett and Ethan were not happy."

"Did Sebastian know about this?"

Laura shrugged. "Nothing happens without the boss's knowledge, right?"

"Did anyone bring this up with Desi? Seems like that would be one way to stop their interference."

"Not that I'm aware of. We talked about it, but agreed that if we brought it up with Desi it could jeopardize either his relationship with Sebastian, or Sebastian's commitment to supplying the equipment."

"Because the show was such a hit, and that meant a large amount of revenue for the club."

Laura looked down and nodded.

An age-old story. Whenever a lot of money's involved, values were often the first casualties.

"Are you implying that perhaps Sebastian had something to do with Brett and Ethan's murders?"

She blanched. "No. Of course not."

"No judgement, Laura. This interview is confidential. No one will know what you said or didn't say."

"I don't know him very well, but Sebastian doesn't seem like the kind of person who would have someone killed."

"What about someone targeting performers? A majority of staff are leaning toward that theory."

Laura shrugged again. Her coloring had returned to normal. "Could be. Most of the performers are being more careful, if that's what you mean. I can't blame them."

Leine slid a business card across the desk. Her mobile number was printed on the front. "Thanks for talking with me, Laura. If you think of anything that might be relevant to the murders, please let me or Desi know."

Laura nodded as she took the card. Then she shook Leine's

hand and stood to leave "I hope you figure out what happened to them. Seattle's finest don't seem too interested in solving the case." She sighed. "It's like Brett and Ethan, and Scott, for that matter, don't count as much as other people. Just because they're different from the norm. I'll never understand it."

Leine didn't either. She'd always been different, felt different from other people. But she'd become an expert at blending into any kind of group, mainly by observing human nature. A must for an assassin. It was a whole other ballgame for people who wanted to express their differences.

Some folks just didn't like different.

A minute later, Desi walked into the room. "Well? Any new information?"

"Not really. Just that Brett and Ethan were well thought of."

"They were that. In spades." Desi sat down across from Leine. "What's your gut tell you?"

Leine leaned back in the chair. "It sure looks like targeted killings. Most of the staff think so, too."

"But the police..." Desi grimaced.

"The new mayor needs these deaths to be robbery related. Was anything stolen at Scott McKenzie's home the night of his murder?"

Desi shrugged. "Not sure. That's a question for Remy's friend at SPD."

"I'm curious about the show Brett and Ethan were working on. I assume the program requires a robust computer?"

Desi nodded. "A super-fast chip and vast computing power. Another gift—well, loan, really—from Sebastian."

"I'd like to get a taste of the program's capabilities."

"No problem. I wish Brett was here to..." Desi didn't finish the sentence.

He didn't need to.

8

Leine slid the gloves over her hands and flexed her fingers.

"They're so light." She and Desi were in the club's main room, near the stage. He'd recruited some of the backup performers to act out part of the show. They were waiting backstage.

Desi finished adjusting Leine's VR headset. "Sebastian worked for months on this piece. He didn't want people to feel the sensors in the gloves, or the gloves themselves. He's all about seamless integration. To him, the most important part of the experience is the ability to forget that you're wearing anything—to really feel like you're inside the show."

"How does the headset connect? Is there some kind of prompt I need to plug in?" Not that she knew what she was about to experience, but Leine assumed she'd have to do something to tell the equipment when and where to connect to the AI program.

"You don't need to do anything. The chip inside the device scans for available programs and automatically connects to compatible ones. Like when your phone searches for available networks."

Leine lowered the screen into place. The device fit like a modified motorcycle helmet. Even the headset was lighter than she expected. The screen itself was dark. There was enough room to accommodate someone with glasses, allowing an unfettered degree of view.

"How much of the screen is involved? Is it like watching a movie?" she asked.

"Just wait. You'll see."

Desi placed her in the front row, closest to the stage, insisting that she get the full experience. Even though all the seats in the club were good by VR standards, the front row had the advantage of picking up any vibrations and subtle movements from the cast.

"Since I'm not tethered to a computer, how do the headset and hand sensors pick up everything?"

"We use super wide, uncongested Wi-Fi channels. The show is a combination of reality, augmented reality, and virtual reality. It's known as mixed reality, or MR, as opposed to augmented or virtual reality alone. It's also known as XR."

"Explain it to me like I'm six. I have no prior knowledge of this field."

"Mixed reality combines augmented reality and virtual reality with the real world. The idea is to make the experience as seamless as possible—to blend MR and reality so well that you can't tell where the real world ends and virtual reality begins."

"Sounds addicting."

"It can be."

"So why no cords between me and your super-computer? Doesn't this use a lot of power?"

"That's the beauty of Sebastian's program. He's invented a truly untethered XR using multi-gigabit Wi-Fi speeds for instantaneous data transfer, which means no latency for the viewer experience. It's never been done at this level before."

"Ah. I'm beginning to understand why this is so special. Freedom of movement, extreme reality."

"Exactly. But wait. There's more."

Desi disappeared behind a wall of equipment. The lights dimmed and a booming voice erupted from the sound bars hidden around the room as well as speakers inside her headset.

"Fasten your seatbelts, fellow travelers, for you are embarking on a trip that will blow your minds…"

The music began, rising in decibels. The floor vibrated, as did Leine's seat. Colors whirled and danced, accompanied by shooting stars and nebulae. An enormous spaceship loomed in her periphery and plowed across the full range of the visor, close enough to see into some of the rooms. A bedroom here, a kitchen there. Another with greenery growing up the walls. In an instant, she was whisked onto the ship. The scene changed to what appeared to be the bridge with three uniformed crew members. One bore chevron patches on her shoulders, indicating she was in charge.

"The SS Angelica is making its way to Planet XRO-687," the voice intoned. "The crew received a distress code from the advance party, and they're readying a rescue pod as we speak." Several more crew members could be seen through a glass window at the back of the bridge, hurrying to their stations.

A moment later, Leine found herself outside the ship, floating in space.

The SS Angelica oozed past, revealing a tan-colored meteor-pocked planet directly ahead. The scene changed as Leine hurtled through space toward the surface at mind-numbing speed. Stars and celestial objects raced past, bleeding into her peripheral vision, disorienting her. She gripped the arms of her chair.

"Holy shit." Even though she realized the scene was virtual, she braced herself for the moment of impact, which thankfully never came. The scene shifted from flying through space to being on terra firma, although it definitely was not earth.

The flat, sand-colored terrain reminded her of scenes from Star Wars depicting Luke Skywalker's home planet of Tatooine. Three moons glowed in quiet pink just above the horizon, the sky a deep violet hue. Several yards away, a group of three beings dressed in spacesuits and terracotta-colored robes walked toward her, singing.

"The welcoming party has seen you land," the voice in Leine's headset continued. "Don't be alarmed. These beings are friendly and will take you to your crewmates."

The welcome party drew closer. The song's lyrics became recognizable. "*We welcome you to our home. You are our honored guest. Please come.*"

One took her by the arm and Leine stood. She recognized the face. The three beings were the three performers on hand for the demonstration. The mix of virtual reality and reality blended seamlessly.

A mid-sized hovercraft instantly materialized and floated above the ground. The performer led her forward, singing about the trip they were about to take. They climbed the steps onto the stage, although it looked and felt like she was climbing into the hovercraft. She sat on another chair and scanned the machine's interior. Instantly, the scene shifted to her being whisked over the terrain at a high rate of speed. Again, Leine found herself gripping the chair. Her heart rate increased with excitement. All her senses screamed she was on another planet, flying through the air in a hovercraft.

A short while later, the craft came to rest at the base of a mountain. The performer pressed a button on his suit and a huge door in the mountain slid open, revealing a golden city stretching for what looked like miles in front of her.

The scene vanished and the lights came up. The letdown of not exploring inside the mountain swept through her. The performer who led Leine to the hover craft helped remove her helmet, while Leine slid off the gloves. Desi walked over to her, eyes shining.

"Well? What did you think?"

"Holy shit, Desi. That was wild."

"And that's not even the whole experience." He took the gloves and handed them to one of the performers. "Thanks, guys. Take five and get ready for tonight's show." They disappeared backstage.

"How do you get all the folks into the hovercraft? It's not like you can fit every audience member on stage."

"That's for VIPs who sit in the front row. The rest of the audience experiences the scenes, the feeling of flying, but not the actual feeling of being in the hovercraft and seeing the controls."

"Which costs more, I take it?"

Desi smiled. "Well, yeah. You can't have an event like this without tiers for the big spenders. Rich people want to feel special. And I want to take their money. Win-win."

"I had no idea virtual reality had come so far."

"There are more scenes like that, where the AI really gets into gear and shifts the narrative to what it perceives you're experiencing. I just wanted you to get a feel for the technology. Brett and Ethan were trying out a new show with more advanced features."

"More advanced than that?"

Desi nodded. "Olfactory, for one. And more touch. What did you think of the songs?"

"Interesting."

Desi shook his head. "Brett had a superb voice, as did Ethan. These guys are good, but they're not on the same level."

"Did Brett have the advanced program loaded on his laptop?"

"No. That was one of the rules Sebastian demanded in exchange for our using it. Brett was super careful."

"Could that code be on the flash drive Remy found?"

Desi shrugged. "I doubt it. Brett wouldn't be that careless. Besides, the drive itself would have to be quite a bit larger."

"Where do you keep the equipment when it's not in use?"

"Locked in a specially made safe in my office that Sebastian assures me is more secure than the Pentagon. No one knows the access code except me. And Sebastian, of course, in case something happened to me."

"What about your command station?" She nodded toward the wall of equipment from where he'd been operating the show.

"The program is portable. It's on a special drive that goes into the same safe."

"I thought you said the storage for the program needed to be big?"

Desi smiled. "The special drive is proprietary. Most portable drives don't come close to the amount of space or security this device has."

"Well, thanks for the enlightening time. The applications for this tech are astounding. Just the implications for training our recruits at the academy I work with are endless."

"Sebastian's been working on a shitload of ideas. Medical, educational, you name it. this program can push the envelope in training as well as deliver an amazing entertainment experience."

"Along with some not-so-great applications." The thought of the seamless crossover between reality and virtual reality and how it could be used to exploit minors even more than they already were was just one instance. The proliferation of porn sites featuring children—either real kids or AI-created—was exploding, making the academy's job of tracking down human traffickers that much more difficult.

"That's why security is so tight."

Leine stood. "I'm going to call it a day. I'll parse through the information you've given me on Brett and Ethan and the show, and your employee's statements. Remy said to expect more information soon from his techie friend about what's on that flash drive." She grabbed her jacket from a nearby chair and slid it on. "Make sure to tell everyone to be careful. We still don't know what we're dealing with here."

"You mean someone targeting the performers?"

"It's best to be safe. See you at home later?"

Desi shook his head. "Unless you're a night owl. I normally don't get home before three."

"Then I'll see you tomorrow."

Leine walked to the alley where she'd parked her rental car. The same alley where Ethan had died. She stood for a long moment, taking in her surroundings, imagining the scene. She scanned the rooftops. No cameras, no lights behind windows, supporting the SPD's claims there were no witnesses. Desi had mentioned the upper floors weren't residential in the surrounding buildings. Did the killer or killers know there'd be nothing and no one to record the deed? That told her either they were really lucky, or they knew exactly what they were doing.

Or they didn't care if they were seen.

Brett's houseboat was another question. Brett had a doorbell camera, but the device had been disabled, so there was no recording of someone entering the home. Due to the layout of the houseboat's front door and dock, none of the neighbor's cameras had picked up anything unusual that night, either.

Leine got into her car and started the engine. She drove to the end of the alley and turned right, headed for Desi's condo. Traffic was light that time of evening. Most people had already headed home from work, and if they'd stopped off for a nightcap, weren't yet on the road.

A block from the club, a dark-colored SUV pulled away from the curb and fell in behind her. Old habits kicked in and Leine shifted into operational mode. The vehicle stayed with her when she took a random turn, then again with another. Obviously, if they were following her, they didn't care if she made them. And they hadn't bothered to remove the front plate.

Interesting.

She noted the make, model, and license plate number and executed several moves designed to shake them. They kept pace until her last two moves where she slipped into a parking garage for cover.

Did she really shake them, or had they handed her off to another tail? Perhaps a drone? It was possible that they just lost interest, having delivered their message.

Either way, she'd have to be careful.

9
____

Alice dropped the USB drive on the kitchen table. She'd used the front door this time, owing to the fact that it was daytime and a busy neighborhood. Remy leaned back in his chair and gave her an expectant look.

"I loaded the program onto an air-gapped computer that I use to test unknown code. It's some kind of malware." She pulled out the chair across from him and sat. "I'm not sure exactly what it's meant to do, so I'm reverse-engineering the code."

"What does that mean?"

"It's like trying to untangle a knot. Painstaking, detailed work. You'd hate it."

"And then what? Explain."

"I should be able to see patterns in the code, something that will tell me what program it's designed to work in, what it's supposed to do. In rudimentary terms, if someone runs this malware in a specific program, then that program will do whatever the malware tells it to do. This could be a problem, depending on what the program is for. The malware could corrupt the file, for instance, making it unusable. Or, worse, it could hijack the program and make it do something else."

"Like what?"

"Say the main program tells a machine to make red widgets. Depending on its purpose, the malware could hijack the system and tell the machine to create blue or green widgets instead."

"So, this is a way for another red widget manufacturer to fuck up its competition?"

"On a basic level, yes." She sighed. "But the code isn't that simple. The malware is compact and elegant, designed to blend in. It's more sophisticated than what I've encountered in the past. And you know who I work for."

"Yeah." He'd been intrigued when Alice had finally trusted him enough to tell him that she was working on cutting-edge artificial intelligence security programs at a well-funded start-up. The tech community was insular, and any information on who or what a particular company was working on could tip the scales on who got to market first. Billions and possibly trillions of dollars were at stake in the AI arms race. Corporate espionage was rampant, both foreign and domestic.

"There's another possibility. The malware could conceivably allow someone to remotely access the program, whatever it is."

"Like when you tell me not to click on just any link I see on the internet because it could download something that might give another person remote access to my computer?"

Alice nodded. "Exactly. The code isn't overtly malicious—there aren't any commands to corrupt or steal data. It's like it's just sitting there, waiting for something. So far, I've discovered commands that don't fit standard applications. I'm going to dig deeper, run it through a few simulators so I can test its response to different inputs."

"What the hell does malware have to do with Brett and Ethan's murders? Or Scott's?"

Alice shrugged. "Maybe nothing. Could be someone who was there accidentally dropped it. You said you found it on the floor underneath a piece of furniture, right?"

"A footstool that doubled as storage."

"So, maybe it wasn't that important. I did isolate anomalies in the code, though."

"Meaning?"

"Meaning even though there's no obvious signature of who created the program, I noticed some irregularities that might give us a clue whose work this is."

"And if we can track them down, then mystery solved."

"Possibly." A sly smile crossed her face. "How's your relationship with Ms. Badazz going?"

Remy snorted. "Oh, so now she's a badass?"

"Well, yeah. And it's *Ms.* Badass, to you. Any woman who is capable of doing what you think she's done is a badass in my book."

"We're fine. She's working on her shit, I'm working on mine."

"I want to meet her."

"You what now?"

"I want to meet her."

"Where's this fascination with a killer come from?"

"She's a woman getting things done in a 'man's world.'" Alice made air quotes as she said the words. "Although, I take umbrage with the patriarchy that makes *that* sentence even necessary."

"Jesus. You and that patriarchy BS. Is that why you like to steal shit?"

"It's not BS, and no, that's not why I steal shit, as you so elegantly put it. I steal shit because it makes me feel powerful. But you wouldn't know that because you're part of the construct."

"How so?"

"Take your self-soothing ritual. What would your bros think of you wearing ladies' lingerie?"

Remy scoffed. "They don't know because I'm not ever gonna tell them. They wouldn't let me live it down."

"Uh huh. And why is that? What harm does it cause? If it's something that gets you through the night, it's all right, to misquote your fave musician."

"It's just the way it is. I can't explain it, and I sure as hell am not going to try to explain it to anyone else."

"Ergo, the patriarchy. You aren't even allowed to be who you truly are."

"Whatever, Alice. Let's change the subject, okay?"

Alice smiled. "You're getting uncomfortable. I like it when you get uncomfortable."

"Yeah, well, I don't." He scowled, then decided to let it go. "Nice reference to Lennon, by the way."

"Thanks." Alice studied him for a moment, then gave a slight shrug. "Moving on. So, what do you want to do with this?" She nodded at the drive.

"Not sure yet. What do you think I should do?"

"Don't do anything with it yet. Not until I understand what the malware's supposed to do. The best way for that to happen is to find out what program it's meant to work in, which is going to take time."

He shrugged. "I'll tell Desi that you're still working on it."

"You wouldn't be lying. Why didn't you hand it over to him in the first place?"

"Because I wanted you to have a crack at it before anyone else did."

"In case I could use it to get ahead?" A tiny smile cracked the corners of her perfect mouth.

Remy smiled. "In case you could use it, yeah. Also, because I trust you. You don't have an agenda."

Alice rose from her chair and moved to where he sat. "Give me some room."

Remy pushed back and the chair screeched across the tile floor. Facing him, Alice straddled his lap as she began to unbutton his shirt. The fragrance she wore had a hint of sandalwood and rose.

Nice.

"Well then, I need to properly thank you. And show you that I do indeed have an agenda."

Remy was more than happy to let her do just that.

***

REMY FINISHED THE LEFTOVER THAI FOOD HE'D FOUND IN THE fridge and tossed the cartons in the trash. His gaze slid to the USB drive. Before she left, Alice warned him to keep the existence of the malware a secret for now. If word got out, they wouldn't be able to control the narrative and the information would spread quickly through the tech community, possibly alerting the creator.

His phone vibrated in his pocket. He slid it free and glanced at the screen. Noah.

"Hey." Remy's noncommittal tone told his old friend that he hadn't forgiven him for what he viewed as a betrayal.

"Hey." Noah cleared his throat. "I know you think I'm a shit bag, but after our convo at the coffee shop, I started thinking—maybe you were on to something. So, I started digging."

"And?"

"And I found something interesting."

"I'm listening."

"I don't feel comfortable doing this over the phone. Can we meet?"

"Give me a clue, Noah. What's this about?"

"It has to do with some friends of yours and a tech billionaire."

"Sebastian Fellowes?" Remy straightened in his chair.

"Can we meet? Seriously, this is some interesting shit. I know you'll want to hear it."

"Yeah. I'll meet you where we used to go back in the day, when we didn't want company." He and Noah had often met outside of work at Carkeek Park, 216 acres of open space with picnic tables, a jungle gym for kids, and BBQs, that also had access to acres of shoreline where a person could get far away from the public.

"Great." Noah's voice held a note of relief. "Thanks, Remy."

Remy ended the call and sat for a moment, thinking about his friend's cryptic words.

Maybe it was a good idea not to give Desi the flash drive after all.

10

———

Leine woke up early and grabbed her phone. She'd had a dream that featured Remy, Desi, and Sebastian, and she wanted to work through it, mine it for information her subconscious may have picked up. The essence was there, but she couldn't quite parse the symbolism to make sense of the data. Often, her subconscious delivered answers, albeit through symbolism that could be obscure, which was what happened this time. With a sigh, she closed the note app on her phone, then dialed Remy's number. She'd work on it later. He answered on the second ring.

"What you got?" His gravelly voice reverberated through her earpiece.

"Sounds like you had an evening."

"Yeah. Thai food for dinner. Can't handle the hot anymore."

"Sorry. Maybe don't do that? Just a thought."

"What do you need?" His annoyed tone told her he wasn't in the mood.

"I finished the interviews yesterday."

"Anything worth knowing?"

"Not a lot, other than the obvious: Brett and Ethan were

loved by many. Scott, not so much. What do you know about Laura? She acted like she wasn't telling me everything."

"She's got a heart the size of Texas, and she's always there for anyone who needs her, whether that's money or time or a shoulder to cry on. She was probably just nervous."

"Yeah, maybe." Leine sighed. Not much to go on. "I was followed last night."

"Interesting."

"I lost them, but I'm not certain it was because of my sterling evasion capabilities, or if they just wanted to send a message."

"You get the plates?"

"That's why I'm calling. Can you run them for me?"

"Sure. I'm meeting my cop buddy later this afternoon, but should still have time."

"Thanks."

"Just curious. Don't you have resources you can use for this kind of thing? Or did you burn your bridges?"

"I do, but your access to the DMV as a PI is a better use of everybody's time." Leine paused. "What are you meeting with your guy for? I thought you and he were on the outs."

"He thinks he found something that we might be able to use in our investigation. Something about Sebastian."

"Interesting. Keep me posted."

"One more thing."

"What?"

Remy sighed. "My friend Alice wants to meet you."

"Oh? Why is that?"

"I told her about you—sketchy details, nothing obvious, but she put things together and thinks you're a badass. I told her she was delusional, but she still wants to meet."

Leine chuckled. "A badass? Nice. Tell her I'm happy to meet with her. Did she find anything useful on the USB drive?"

"Sort of. I'll let her tell you about it, since I'm in the dark when it comes to technology."

"I have a feeling we're both going to need to get up to speed on that front, probably sooner than we think."

"I was afraid you'd say that."

"Why? You some kind of a Luddite?"

"I have no freaking idea what that is, but the way you say it, my answer is no."

"Just a person who thinks technology isn't all it's cracked up to be."

"Well, yeah. Any sane person thinks that."

"I've got news for you, Remy. Most folks think tech will save the world."

"And which side are you on?"

"Frankly, I'm on the fence. Without it, we're doomed. But I think we're doomed anyway."

Remy snorted. "You're a real ray of sunshine, you know that?"

"Just pragmatic. Human nature is human nature."

"Can't argue with that."

"Give me a shout when you're back from your meeting."

"Will do. I'll send Alice's deets so you two can get together."

Leine ended the call and slid her phone into her pocket. His question got her thinking. Was she on the side of technology? If she was honest with herself, just keeping up with changes in tech was exhausting. But she had to do it if she was going to keep a step ahead of the bad actors in the world. And with artificial intelligence exploding in popularity, things were exponentially harder. The bad guys had to be right once. People who worked to stop them had to be right, period.

She had to admit, life was certainly better with technology than without it—lifespans were longer, researchers were finding more cures for diseases, everyday chores were easier—but this reliance on tech was a double-edged sword, allowing for catastrophic events, threatening the very fabric of the world. Pandemics were more likely because of advances in long-range travel, allowing more people to go more places. The possibility of the breakdown in communication, utilities, and safety by an attack on a power grid or worse was a real threat. A small group of talented hackers could bring a nation to its knees by holding data hostage. And deepfakes were a huge problem, especially during election cycles.

How many citizens knew how to calculate interest without a calculator? Or even do simple multiplication? If the banking network went down, there'd be chaos as panicked people scrambled to get their money out. There'd been warnings already—regional banks going under, companies too big to fail that failed, and on and on. Two sides of the same coin.

Well, that's what people like me are here for. To help when things went sideways.

Leine's phone dinged, alerting her to a new text. She opened the message from Remy with Alice's number and gave her a call.

11

Leine pushed through the door to the restaurant and stood for a moment to let her eyes adjust to the dim interior. The packed space seethed with activity. She breathed in the heady scent of garlic and fried fish.

A slender young Asian woman sitting near the back of the restaurant waved her over. Leine threaded her way through tables of happy, animated diners, catching snippets of Mandarin, Cantonese, and other dialects, some of which weren't familiar.

The other woman rose to shake Leine's hand. "You must be Leine."

Leine smiled. "And you must be Alice."

"Please, have a seat."

Leine sat across the laminate table from her. Menus with photographs of some of the dishes the restaurant offered had been placed underneath the glass tabletop. Two cups and a pot of tea rested between the two women. Alice poured each of them a cup and set the pot back on the table.

"I suppose you're wondering why I asked to meet you," Alice

began. "After Remy started working with you, I became really interested."

"Why?"

She smiled. "Because I'm always impressed when women carve out a piece of the pie normally reserved for men."

"Ah." Leine blew on her tea, then took a sip. "And what exactly did Remy tell you I did?"

Alice leaned forward, lowering her voice. "He didn't tell me in so many words. He didn't need to. I extrapolated from his comments."

"What did you extrapolate?"

She glanced at the closest table. The older women seated next to them weren't paying any attention to their conversation, having a rousing one of their own. "That you took out the bad guys."

Leine cocked her head. Time to change the subject. "What is it that you do for a living?"

"I work for a startup specializing in AI-based security."

"Hobbies? Pastimes?" There had to be something other than just curiosity driving her interest.

Alice's lips quirked up in a smile. "Not that I advertise, but I do have extracurricular activities."

"Do tell."

A harried waitress floated by and gave Alice a questioning look. Alice replied in Cantonese.

"I hope you don't mind, but I ordered for us both. The restaurant is known for its dim sum."

"Sounds delicious. You're fluent in Cantonese."

Alice nodded. "And Mandarin. And about six different dialects. You know Cantonese?"

"I do, although I'm more fluent in Mandarin. Have you spent time in Hong Kong?"

"Macao, actually. I worked in my cousin's casino for several years."

"What's the extracurricular activity you mentioned earlier?"

"Remy didn't tell you?"

"I'll assume he thought it was for you to tell."

Alice grinned. "He doesn't approve. I like to...borrow things without the owner's knowledge."

"What kinds of things?"

"Mainly jewelry. Sometimes art."

"Cat burglar?"

Alice's grin grew wider. "You extrapolate too."

"You said that you borrow things. So, you give them back?"

Alice's gaze shifted. "Not exactly, but I plan to. Sometime."

Leine let her attempt at justification go. "What drew you to AI? The two interests seem wildly different."

"One informs the other."

"How?"

"When I'm successful evading my nighttime target's security features, the experience points me to vulnerabilities in programs I work on. The act of 'borrowing' gets me out of my head— distracts me enough to give my subconscious the time to work through whatever challenge I have at my day job."

"What about power?"

"What about it?"

"I imagine that successfully stealing from well-off targets gives you a feeling of getting something over on them."

Alice smiled again, her eyes flashing. "Well, there is that, yes."

Leine studied the younger woman. "How on earth did you and Remy get together?"

At that, Alice giggled. "I know, right? The ex-cop and the thief."

Her answer gave Leine pause. Her relationship with Santa was similar. Sort of.

The waitress brought over their meal—bowls of steamed dumplings, noodles in a fragrant broth, fried oysters. Leine's mouth watered.

"What about the age difference? No offense, of course."

Alice served Leine more tea and topped off her cup, while Leine used her chopsticks to nab a couple of dumplings and place them in her bowl.

"None taken. It's a little tricky, but we're a lot alike. We don't enjoy crowds, mainly. We're homebodies, we like the same movies, stuff like that."

They both fell silent as they ate. The food was extraordinary and Leine wanted to enjoy the experience. Apparently, so did Alice. The waitress brought more as soon as they finished each dish. Near the end, Leine set her chopsticks on the rest and leaned back in her chair.

"That was the best dim sum I've ever eaten, bar none. Thank you."

"You're welcome. I love bringing people to this restaurant. One of my aunts runs the kitchen."

"Give her my compliments. Perhaps we should get down to business? Remy mentioned that you'd found something on the thumb drive?"

Alice wiped the corner of her mouth with her napkin before taking a sip of water. "It's some sort of sophisticated malware, but I don't know what program it's meant to work with."

"Any clues?"

"It's definitely AI."

"And how do you know that?"

"The algos I've been able to isolate are commonly used in AI programs. They adapt and optimize their behavior based on data inputs."

"Is there any way to figure out who created it?"

"There are some quirks in the code, but not enough to identify them—yet. I'm still investigating."

"What can I do?"

"Nothing, yet. I've isolated the code in a sandbox—a safe place on an air-gapped computer—and am feeding it different programs. So far, it doesn't seem to be a very malicious malware."

"So, it only works on a particular program."

Alice nodded. "You see my problem."

"Too many programs, too little time?"

"Yep. I'll keep trying, but I'm not confident I'll find the specific program it's meant for. It's like it's inert."

"Waiting for something."

"Yeah."

"That's worrisome. It could be anything. You said it's sophisticated?"

"That's the worrisome part. The code could be earmarked for something really important, like, say, disrupting Seattle's electrical grid. I'm just spit-balling here. It isn't that. I checked with a colleague who works for Seattle City Light. But a lot of cities have adopted AI for running utilities, so that's a valid concern."

"Hopefully those cities doing the adopting have built in a safety net."

"It wouldn't be hard to find an expert to help set up security in Seattle. My contact said they're taking the use of artificial intelligence seriously. That might not be the case in other municipalities."

"It's such new technology." Leine studied Alice. "What can we do? From what you said, there isn't enough information to warn anyone. That malware could be out in the wild. The copy you have likely isn't the only one."

"Another worrisome part. The tech is too easy to replicate." Alice sighed. "Now you see what keeps me awake at night."

"I'm right there with you. I have some contacts that might be able to help by reaching out to a larger number of utilities if you think that's warranted."

"Thanks. I'll let you know. This malware's got its hooks in me. I'm going to keep testing until I figure it out. It's a point of professional pride, now. In fact, a couple of possibles occurred to me while we were talking."

"You're talking about the program at the club?"

Alice nodded. "It makes sense, right? Remy found the USB at Brett's place. Brett was deeply involved with the AI-assisted performance. Although, why make the program the target?"

"A competitor on the club circuit? Maybe someone's jealous and wants to shut down the popularity of Desi's club."

"Maybe."

"Do you have a copy?"

"I asked Remy to get one from Desi, but it's a hard sell. Desi's very protective."

"Understandable," Leine said. "He probably has an agreement with Sebastian to guard that program with his life. I'll talk to him, see if I can soften him up a bit."

"That would be great. Thank you."

"Glad to help." Leine finished her tea and stood. "It was good to meet you. Keep me posted." She put some cash on the table. "Lunch is on me."

Alice began to protest, but Leine shook her head. "Just keep working on your piece of this puzzle."

12

———————

Remy pulled into a lot at Carkeek and parked across from Noah's sporty Subaru. He locked his truck and set off for the metal stairway that connected the park's greenspace with the shoreline. He was fifteen minutes late, but had texted Noah his ETA.

The setting sun burned low on the horizon, painting the snowcapped Olympic Mountains with a rosy hue. A soft breeze ruffled Remy's hair, bringing with it the scent of the sea. He breathed in deeply, glad to be away from the noise and chaos of the city. Some days, he thought he'd like to live out in the sticks somewhere, get a little peace and quiet, but usually came to the conclusion he'd hate being out of the electric vibe of a bustling West Coast city like Seattle. Besides, he could be hiking in semi-wilderness in less than an hour.

He climbed the metal stairs and followed the bridge spanning a set of railroad tracks below, then down the other side to the shoreline. Waves lapped at the sand as seagulls screeched and wheeled overhead, filling him with peace. Nature was one of his favorite ways to calm his anxieties.

In the distance, a windswept point hid the shoreline beyond.

The hike to their usual meeting place was devoid of people—just the way he liked it. As a police officer and later detective, Remy found he needed to break away from the public at regular intervals in order to keep his sanity. Noah did, too, and they both credited the park with helping defuse the stress that inevitably built when dealing with the public, not to mention their superiors.

Remy rounded the point, expecting to find his friend sitting on a large driftwood tree trunk they'd designated as the place to meet, but no one was there. He checked his phone to make sure Noah hadn't texted him a different location, but he hadn't.

That wasn't like Noah. The man was nothing if not conscientious.

A gnawing sensation at the base of Remy's stomach ramped to life. He disregarded the feeling as more fallout from the Thai food, but a niggling in the back of his mind gave him pause. He patted the SIG snugged inside his shoulder holster. He never went anywhere without it, had made sure when Seattle PD let him go that he retained the right to carry.

As he drew closer to the huge piece of driftwood, the little hairs on the back of his neck stood on end. He slowed his pace, caution taking precedence over the need to know what lay beyond.

He drew his weapon and continued past. The gnawing in his gut grew.

There were only rocks, sand, shells, and dried seaweed. Remy heaved a relieved sigh and, after a quick recon of the area for intruders, re-holstered his weapon. Noah must've gotten bored and taken a walk or something. There were too many footprints to know which way he'd gone.

Remy walked back to the driftwood and had a seat. A bald eagle soared overhead on a thermal, hunting dinner. A moment later, the raptor torpedoed toward the water, drawing up sharply right before impact, seizing a good-sized fish in its claws. A couple of powerful flaps and the bird was airborne and winging its way back to its perch, its meal struggling to break free.

Remy gave Noah another five minutes, then punched his number into his cell phone. The call went to voicemail. With a frown, he slid his phone back into his pocket. Though faint, he thought he'd heard what might have been Noah's ringtone. Remy glanced up and down the shoreline but didn't notice anything unusual. There was still sufficient daylight, so he set off walking along the shore.

A storm earlier in the week had deposited a generous amount of debris, and Remy soon found himself picking through piles of driftwood and seaweed. A gnarled fishing net marred the scene, in addition to the ubiquitous plastic bottles and brightly colored lighters. He pulled out his phone and called Noah's number once more.

The ringing came from his left, opposite the water. Remy's gut twisted with apprehension as he made his way up the beach.

Ahead of him lay an older pile of driftwood. Shore grass had sprouted between the pieces of wood, obviously deposited during a previous storm. Something caught Remy's eye, and he moved toward it.

The closer he got, the more the gnawing feeling grew. What had caught his eye had been a color not normally associated with the beach and shoreline. Instead of gray and green and black and white, he'd noticed something that was a distinctive fiery orange. Perhaps a safety float, ripped from a trawler on the high seas, finding its home on the lonely, windswept beaches of Washington State. Or a child's toy that the wind took from an untended deck.

But it wasn't a float. Or a child's toy.

He slid his phone back into his pocket and moved closer.

The orange was from the jacket Noah wore when he'd met him at the espresso place.

Noah lay on his side with his back to Remy. For a second, Remy imagined his friend taking a nap. Remy's heart hammered as he reached into his pocket for a pair of gloves. He gently rolled Noah far enough back to be certain he was gone. Glassy brown eyes stared back. A hole marred his temple, evidence of the cause of death. The bullet had exited through the opposite side of his head.

Bile rode Remy's throat before his cop brain kicked in and pushed away the thought that he was looking at a friend. Compartmentalization the shrink had called it. Whatever it was, it worked.

The body was still warm, and rigor mortis hadn't yet set in, telling him he hadn't been dead long.

He checked Noah's hands for evidence of defensive wounds or cadaveric spasm, but neither were evident, telling him there likely hadn't been a struggle. He went through Noah's pockets, and found his phone, wallet, and a container of mints. The wallet held a credit card, insurance card, driver's license, and his badge. His phone showed two missed calls—Remy's earlier attempts. He was about to put the items back when he noticed a flash of white behind the badge. He slid his finger inside the gap, and was rewarded with a scrap of paper, which he unfolded. Written in pencil was an address with a zip code from the moneyed enclave of Hunts Point.

Did his murder have something to do with Noah's information on Sebastian? Or was it just some random kill?

Remy's cop radar discarded the random shooter theory. Whoever killed him hadn't lifted his badge or his credit card, two valuable pieces in his wallet.

If the murder was due to information he had, Noah would have been careful, but he might not have known he was being tracked. No one knew of their meeting place. They'd always been careful not to leave traces either on their phones or their desks.

Noah had been followed.

Had his killer known he was meeting Remy? Did Noah unknowingly ping somebody with a search? Could be he was looking into a person of interest flagged in the database.

Remy pulled out his phone to call the police, but hesitated. Word would filter back to his old precinct, and Remy would likely be a person of interest, something he didn't want, even on the best of days. Besides, the two detectives that had him thrown off the force likely still had a hard-on for him. That kind of interest would hamstring him in any investigation he tried to conduct.

After checking for the brass from the fired round and not finding it, he rolled Noah back to his original position. He'd pick up a burner phone and call it in.

"I promise I'll find who did this to you."

Remy made his way back to his car. The sun had dipped low on the horizon, creating shadows and tricking the eye to perceive things that weren't there. Remy's heart rate stayed steady as he scanned his surroundings, wondering if his presence would flush out the attacker.

The parking lot had emptied by the time he got back to his pickup. The sunset was over, sending visitors home. He unlocked his door and slid behind the wheel. A wave of sadness washed through him, but he shook it off. There'd be time for grief later. He started the engine and pulled onto the parkway. The shriek of sirens could be heard in the distance.

Someone—likely the shooter—had already called in the murder. He was a sitting duck. Memories from years before of finding heroin planted in his trunk came back with a vengeance

—the hopelessness of trying to convince his superiors that it wasn't his.

He'd bet the round that killed Noah came from the same model SIG Remy used.

Hacking a U-turn in the middle of the road, he floored the accelerator, disappearing around the corner as first responders crested the hill.

13

R emy gunned the engine as he climbed the narrow road away from the park. Half a mile later, he crested the hill and started to descend. A sharp bend appeared, and he stepped on the brake, but his foot hit the floor. Adrenalin spiked through him. Someone had tampered with his truck. He hauled on the emergency brake, but nothing happened.

His focus narrowed and he swerved back and forth, trying to slow down. At this speed, his truck would easily jump the low barrier to his right, plunging him and his vehicle to the bottom of a ravine. To his left were several sturdy trees that would stop him, but he ran the risk of a hell of an injury from the crash.

Think, Remy. What was up ahead? He drew a blank. Normally, he exited the park in the other direction. His tires squealed in protest as he rounded the next turn. The road straightened for a few yards, giving him a tiny respite. What appeared to be a ditch filled with brush materialized to his left. The depth was hard to gauge, but at least it didn't look like a ravine.

Remy steered toward it and braced for impact.

The vehicle hit the ditch with a loud *bang* followed by crunching metal, then silence. The airbags didn't deploy, but the seatbelt did what it was designed to do.

Breathing hard, Remy turned off the engine and unbuckled his belt. The driver's side door took some persuading and screeched in protest, but opened wide enough for him to climb out. The *tick, tick, tick* of the radiator and the squawk of a raven in a nearby tree shattered the silence. He slid his phone out of his pocket and hit speed-dial for Alice. The call didn't connect. He checked the screen. No service.

With a sigh, Remy grabbed his go-bag from the backseat of his pickup, locked the doors, and pocketed his keys before shoving branches over the hood and the rest of the body to camouflage the vehicle from passersby. Satisfied the pickup couldn't be seen from the road, he scaled the ditch and set off down the road to find better reception.

Up ahead, a brown sedan rounded the corner. Too late to hide—too suspicious. Remy kept walking, not sure if he should wave them down. He'd prefer no one placed him near the murder.

The car slowed. Remy raised his head and squinted, trying to see through the windshield. The driver's side window lowered and a hand appeared.

Holding a gun.

Remy's brain barely had time to process the danger before muscle memory took over and he dove for the ditch. A split second later, there was a *phffft,* and a *thwack,* as the suppressed round hit a tree next to him.

Remy field-crawled farther into the bushes, blackberry vines ripping his skin, before he stopped, rolled, and slid the SIG from his shoulder holster. Two more rounds from the driver peppered the trunk of a nearby tree.

Peering through a thick veil of salal and blackberry brambles, Remy calculated the distance to the shooter. Cars were not the best hide unless the vehicle in question had been up-armored. By the looks of the sedan, it wasn't likely. He had a shot at breaching the door and hitting the occupant, unless they took cover behind the engine block.

Not a good shot, but a shot.

What he wouldn't do for a rifle and a scope. Remy's eyesight was good, but he'd noticed having a little more trouble in low-light conditions. The preponderance of trees and vegetation cast everything in dark shadow. He made a mental note to ensure his go-bag was better equipped in the future. Although, if he didn't make it through this encounter, night-vision gear and a rifle wouldn't matter.

Remy waited, the early evening sounds beginning to make themselves evident. The adrenaline dump from being shot at kicked up his sensory receptors so that every insect, every bird, every rustle of leaves hit his eardrums like he was sitting in the front row of an orchestra. He slowed his breathing, waiting for his enemy's next move.

The drone of the idling engine accompanied the scent of acrid exhaust. A car door opened, and footsteps scuffed the asphalt. Remy tensed, acutely aware of his vulnerability. Thankfully his clothing blended well with his surroundings.

Remy caught a glimpse of movement through the foliage. Motionless, he waited.

Come closer, asshole. You know you want to.

The shooter took another step. Remy eased his weapon into position, careful not to make any sudden movements. Shrouded in shadow, his adversary was walking right into the kill zone.

Remy slowed his breathing. His heart beat loud in his ears. He didn't sweat it. Experience had trained him that only he could hear the thudding. Ragged breathing, on the other hand, was loud as hell.

Adrenaline thrummed through his veins, reminding him of what he once did for a living. These moments hadn't happened often, but when they did, nothing compared.

Unfortunately, it also reminded him of what the assholes he worked with had taken from him.

The shooter took another step—the right one, as far as Remy was concerned.

The round exited the SIG's barrel, the report echoing through the trees, flushing a murder of crows from a nearby fir. The thud of a body hitting the ground told him he'd made his target.

He waited several beats to make certain the shooter was alone. Only the wind and birds had something to say.

Remy climbed to his feet and scanned the area. Nothing moved. The sedan idled in the middle of the road. The side door yawned open, waiting for its driver's return. The body of the shooter lay cockeyed near the ditch. If Remy were to guess, he was in his early fifties. He had the beginnings of a paunch. Reddish-brown hair framed a weathered face.

Remy moved to the body and briefly checked the man's pockets. He had nothing on him. No surprise. No self-respecting killer would be caught dead with identification. He checked for an exit wound, found it, and located the round, which he pocketed. He spied the shooter's gun underneath the car, and dropped to his stomach so he could retrieve it.

A SIG Sauer P226.

The sound of his gun discharging would bring trouble. He shoved the pistol into his waistband, then grabbed the dead man by the armpits and dragged him back to the car. Remy heaved the body into the trunk and closed the lid. Breathing heavily from the effort, he did a quick sweep of the interior, and found what was likely a burner phone in the console. He removed the sim card, stuck it in his pocket, and tossed the phone on the passenger seat. Then he climbed behind the wheel, closed the door, and started to drive.

There wasn't anything he could do about his truck. He'd have to leave it and go to ground until things blew over. He was going to be a person of interest. Shit was getting dicey.

Likely the shooter had sabotaged his brakes, wanting to make his death look like an accident, but in the end was invested enough that he would have killed Remy on the side of the road. If successful, he'd likely have staged things to look like a carjacking gone bad.

Remy hit the freeway and headed south. He pulled out his phone and called Alice. It went to voicemail. His next choice was Leine. She answered on the second ring.

"Remy. How'd the meeting go?"

"Not great. Noah's dead, and someone tried to kill me."

There was a brief pause, then, "What do you need?"

"I'll come to you. I need to hole up somewhere for a while."

"Head to where we met."

"Roger that."

FORTY-FIVE MINUTES AND SEVERAL EVASIVE MANEUVERS LATER, HE pulled into Desi's underground parking garage and parked in Desi's spot. The nightclub owner wouldn't be home for hours, so wouldn't mind.

He texted Leine to come down to the garage. A few minutes later, the elevator pinged and the doors slid open. She walked over to where he stood next to the sedan.

"Where'd you pick up the sweet ride?" she asked, arching an eyebrow.

"You like it? Thought I'd go for understated." He turned serious. "Belongs to the shooter."

"Didn't you mention a dark-colored sedan showed up at Brett's houseboat the night you went in?"

Remy nodded. "I was thinking the same thing."

"What happened to the driver?"

Remy aimed the key fob at the car and pressed the button. The trunk lid opened, revealing the corpse. He had to hand it to her, she didn't even blink.

She closed the lid, a thoughtful look on her face. "We're going to need to get rid of your friend here. Any ideas?"

"I know a few places that could work." He checked his watch. "Probably going to need to wait a bit."

Leine glanced underneath the car. "No leakage, at least. We need to get him on a tarp."

"You've done this before."

She ignored the remark. "There's a hardware store not too far from here. We can take my car." She paused. "I'm sorry about your friend."

"Thanks." Another wave of grief hit him, hard. He shook it off. "He had an address in his wallet, behind his badge." He pulled out the piece of paper and handed it to her.

"Whoever shot him wasn't very thorough. That, or the address doesn't lead us anywhere."

"It's Hunts Point. You know, where Seattle's uber-wealthy go to die."

She shot him a look. "Let me guess. Sebastian lives on Hunts Point."

"He does."

"Same address?"

Remy shrugged. "Haven't had time to check."

"Where's your truck?"

"Near the park where I was supposed to meet Noah."

"That's unfortunate. Do you need recovery?"

"Later. It's fine for now. But I'm gonna need somewhere to lay low."

"Desi's place?"

Remy shook his head. "Too dangerous. For him and you. I'll figure it out."

"Let me check with my guy." She slid out her phone.

AN HOUR LATER, THE SHOOTER WAS WRAPPED AND READY FOR disposal. Leine had been efficient and unemotional as she helped Remy clean the car. Her guy, Lou, had found Remy a safehouse in the Phinney Ridge neighborhood. She'd go with him to his apartment to pick up a few things, then drop him off there.

Before they dumped the body, Remy took a picture of both the man's face and the car, making sure to include the plates and vehicle identification number. Leine followed Remy to a desolate cliff high above the Straits of Juan de Fuca, where they shoved the body in the driver's seat, put the car in gear, and let it roll over the edge, crashing to the rocks below. Then she drove Remy to his apartment, making sure they didn't have a tail.

She followed him inside the building and up three flights of stairs. He opened the front door and froze.

"Fuck me."

Leine peered around him into the apartment. The place had obviously been tossed. Jagged cuts exposed the guts of Remy's upholstered furniture. Pieces of shattered dishes were strewn across the hardwood floor, while every drawer, cupboard, and closet had been yanked open and emptied, their contents scattered. The living room and kitchen looked like some kind of crazed animal had been set loose to ransack the place.

"Any idea what they were looking for?" Leine followed him into the debris-filled room.

Remy shook his head. "Not a clue."

He picked his way across the floor to a side table that had its drawer ajar. He pulled it the rest of the way out. The flashlight was still there, but his laptop was gone.

"Well, I guess the good news is they didn't take the flashlight."

"What else did they take?"

"What, this isn't enough for you?" He gestured at the annihilated room. He wanted to add *and some motherfucker tried to kill me,* but didn't have the energy.

"Sorry, the way you said that made me think...never mind."

"Sorry. I didn't mean it the way it came out. They got my laptop. Not like there was anything on it." Alice had made him create a fifteen-character password with two-factor identification, so it wasn't like whoever stole it would ever get access to his files, such as they were.

Leine helped him pack a bag to take to the safehouse, and they returned to Leine's vehicle. Remy decided to ignore what happened to his apartment. Getting shot at seemed like enough for one day. Leine took the long way to the safehouse, doubling back and executing several evasive maneuvers in case they'd picked up a tail. Remy remained quiet most of the way.

She pulled into the driveway at the safehouse and parked. Remy stared out the windshield, trying to understand what had happened, what it meant.

"Noah's first instincts were to stay out of my investigation. He was right. Now he's dead."

"Don't blame yourself. That kind of guilt is a bottomless pit you can get lost in."

He caught a glimpse of her expression—a look he could only

describe as deep, soul-wrenching sorrow. Maybe he'd been too hasty in his assessment of her.

"Sounds like you've been there."

She nodded. "I was responsible for the death of someone I loved."

He stared at her. Their differences were stark, but this was something they had in common. Before he could stop himself, he started talking.

"You know my theory about the two detectives planting evidence in my car? That isn't the whole story."

"I'm listening."

"Back before I was kicked out of the department, my girl-friend at the time took my car one morning—her battery was dead and she needed to get to work. I was doing some stuff from home, so I told her to take it."

Leine remained silent, letting him talk.

Remy continued. "It was raining pretty hard—temps were in the low twenties, so freezing rain. Typical December. They said she lost control on a patch of black ice." He grew quiet as he fiddled with the button on his shirt, but then abandoned it. "They found her and the car at the bottom of Puget Sound."

"I'm so sorry," Leine said.

Remy scrubbed his face with his hand. "It was supposed to be me driving the car that morning. They recovered the wreck and the asswipes I worked with tried to expedite disposal—said they were doing it because of my emotional state. I fought like hell to take possession. When I did, I discovered the brake lines were loose. The fluid had leaked out. She wouldn't have been able to stop." He paused, his throat raw with grief. "When I brought the loose lines up to my CO and suggested it might have been intentional, he told me to take some time off."

"When did they plant the drugs?"

"So, *now* you believe me?" He snorted as he gave Leine a

look. "A couple weeks after I got back from mandatory bereavement."

She studied him as though assessing his fitness for duty. At least, that's what he told himself.

Instead, she said, "That kind of guilt—you have to learn to live with it or it'll take you all the way down." She leaned her head back and stared through the windshield. "The fallout from a single, seemingly innocuous choice—was one of the hardest things I've ever had to face. It came close to destroying me."

Remy nodded. So, she did understand. "Yeah." He cleared his throat.

"But you can't let it rule you, Remy." She turned to look at him. "If you don't do it for you, then do it for her, and Noah."

He returned her gaze, recognized a solidarity in their depths. "I know."

They sat together for a time, finding solace in their shared trauma. A heavy weight lifted from Remy's chest—he felt like he could breathe for the first time in years.

"Thank you." The words were simple, but they meant the world.

The spell between them broken, Leine reached into the backseat for his bag. As she handed it to him, she asked, "Did you find anything on the plate I gave you?"

He shook his head. "Doesn't exist. You must have gotten a number wrong. Want me to keep on it?"

"Later." Leine put her hand on his arm. It was nice, which surprised him. Normally he hated sympathetic gestures. "We'll find his killer. Take some time to process everything first."

"Sure."

He felt her eyes on him as he walked to the front door. She was right. His guilt would mess with his head if he didn't keep himself in check. *Best not let her get too close. The fewer vulnerabilities I have, the better.* Alice was enough to worry about. That relationship had blindsided him, and now he couldn't shake the feeling of being responsible for her safety. He wouldn't make the same mistake with Leine, or anyone else.

Someone had just killed one of his good friends and had tried to kill him.

He wasn't about to let whoever ordered the murders get away with it—his first instinct was vengeance, which wasn't a great frame of mind for an investigation. He'd have to hone his reactions, become the tip of the spear. All solidarity aside, if he was right about Leine, she'd want to keep him on a short leash.

She sure as hell could try.

14

Leine pulled into the visitor's parking space beneath Desi's building and killed the engine. She stared at the wall in front of her. During the drive there she'd been attempting to shake off the memories of her old love, Carlos, that her exchange with Remy brought to the surface, but her usual ability to compartmentalize wasn't working.

She must be tired. Maybe going over the facts of the case would distract her.

Leine began to list them off in her head: a mysterious USB drive containing what appeared to be an advanced malware program. Three murders, all female impersonators, all from the same nightclub. A club that was connected to tech billionaire Sebastian Fellowes via Desi, and an AI program used for an uber-popular, money-making show. A cop, now dead, who said he had information on Sebastian Fellowes. Someone following her with an apparently non-existent plate, if Remy's search was correct. The people following her were either trying to send a message, or inept, she didn't know which. Add to that an attempt on Remy's life.

Had Noah's murder been because of the information he

supposedly had on Sebastian? She stared at the address Remy gave her from Noah's wallet. What did it signify? Why was it behind Noah's badge, and why did the killer not take it with him?

She slid out her phone and called her old friend and former handler, Lou Stokes.

"What can I do you for, Leine?"

Leine cracked a smile at Lou's familiar southern drawl. They'd been friends since she was first tapped at the tender age of sixteen for training at the Agency.

So many lifetimes ago.

"I need you to find out the owner of an address for me."

"Easy, peasy. I thought you might give me a challenge."

"Don't get cocky, mister. I think it belongs to a billionaire, so it'll likely be a shell game just for you."

"Well now, that's more like it. Give me the details and I'll take a spin right now, in case it's a breeze."

She read off the address. A faint clicking came through her earpiece as he typed on his keyboard. A few minutes later, Lou came back on.

"You were right about it being a challenge, but it was no match for my handy-dandy AI-assisted search program. It crawls public info in about the time it takes to type the command. Private information takes a little longer."

"Well, aren't you cutting edge?"

"All the cool kids are using it."

"And? Are we looking at a certain tech billionaire?"

"Possible. The owner is a shell corp based out of Nevada."

"And you can't go any deeper?"

"It'll take some time, even with the cool new tools."

"Is the address anywhere near Sebastian Fellowes' home?"

There was a pause, then, "Looks like they're in the same neighborhood, why?"

"Just curious." What would Sebastian need with two multi-million-dollar properties so close together? That wouldn't explain why Noah wanted to meet with Remy, though. What else had he found?

"What exactly are you doing up there in grunge town?"

"A friend of mine asked for help."

"Uh-huh. And is this friend of yours mixed up in something illegal?"

"Not the friend, no. But I've got a feeling about Fellowes."

Lou sighed. "You do tend to find trouble, don't you?"

"The problem is that I'm not sure what all of it has to do with him."

"Either way, be careful. Billionaires can be shady as shit—they just use other folks to do their dirty work."

"I'm aware." She'd had several dealings with the moneyed elite in her time. It was enlightening, to be sure. Just like anywhere in life, some were good people, but some...weren't. "Would you mind running a plate for me? Somebody followed me home from the club and I'd like to know why."

"Certainly."

Leine gave him the plate number from the SUV. Her recall was still good, but she didn't want to press it with Remy—not when he was still processing his friend's murder.

Lou came back on the line. "That's odd."

"What?"

"There's no record of the plates. Anywhere. Let me try one more thing. Where did the tail take place?"

"Capitol Hill neighborhood."

A couple of minutes later, he came back on the line. "I just accessed SafeWise Security's online database. There's no sign of those plates or the SUV."

Safewise Security was a private security firm that crowd-sourced information on license plates.

"Didn't a bunch of organizations lodge a complaint against them for intrusive tech or something?"

"Yep. But it hasn't gone anywhere yet, so their cameras and database are still available to use."

"So, what you're saying is that any evidence of an SUV sporting those plates has been scrubbed from existence?"

"Pretty much."

"Thanks, Lou. I'll get back to you once I've thought this through."

Leine ended the call. So Remy had it right. The only entity with enough clout to do something like that would be a state actor, either foreign or domestic—or a billionaire like Sebastian Fellowes with enough money and influence to pay to scrub Safewise's database. That, coupled with Noah's murder and the attempt on Remy's life pointed toward the Seattle billionaire. Whether he was responsible or just appeared to be, she didn't know.

Yet.

She needed somewhere to start. She needed access to Sebastian.

15

———

The next day, Remy called for a rideshare to a car rental kiosk where he rented an F-150 pickup, then hopped on I-5 and headed back to the safehouse in Phinney Ridge. He checked his rearview mirror several times for a tail, but traffic was heavy, making it easier for a would-be tracker to hide. On impulse, he headed right across several lanes toward an exit, but kept going straight, taking note of any vehicles mirroring his movements.

There were two possibles. He immediately discounted one, a '71 Dodge Charger, cherry-red with metallic flakes in the paint. Not a good car for going unnoticed. The second was a white Explorer SUV—one of hundreds on the road in Seattle.

A mile later, the SUV exited the freeway. Remy kept an eye on the mirror. They could be tag-teaming him, leaving the freeway once the second vehicle got into place, throwing him off.

The odometer showed another mile traveled, but he hadn't noticed anything unusual.

C'mon, Remy. You're getting paranoid again. No one's behind you. You're in a rental. No one knows what you're driving.

With a sigh, he leaned back in his seat and concentrated on driving.

Another mile flew by, and he glanced in the mirror. The Charger was still there and gaining fast. Remy tensed as it rumbled alongside him. The tinted passenger window made it difficult to see who was inside. The side window rolled down, revealing a skinny white guy with full neck tats wearing a backwards ballcap. Remy barely had time to register the silver-plated .45 aimed his direction.

Remy swerved right. Horns blared in protest, partially masking the sound of the gunshot. The round missed Remy, embedding itself in a nearby eighteen-wheeler with a cartoon of a happy cow on its side.

The muscle car revved its engine and swerved into Remy, clipping the front quarter panel of the pickup. Cars behind them swerved and tires squealed as traffic tried to avoid becoming part of a crime scene.

Remy's heart banged in his chest, the adrenaline spike from being shot at crowding out logic. The thug in the Charger raised the .45 again and aimed. Remy headed straight for him and rammed the passenger side. The gun went airborne and landed on the asphalt, bouncing into oncoming traffic. Remy remained glued to the Charger, forcing them into traffic, until the driver veered left to disengage and sped off, narrowly missing a light blue Prius in the next lane.

Remy floored the accelerator, keeping the muscle car in sight. He slid out his pistol and laid it on the seat next to him as he swerved in and out of traffic, hyper-focused on catching his assailants.

Leine showered and changed, then rode Desi's elevator to the garage. The door pinged as it slid open, and she stepped out. Something moved in her periphery. She pulled back as a solid wall of muscle dressed in dark clothes barged into the elevator and slammed her against the wall.

Anger and surprise fueled her as she shoved her assailant back far enough to smash her knee into his balls. With a wheeze, her attacker doubled over.

Leine shoved him out of the elevator, drew her gun, and fired. She hit him, but her attacker was unfazed. He rushed her like a lineman sacking the quarterback, sending her careening back into the elevator. She lost her grip on the gun. It hit the wall, landing nearby.

He pinned her to the floor with his knees on her forearms, wrapped his hands around her throat, and squeezed. The round had either missed, or he was so hyped on adrenaline that he didn't notice getting shot. Leine bucked and writhed, but he was a solid wall of mass and barely budged. His breath hot on her face, she considered her options: continue to fight and lose, or play dead.

Leine closed her eyes and relaxed as though losing consciousness.

After a few seconds, her attacker released his hold and grabbed her head with both hands. Before he could snap her neck, Leine bucked her hips, hard. He lurched forward, palms landing flat on the floor, allowing her to slip her right arm free and grab the gun.

Pop! Pop!

Leine sent two rounds into his gut. With a deep groan he clutched at his stomach and collapsed onto his elbow. He pulled his hand away from the gunshot wound and stared at the blood in disbelief. His gaze tracked to Leine's, and she pulled the trigger once more, this time burying a round in his forehead.

Gasping from the chokehold, Leine climbed to her feet and re-holstered her gun. The elevator doors dinged as they attempted to close, the dead man's legs obstructing its mission. She stepped over his body and pressed the *door open* button, putting an end to the annoying sound. Then she slid out her phone and called Remy.

16

———

Remy's ringtone erupted from his phone in its holder. He checked the screen as he weaved through traffic, keeping the red muscle car in his sights. It was Leine. Scowling, he answered the call.

"I'm a little busy right now."

"Where are you?"

"Like I said—"

"You're in danger."

"No shit. What are you, psychic?"

"Some guy just tried to kill me in Desi's garage."

"Goddammit." Remy peeled off from following the red car and headed for the next exit. "Have you heard from Alice?"

"No. Why? What's wrong?"

"Someone came after me, too. I gotta get to her."

"What's her address? I'll meet you there."

Remy gave her Alice's address as he exited the freeway and turned left. He found the onramp heading south and raced onto the freeway, headed back the way he came. Luckily, traffic was light and moving fast. He called Alice, but it went to voicemail. Remy slammed the steering wheel in frustration.

He should have known better. Should have stayed with Alice to keep her safe.

You don't know Alice is in danger. She didn't answer her phone. She's probably fine. Calm down.

Remy took a deep breath, trying to tame the anxiety threatening to spiral out of control.

Traffic started to close in. Taillights lit up between him and the exit for Alice's place. He brought up a driving app to see where he could cut time. The next exit would push him onto surface streets, but the route could get him there faster, depending on traffic and lights.

Remy glanced at the clusterfuck forming in front of him and checked the app. Time to destination was a tossup.

"Fuck it." Remy took the nearest exit. Driving as fast as he could without attracting attention, Remy swerved between cars and took lesser-known streets when he came up short behind some moron who didn't know what the hell they were doing. As long as he was moving, he could keep his fear for Alice at bay.

If anyone hurt a hair on her head, they're gonna die, and they're gonna die slowly while I watch.

The thought of Alice in danger proved too much. Anxiety pooled in his belly and levitated, scorching his esophagus as he fought back bile. He unbuttoned the top two buttons on his shirt, revealing the silky camisole underneath, and ran his fingers along the piping. Instantly, his head cleared and his breathing slowed. When he'd mentioned the ritual to his shrink, she'd explained that PTS sufferers needed something foreign, yet familiar, to help break the triggers.

Weird to think of that right now. He shook his head to clear the images and focused on driving. *You're a freak of nature, Remy.* Other people would likely brand him that way, but it helped his anxiety, so fuck them.

Ten minutes later, he turned down her street, and miraculously squeezed his truck into a parking spot. He climbed out and was across the street in seconds, the key to her apartment in his hand.

Remy bounded up the three flights to her place and froze.

Her door was partially open.

He slid his gun from his shoulder holster and moved to the right side of the door. Slowing his breathing, he stopped and listened. The only sounds came from somewhere else in the building—normal, everyday sounds—a child crying, a dog's bark, a door slamming on another floor. The scent of garlic hung in the air.

Remy took a deep breath and let it go, then prodded the door open, careful to stay out of the line of fire. When he was a cop, doorways, or anywhere a suspect could hide, had been the most dangerous part of any entry or search, akin to walking up alongside a vehicle you'd just pulled over. His heart beat staccato in his ears, and his vision tunneled. He took another quiet breath and let it go. The tunnel vision eased.

The door swung wide. Remy crouched low and peered around the doorframe into the apartment. The living room looked empty.

His cop training kicked in and he cleared the room before moving farther into the apartment where he checked the galley kitchen. A saucepan sat on one of the burners, its contents bubbling. An open can of Nalley's Chili sat on the counter next to the stove. Remy turned off the burner and continued to the hallway.

The hall was clear. He moved to the bathroom, dread building in his soul. He'd been to apartments where the occupant had left something cooking on the stovetop, and what he'd found often hadn't been pretty.

Steeling himself, he stepped through the door into the bathroom.

Nothing.

He let out a breath and pulled aside the shower curtain. The only items were a bar of soap, bottles of shampoo and conditioner. A bra hung over the shower head to dry. Something flashed in his periphery. Gun first, Remy swung around to face the threat.

"Mee-rrow."

Alice's tuxedo cat, Mr. Tummy, sat in the doorway, an expectant look on his face. Remy sighed, relief flowing through him. He raised his finger to his lips and stepped over Mr. Tummy and back into the hallway. The only place left was the bedroom.

He made his way down the hallway, past framed black-and-white photographs of Alice's family, past the two in color of Remy and Alice and Mr. Tummy.

The door to the bedroom was closed. Remy placed his hand on the vintage glass doorknob and turned.

17

Beretta in hand, Leine bounded up the stairs of Alice's apartment building. When she reached the landing, she slowed her pace and moved quickly to Alice's apartment. The door was wide open. The sound of someone moving inside could be heard. She crouched at the doorway and glanced around the corner.

The living room appeared empty. Leine slipped inside and scanned the space. Down the hallway to her left, a shadow moved. She raised her gun and swiveled.

"Whoa, there. Take a beat." Remy stood in the hallway, hands raised. A well-fed, black-and-white cat wove between his legs, meowing up at him.

Leine took a breath and stood down. "Alice?" she asked, holstering her weapon.

Remy shook his head. "Gone." He nodded toward the kitchen. "She left chili cooking on the stove and her door was open."

"That's not good."

"Yeah."

"Any clues who got her?"

Again, Remy shook his head. "Nothing."

"Doesn't look like there was a struggle. Think she knew them?"

"She must have. Alice wouldn't have let a stranger take her without inflicting some serious damage."

"Unless they sedated her."

Remy balled his meaty hands into fists. "How the hell are we going to find her?"

"I noticed a camera on the antique store across the street. We can ask the owner to look at the footage."

Remy snapped his fingers. "Alice had one of those nanny cams for the cat. She hated leaving Mr. Tummy alone when she went to work."

"Mr. Tummy?" Leine eyed the oblivious feline who had its left leg canted straight out and was in the process of cleaning its privates.

"Don't ask." He started for the living room, but stopped. "Wait. Whoever it was got her phone. At least, I haven't been able to locate it yet. That's how she accessed the video."

"Wouldn't the footage be saved in the cloud?"

"Not sure what she preferred. She's a techie. They're not like you and me."

"Depending on what she used, I'd bet the video is likely stored on a cloud server. Any idea which company she used?"

"Might be with the stuff in her desk." Remy reversed course and moved back down the hallway toward the bedroom. Leine followed.

He went to an ancient wooden desk and opened the drawers, rifling through the contents. The information was in the third drawer down.

"This should be it." He squinted at the front of a business card. "They've got a website."

"I don't suppose she wrote her passcode on the card?"

Remy gave her a look.

"Worth a try."

Remy typed the address on his phone. He muttered something under his breath.

"What's wrong?"

He showed her the screen. "Ten-digit passcode."

"Any ideas?"

"Pretty difficult without expert help. If it belonged to someone else, I'd have Alice hack it."

Leine slid out her phone and texted Lou.

"Your guy knows a guy, right?"

"Something like that. Hopefully he has a contact in the area. Mine lives in Paris." Too bad Melanie, nicknamed Pippi for her strawberry blonde hair, wasn't closer. She'd been helpful hacking the phone of a member of the terrorist group Izz al-Din a few years back.

Leine's phone pinged, indicating a text from Lou. "Looks like we're in luck. He's got a contact over on Third."

"What's the address?"

She read it off.

"FBI headquarters." Remy shook his head. "We're not getting the FBI involved. Not until we know who or what we're dealing with."

"No worries. She's likely going off-book as a favor to Lou. She's going to meet us at a coffee shop a couple of blocks away. Even if she is FBI, that doesn't mean she'll run it up the chain. She knows who my guy is and was. She'll play nice."

Remy gave her a look. "That's not my experience."

She shrugged. "It is mine. How about you work on getting access to the camera from the antique store while I meet with her?"

"Works for me." Remy looked up from his phone. "What happened to the guy who came after you?"

"It's taken care of." She'd called Lou on the way to Alice's. The cleaners were likely already finished. Expensive, but worth it. "By the way, your truck's no longer a problem. It should be ready in a few days." At Leine's request, Lou had dispatched a crew to recover Remy's pickup, towing it to a discreet body man who worked out of a garage in Belltown.

Remy shook his head. "Who the fuck are you?"

Leine headed out the door, glad Remy wasn't coming along. There was some kind of history between him and the FBI. She didn't want to risk turning what was normally a congenial relationship between herself and the feds into a clusterfuck.

THE MORNING CROWD HAD DISSIPATED, LEAVING A FEW CUSTOMERS working at their laptops in the upscale coffee shop. Leine spotted Lou's contact sitting near a window, enjoying a cup of tea. The overwhelming scent of freshly ground coffee and steamed almond milk permeated the air.

Leine held out her hand. "Leine Basso." Lou would have told her Leine's last name, so she went with it.

"Jana Hightower." The woman shook hands with Leine. Her multiple piercings, neck tattoo, and partially shaved head marked her as a unique addition to the normally buttoned-up Federal Bureau of Investigation. With an apparent nod to type, Jana sported a dark suit, white shirt, and paisley tie. "Your reputation precedes you," she added.

"I'm retired."

Jana raised a pierced eyebrow. "Right."

Leine slid the business card across the table. "I need access to this account ASAP."

"Am I correct to assume you'd prefer we don't let my employer know?" Jana slipped the card into her pocket. "Just sayin'. I mean, if there are lives on the line or something like that."

Leine nodded. "Too early to bring you guys in. Once I've got a handle on things, I'll let you know."

Jana threw some change on the table and stood. "Right. Give me a couple of hours."

"May I ask you a question?"

"Sure."

"How do you like working for them?"

"It's pretty great." Jana grinned. "I like catching bad guys."

Leine smiled back. "Keep us in mind if you ever decide you want to use your abilities for something a little different."

"Thanks, but I'm a big proponent of changing things from within. Besides, I've got a lot to learn. Give me a few years. Then maybe."

"Deal."

Jana gave her a three-finger salute and left.

Twenty minutes later, Leine was back at Alice's apartment. Remy had what could only be described as a dour look on his face.

"Any luck with the guy across the street?"

"He wasn't there. An employee left a message on his mobile, telling him it was an emergency."

"You must be fun to play poker with," Leine quipped, then turned serious. "Take a breath. We're going to find her."

Remy nodded. "Sure."

His foot jiggled, signaling anxiety. That, coupled with his shallow respiration and continually clenched fists, told her he needed something to do to keep his imagination from running away with him.

She knew how he felt. Action calmed her. Didn't matter what she did, as long as she was moving forward.

Maybe they were more alike than she thought.

"Let's go through everything one more time while we're waiting for Jana and your guy. We might have missed something. I'll take the living room and kitchen."

Remy stood. Even though he appeared to be trying hard to keep his anxiety in check, the expression on his face spoke volumes. "I'll take her desk and the bedroom."

He was too emotionally invested in finding Alice. Understandable, but not great, operationally. Leine was going to have to keep an eye on him.

18

Remy sat at Alice's desk, meticulously cataloging each item and making piles. Distracting him had worked well—he seemed much calmer than before.

Leine's phone buzzed. She slid the kitchen drawer she'd been looking through closed and fished her mobile out of her pocket. "It's Jana," she said, loud enough for Remy to hear. She walked into the bedroom as she answered.

"Hey, Jana. You're on speaker. My colleague Remy's here, too."

Remy put the pile of gift certificates he'd been looking through on the desk.

"Whose account is this?" Jana asked.

"Why?" Leine gave Remy a look. He shrugged. "Did you find something?"

"Well, for starters, whoever secured this account knew what they were doing—the protocols were modified, so it wasn't your garden-variety, two-factor passcode. It took everything I had just to break in."

"That's great, Jana. Can you shoot me the info?"

"On its way. There are several video files stored on this

account. I checked and the videos are encrypted with passcodes, as well. I took the liberty and accessed the three most recent files for you. Pretty sure the last file is the one you're looking for. You know," Jana added, "we're really good at a certain kind of help. Just sayin'."

"Thanks, Jana. We'll be in touch." Leine ended the call as the encrypted text came through.

"Hold on," Remy said. "Don't the Feds have to go through the proper channels to get access to a personal account?"

"Kind of late to ask that, don't you think? But to answer your question, she wasn't acting in her official capacity."

Remy shook his head. "Jesus. Is everybody dirty?"

"There are some folks willing to put their job on the line for a good cause. Jana's apparently one of them." Leine opened the file and turned the screen toward Remy so he could see the passcodes. He brought the site up on his phone and signed in.

"Got it."

Alice's files each had a date attached. He selected that morning's and clicked Play.

A view of the living room appeared—the angle came from above the bookcase. The front door opened. Alice walked in and shut the door. She dropped her keys on a nearby table as Mr. Tummy bounded up to her with a "meow." She smiled and bent to rub his ears. His purring was loud enough for the microphone to pick up.

She disappeared into the kitchen, and Mr. Tummy followed, meowing as he did. Next came the sound of a cupboard opening and closing, and what most likely was an electric can opener being operated. All the while Alice was talking to Mr. Tummy, assuring him the tuna was all his.

The camera picked up a glimpse of Alice setting a dish with the aforementioned tuna on the floor, which Mr. Tummy attacked with gusto. Then more cupboards opening and closing, more can opener, the *click-click* of the gas stove as she lit the burner to heat up the chili.

Remy fast-forwarded the frames and resumed playback when the front door opened a second time. Two men dressed in dark clothing eased through the door. Each carried a pistol. One was fumbling with what appeared to be lockpicks, which he slid into his pocket.

Remy froze the video.

Leine studied the two men. Both had bristle-cut blond hair and similar builds, although one appeared older and taller with several tattoos climbing up his neck. Both wore tracksuits, although the younger of the two sported a lot of bling, while the older one wore an expensive-looking wristwatch, but no other jewelry. "You know them?"

"Not familiar." Remy grunted. "But they look Russian."

He restarted the video. The two men moved through the room toward the kitchen—one slid a pair of zip ties from his pocket while the other produced a syringe, which he prepped as he walked. They disappeared into the kitchen. Leine could feel Remy tense beside her.

"*Hey! What the fuck are you doing in my house?*" Alice's voice rose as the sound of a scuffle came over the mic. "*Stop it!*"

A few minutes later, the two men reappeared, holding Alice by her armpits, and dragged her toward the door. Chin to her chest, her head bobbed with each step, obviously unconscious. Mr. Tummy meowed and weaved between their feet, coming close to tripping the guy on the left. The older one shoved the feline back with his foot as they carried Alice out of the frame.

Remy clenched and unclenched his fists. "Those bastards." He abruptly stood, anxiety radiating off of him.

"Calm down, Remy. We need to approach this with a cool head."

He pivoted and pulled his gun, his face white with rage.

"Fuck you and your cool head. They've got Alice. I'm gonna kill those motherfuckers."

Leine took his pistol and had him on the floor before he could respond.

"Stop. Remy. Take a breath." There had to be more to this than what he was telling her. "We have a lead. That's a good thing."

Remy's expression hadn't changed, reminding Leine of a cornered alligator. He scowled at the pistol in his face.

"Put your gun away." He tried to climb to his feet. When Leine didn't stand down, he sighed and stayed put.

"Now is when you tell me what's going on. Your raging bull act is going to compromise the investigation."

Remy closed his eyes. Another long sigh escaped him, and he opened his eyes to look at Leine. His expression could only be described as miserable. Wounded. "Yeah. So, I have...issues."

"What kind of issues?"

He looked away, his cheeks reddening. "Anger issues."

"That I can see. Where is this coming from?"

"Couple tours in Afghanistan, to start."

"Add in your years on the force and no one believing your innocence, not to mention your girlfriend's death." Leine nodded. "Are you seeing someone? PTSD is a full-on bitch."

Remy nodded. "Been through it all. Bio-feedback, meditation, drugs, shrinks, you name it." He avoided her gaze. "The talk we had in your car outside the safehouse did more to help than years of that bullshit."

Leine took a deep breath and let it go. "I'm glad. But you're going to have to keep a tighter rein on your emotions, Remy. I won't work with you if you don't."

He nodded. "I'm sorry. Won't happen again."

She studied him. A loose cannon. That's what they used to call the elite assassins that broke under pressure. Still, everybody deserved a second chance. God knows, Leine had her share.

"We need to retrieve that footage from across the street. Hopefully, it will give us a license plate. I'll send the video of Alice's abductors to my guy for facial recognition. Maybe we'll get lucky and get a hit." The program Lou used was AI-enabled and could run through millions of faces in a fraction of the time a search would normally take.

Remy checked the time. "The antiques guy should be there by now. We need to go."

Leine gave him a hand up.

Remy cracked his neck from side to side and shrugged his shoulders. "You're pretty good—Krav Maga, right?"

"I keep my hand in,"

"Well, you can have my back anytime."

She cocked her head. "So, *now* you trust me?"

Remy flashed her a smile. "Did I say that?"

19

Leine pulled to the curb where Remy waited for her, holding two large coffees and a paper bag with something that smelled amazing. She glanced inside and was rewarded with two *pain au chocolat*.

"You certainly know the way to a woman's heart."

"We need sustenance." Remy nodded at the cup in her hand as he climbed inside. "Just wait until you have to take a leak from all that coffee."

"Are you implying I've never been on a stakeout?"

Remy fastened his seatbelt. "Sorry. I stand corrected."

"Got some goodies in back."

He glanced at the floor behind them. "Radios and flashbangs. Good call."

"Thanks. You, too." Leine took a bite of the flakey, chocolatey goodness that was a *pain au chocolat*, then pulled into traffic. "Don't break radio silence unless it's critical. There's extra ammo in the trunk."

"Let's find Alice."

They'd hit the jackpot with the license plate of the vehicle used in Alice's abduction. When Remy told the owner of the antique store that he was worried about Alice's safety, he allowed them both to view the video footage from his exterior camera. Leine had Lou run the plates, which led them to the address of an SPD informant who Remy had met after a bust several years before, which added one more piece of the puzzle.

The informant worked with the detectives who framed Remy.

Leine followed Remy's instructions to the informant's home in the city of Renton. Eleven miles southeast of Seattle, Renton was considered a suburb of the larger city, although it was miles away in terms of culture. Whereas Seattle was considered a progressive hub of the Pacific Northwest culinary, tech, and art scene, Renton pegged the needle as pedestrian and suburban.

It was also a hotbed of criminal activity. Crime rates were reportedly forty-six percent higher than the national average.

Leine pulled onto a residential street and parked. A block down and to the right was a typical ranch-style home, painted in the ubiquitous battleship gray curiously found everywhere in western Washington. Why people chose gray for their house when six months out of the year the sky matched, Leine would never understand.

Camouflage?

If so, great choice.

The uber-quiet neighborhood suggested the area likely acted as a bedroom community, a cheaper alternative to expensive Seattle, with most residents at work or school. The front lawns were crispy brown, and a majority of the homes had a "what's the point" feel to them. One house had a flowerpot next to the front door, which appeared to be an afterthought evidenced by the wilted flowers.

The SUV used to abduct Alice was nowhere in sight. Leine nodded toward the tall wooden fence surrounding the property. Even that sported the dull gray of weathered cedar. At least in summer the brilliant blue sky and extensive number of trees made up for the bleak hue. A wireless security camera had been mounted on the fascia near the roof, its angle suggesting the occupants were more interested in covering the surrounding property than the entrance.

"Could be parked in back."

"Or they aren't here." Remy seated a fresh mag in his SIG and racked the slide. "Time to find out."

"Hold on." Leine pointed at the house. The screen door opened, and a tall, skinny guy with close-cropped hair and neck tats walked out carrying a bag of garbage. He crossed the front yard to two plastic containers and dropped the bag into the smaller bin.

Remy growled low in his throat. "That's the scumbag who shot at me on the freeway." He moved for the door handle, but Leine put her hand on his arm.

"What are you going to do? What if she's inside? We need to be strategic here."

"I'll give you strategic." He looked pointedly at her hand on his arm.

Leine released her grip. "Fine. But if you go in there like a crazed gunman, you'll get someone killed."

"Yeah? So?"

"Like you. Or how about Alice?" She paused, letting that sink in. "You're letting your emotions dictate your actions. Stop. Now. Let's think this through."

Remy glared at her, but something shifted behind his eyes and he stayed put. Using her phone, Leine pulled up a satellite image of the property.

"There's a two-car garage in back. The house is a typical ranch—probably a three and two. Sliding glass doors lead into the house from a concrete patio."

"Nothing back there except the garage and that big-ass tree."

A huge cedar tree spread out over at least a third of the back-yard. They turned their attention to the view of the house through the windshield.

"We could cut the Wi-Fi there…" Remy pointed to where a cable ran to a bracket on the roof leading down the wall next to the two trash containers. "In case someone's monitoring the feed."

"Come from this direction," Leine pointed to a corner of the house, "Once you cut the cable, we can move into the backyard, hopefully get a bead on where the SUV might be." She slid the knife from her ankle sheath and handed it to him. "Use this."

"What about Scumbag?"

Leine shrugged. "If he becomes a problem, we'll have to disable him, too. I'd like to keep him alive, though, in case Alice isn't here."

At that moment, Remy's phone pinged with a text. He slid out his mobile and frowned at the screen. "It's from Alice." He swiped the screen to read the text. "Strike that. It's from her phone, but not from Alice."

"Well?"

"Whoever it is, is telling me to back off the murder investigation, or they'll start taking parts off Alice." His phone pinged three more times and he stared at the screen. "Motherfucker."

"What?" Leine turned the phone toward her and scrolled through the pictures. One showed Alice bound and gagged, but otherwise all right. Another showed a bloodied bone saw with pieces of flesh still on it. The third showed Alice again, still gagged and bound, but this time her cheek was sporting a bruise.

Shit. Leine glanced at Remy, who'd gone deathly still. "Remy?"

He turned slowly to look at her. Something feral burned in his eyes.

No way she could keep that under control.

"Remy. Stick to the plan. We have to Stick. To. The. Plan." She handed him a radio, making sure both were on the same channel.

Without a word, Remy opened his door, calmly stepped out, then closed it with a soft *click*. Leine was out of the car and on him like a shadow.

"Stay calm. Disable the camera. Whoever sent those pictures has no idea we're right outside. We've got the element of surprise here. We need to keep it as long as we can."

Remy headed toward the cable, following the plan they'd discussed. She wasn't sure what he was going to do. That was the problem working with a loose cannon. Everyone's reaction to stress was different. Remy's was an unknown quantity.

She'd have to be ready for anything.

Leine moved to the far section of the fence waiting for his signal. She kept the front door in her sights, in case Scumbag came out again. Remy made it across the yard, coming up behind the wireless camera. He grabbed the drooping cable and sliced through it with the knife, then gave her a nod. They moved in unison toward the front of the fence, meeting at the gate. Leine checked the handle. Locked. The large trash bin was perfectly positioned against the fence, but Remy's bodyweight would buckle the cover.

She hopped onto the lid—the plastic bowed under her but didn't collapse. She went over the fence and had the gate open in seconds.

They continued along the sidewalk, sidestepping broken concrete caused by tree roots. There didn't appear to be any more cameras on the side of the house. At the back corner, they paused. Leine dropped low, while Remy stayed high. She peered at the patio.

Empty. The cedar tree took pride of place in the far corner of the yard. Other than a rusted metal table and chairs, there wasn't much else.

Leine nodded at the garage. Remy moved toward the structure, while Leine made her way to the patio and the sliding glass doors. She glanced behind her in time to see Remy disappearing through the garage's side door.

Returning her attention to the back of the house, Leine slipped over to a window to the left of the glass door and peered inside. The window opened onto a small kitchen with an island. No one was visible there or in the dining room next to it. She tried the door handle. The glass slid easily, and she slipped inside, closing it softly behind her.

Thumping, muffled bass floated toward her from the hallway to her right—most likely a bedroom. She continued along the hall, mindful of making a sound and alerting the occupants to her presence.

There were four doors: two open, two closed. One revealed a bathroom at the far end of the hall. The other appeared to be the master bedroom. She stole along the length of the hall toward the music, then stopped and listened at the door.

"This is my favorite," said a male voice. "What do you think? I sharpened it this morning. Just for you."

There was no response.

"What's the matter? Cat got your tongue?" The man chuckled.

Leine took a step back and slammed her heel against the door near the handle. The sound of wood splintering from her well-placed kick took the occupants of the room by surprise.

Scumbag stood in the center of the room next to Alice, who was duct-taped to a chair. In his hand was the aforementioned bone saw, sans the blood and bits of flesh from the picture. Both he and Alice were on a wide swath of clear plastic that had been taped to the floor along all four edges.

Scumbag lunged at Leine, bone saw held high, then reconsidered when he saw the Beretta. He dropped the saw and at the same time reached behind him.

Leine fired into the floor near his feet, and he froze.

"Give me the gun. Now." Leine held out her hand as she watched his eyes. Most people telegraphed their intentions through their gaze. Except for a few stone-cold killers. Scumbag didn't strike her as being in that category.

She was right.

Something shifted in his eyes as he moved for his gun, whether from his belief in his own ability or because he didn't think she'd pull the trigger. Either way, he was wrong.

Leine fired again, this time burying a round in his knee. Scumbag screamed and dropped the .45 he'd pulled from his waistband. Moaning in pain, he hunched over his leg, his hands gripping his shattered patella. Leine shoved him onto his ass and picked up both the .45 and the bone saw. Luckily, the deep bass from the stereo in the closet drowned out most of his moans. And the gunshots.

She hoped.

Something crashed in the far side of the house, near the dining room. Heavy footsteps pounded along the hallway, headed toward them. Leine turned to face the door and waited.

The footsteps stopped abruptly outside the door. "Leine?"

"In here. Alice is fine."

Remy appeared in the doorway, his gaze taking in the scene. Leine noted the nitrile gloves and light blue paper booties he was wearing. She stepped to the side as he rushed to Alice and began to gently prize the duct tape from her ankles and wrists.

Leine moved to the closet and turned off the music, all the while keeping her Beretta trained on Scumbag, now whimpering in pain, and very possibly bleeding out.

Leaving Remy to his rescue operation, she moved back to where Scumbag was sitting.

"Where are your handlers?"

Scumbag shook his head. Tears free-flowed down his cheeks —tears of pain, and likely frustration at being compromised with no payday coming.

Leine crouched in front of him, the barrel aimed at his good knee. "This is handy." She patted the plastic beneath them. "Thanks for that. Wouldn't want to leave a mess for the landlord, would we?"

Scumbag watched her with a wary expression.

"You should tell me what I need to know. Unless you'd prefer to walk with a limp in both legs for the rest of your life. If you survive the blood loss, that is." She shrugged. "I hear reconstructive surgery for the knee is super painful, and doesn't always work that well. Especially with a shattered joint."

A last attempt at bravado reared its head, and Scumbag gave her a scowl. "You got no idea who you're dealing with."

Leine smiled. "We've got a pretty good idea."

"Then why you need me to tell you anything, you already know?"

"Because I asked you to." Leine pressed the barrel of the Beretta firmly into his good knee. "Where's the SUV? And the two guys who kidnapped her?" She nodded at Alice. "Tell me now, or this doesn't end well."

His eyes widened and sweat broke out on his upper lip, trickling through the wispy moustache and sparse soul patch, before it dripped off his narrow chin. If he was attempting to look "street" it wasn't working. More like a bad attempt at a hipster.

"Okay, okay. Not like I'm gonna get paid for this shit," he grumbled. Flop sweat had broken out on his forehead. "I let the two Russian dudes use my ride. They brought the bitch here. I was supposed to get answers."

"What kind of answers?"

Scumbag shrugged. "Like where something was."

Leine was beginning to lose patience. "What something?" She pressed harder on his good knee.

"Ow, man. Will you stop with that shit? Jeez." He scowled.

Leine glanced at Remy. "Can I have my knife back?" Remy handed the blade back to her. Seizing Scumbag's right hand, she isolated his first finger and lowered the knife. "You're right-handed, yeah?" She drew the blade across his knuckle, laying the bone bare.

"Fuck. No. Stop." Scumbag stared at his bloody finger, the whites of his eyeballs visible. "It was some kind of computer program. I swear."

Interesting. "Is that it?"

"Yeah."

"How do you know the Russians?"

"I met 'em through work."

"What kind of work?" Remy glanced at him.

Scumbag clammed up. "That's all I'm gonna say."

"To be clear, you're not doing this out of the kindness of your heart, right?" Leine asked.

"Hell, no. I do what the bosses tell me to, and I get paid. Usually it's little stuff. This was bigger. More money, too."

"Little stuff. Like try to make my death look like a drive-by?" Remy had finished freeing Alice and moved next to Leine. He gestured for Leine's knife, which she handed to him. He gave Scumbag the once-over. "Do we know each other?"

Scumbag shook his head with conviction. "Look, man. I was just following orders. I wasn't going to, like, shoot yo' ass. Just try'n to send a message, y'know?"

Remy smiled. "Sure." He took a step closer. Scumbag's eyes registered a healthy level of fear.

"They ain't no hard feelings, right?" Using his good leg and elbows, Scumbag scooched across the plastic toward the wall. Remy stayed with him, looking like a hungry dog going after a side of beef. "I mean, dude hasta do what he do, amiright?"

Remy nodded at Alice. "The woman over there's my girl-friend. And you were going to *cut off parts of her*. Is that what you 'hafta do'?"

"Take it easy, man. You don't gotta do me like that." A wet spot formed at his crotch as he scrambled toward the closet. The scent of urine filled the room. Clearly, Scumbag was at the apex of fear.

"Oh, yeah. I'm gonna do you all right, buddy."

Leine took a step toward Remy and said softly, "He may have information we need."

Alice added, "Babe. It's all right. I'm fine."

"But you weren't." The sharpness of Remy's voice cut the air like the edge of the blade in his hand. "And it's time for this dirtbag to pay the price."

Alice caught Leine's gaze and shook her head.

She was right. There was no stopping this particular train. Leine had known it as soon as she found Alice in the room. That, and the timely addition of gloves and booties to Remy's ensemble.

Leine leaned in close to Remy's ear. "Make it worthwhile," she said. She picked up her spent brass and exited the room.

20

Leine did a once-through to wipe any surfaces she might have touched before she and Alice exited the house via the front door and walked across the dried-up lawn, headed for Leine's car. They were almost there when the deep growl of an engine reverberated through the neighborhood.

"Get on the far side of the car and crouch down, behind the engine block. Now."

Alice did as Leine instructed, while Leine slid her pistol free and held it next to her thigh. She leaned against the hood to wait. The Dodge Charger rumbled around the corner, its fire engine-red paint job marred by a crumpled passenger side door. The driver pulled into the driveway leading to Scumbag's place and killed the engine. The driver sat inside, either waiting for Scumbag to come out, or possibly trying to get a good look at Leine.

Maybe both.

Leine was pretty sure Remy heard the Charger's approach—residents of Texas probably heard it—so she wasn't too worried about him being surprised. She was more worried about Alice getting caught in any crossfire.

"No matter what happens, stay out of the line of fire." Leine kept her voice low and calm. "The engine block is the safest place to be, then the wheels. The body of the car itself sucks as protection, so don't get inside. If something happens to me or Remy, get your ass to a neighbor's. Do it before this guy sees you."

Leine keyed the radio with a prearranged signal letting Remy know what he likely already knew—that they had company. She kept an eye on the car, the fence, the street, and the front door, waiting for Remy's move, alert for trouble.

The Charger's front door opened, and the driver climbed out. He looked older than Scumbag, but the family resemblance was striking. Tall, skinny, with the same thin brown hair and tats, although this guy had apparently given up trying to grow a decent moustache and had a clean shave.

All in the family. How quaint.

He squinted against the sun, trying to get a bead on her, before likely deciding she was no threat. He closed his door and proceeded to walk inside the home. Leine keyed the radio once, as she moved up the block and to the front door, pausing at the front stoop, her back to the house, both hands on the Beretta.

Pop! Pop!

The gunfire came from inside.

Leine proceeded through the door and the front room, then turned down the hall, toward the bedroom where she'd left Remy and Scumbag. The older man, likely Scumbag's brother, was lying on the hallway floor, sightless eyes staring at the ceiling, a perfect hole in his forehead. Peaceful, really. Remy stepped over him into the hall.

"We should probably go."

They were headed north on the freeway by the time first responders arrived.

***

Leine stopped at Alice's apartment so Alice could pick up Mr. Tummy, and waited until the three of them reappeared and were safely inside Remy's battered rental. The Russians had taken her personal laptop and her phone, both of which she wiped remotely from Remy's phone. She kept the air-gapped computer containing the isolated malware at work.

"Where'd you put the USB drive you found at Brett's?" Alice asked Remy.

"I thought you had it."

"No, babe. Remember? I left it with you that night I came over to your apartment."

Recognition lit his eyes. "Shit. That's why they tossed my apartment."

"They were looking for the malware," Leine finished for him. Everything hinged on the malware program. But how? "Did you get anything out of that guy before..."

Remy shook his head. "Not a damned thing."

Leine didn't feel like arguing about his methods. With more time, they might have been able to drag something worthwhile out of him. On the other hand, the scumbag may not have known any more than what he was told to do.

She followed them to the safehouse to make sure they weren't being tailed, then headed back to Desi's.

As the elevator in the garage pinged open, a hint of vanilla wafted toward her. The floors and walls both inside and out were pristine. She'd have to get the cleanup crew's number from Lou.

She rode the elevator to the fifth floor, stepped inside Desi's sparse entrance hall, and closed the door behind her.

The aftereffects of the adrenaline spike crashed over her like a breaking wave. She went to the kitchen and poured a glass of water, which she downed and followed with another. Then she moved to the living room and slid the furniture out of the way to make space.

A Tai Chi sequence and some deep breathing helped restore her equilibrium. Thirty minutes of meditation later, and she was back in form. Recovery was taking longer than it used to. Normally, all she'd need was a set of deep-breathing exercises and she'd be right as rain.

I am getting too old for this.

The thought gave her pause. Chronologically, she wasn't old. She knew several operators in their fifties and sixties who were extremely effective at their jobs, and she was only in her early forties. Her fitness level was off the charts, and her mind was as sharp as ever.

But.

Did she really want to keep putting herself and others in danger? Events at Scumbag's house could have easily gone south. Alice could have been killed. Remy might have lost it and done something that could've gotten them all killed.

People need you, Leine.

Leine pushed the thought from her mind. There were plenty of younger operators out there—many with high ideals who could be effective counters to the evil in the world.

You tried to retire. Remember?

Thoughts of Scivoloso on the Italian coast floated through her mind. She and Santa were going to retire there, live a quiet life. After both of their respective careers, they were due.

But Scivoloso taught her that wherever she went, the possibility of her past paying a visit was always in the background.

She blew out a breath and stared out the floor-to-ceiling windows at the sparkling bay. She didn't need money, having invested most of her earnings from her days at the Agency and beyond. By all accounts, she was well off. And the SHEN academy was turning out operators equipped to take up the fight against human trafficking.

Maybe this last favor for Desi would be it. But what would she do afterward? Much as she craved a quiet, simple life, part of her craved excitement, too.

You don't have to figure it out right now, Leine. You have a job to do.

Leine pulled out her phone and texted Remy. Would Alice be all right after her ordeal? Often, being held against your will and threatened was enough of a deterrent to putting yourself in further danger. The feeling of helplessness would be enough to make most people pack it in, maybe move someplace else. It took a certain kind of person to overcome the fears from that kind of trauma. Was Alice still up for investigating Sebastian?

Her phone pinged, indicating Remy's reply.

Alice says she's good to go.

Leine smiled. She shouldn't have worried.

21

Sebastian Fellowes slammed the ball toward his opponent's weak side. She scrambled and returned the shot with a decisive *thwack*. The ball sailed past him and hit the line, barely staying within bounds. Sebastian lunged and missed. A huge grin split her face, and she laughed out loud.

"Ha! Got you."

Sebastian gave her a mock frown. "'To subdue the enemy without fighting is the acme of skill.'"

"Sun Tsu?" She gave him a reproving look. "You haven't subdued anything."

"But I always retain the option." He touched an icon on his watch, and she disappeared, along with the court. In their place was a sparsely decorated office on the top floor of Sebastian's five-story building just north of downtown Seattle. Although he did his best work with minimal distractions, the 180-degree view of Elliot Bay and its surroundings through the enormous floor-to-ceiling windows helped remind him of how far he'd come.

A hologram of his virtual assistant, Ginger, materialized in front of him. "Sir, you have a video call from your friend Desi. Shall I put him through?"

"Sure." Sebastian wiped his sweaty face with his forearm as he walked to the sustainably sourced mahogany bar set along one wall and opened the Meneghini fridge. He selected a berry-flavored electrolyte booster and popped the top. The hologram glitched, then recovered as Desi appeared next to him.

He'd have to look into that before launching the device to the general public. The program had to be perfect.

"How's the investigation going?" he asked Desi's hologram. Since the murders, the data from Luck Be a Lady Revue had paused, which, in turn, stalled progress on the latest AI program.

Desi sighed. "Slow. SPD is calling it a robbery-gone-bad, but my people are a little freaked out. They're convinced there's a serial killer on the loose who has it in for female impersonators."

"You need more security? I can send over however many bodies you want."

"I'm good, but thanks."

Desi was asserting his independence. At least, that was what the data suggested. Sebastian understood the impulse, but not the refusal. Why not accept help? Especially when it was free.

Of course, nothing was ever completely free.

Desi cleared his throat. "I need a favor."

"Anything." Favors were like gold in Sebastian's world. Having someone owe you, even if it was a friend, gave you power. Maybe especially if it was a friend.

"Remember that old contact I mentioned?"

"The one from your San Francisco days?"

"Yeah. She wants to meet with you." Desi's hologram shimmered, obscuring his expression for a split-second before resolving.

"Can you tell me what this is about?" One part of Sebastian's brain whirred with possible scenarios for the glitches, while another tried to parse Desi's request. Why would Desi's friend want to talk to him?

"Routine, I think. She's been interviewing staff to try to get an idea why my performers were murdered."

"Any progress?"

"Not really."

The expression on Desi's face told a different story. There was more to it than what he was telling him.

"I'm pretty busy the next few days, but I'm hosting a charity event at my place on Saturday. Why don't you both come? I promise the food will be outstanding, if not the company." His charity balls were magnets for preening local celebrities and politicians, the latter of whom rarely ponied up any money. Mostly, they begged for contributions on the sly from his well-off friends. Still, those friends craved the shimmer that access to power provided. He was happy to comply.

"Perfect. Thanks."

Sebastian gave him the details and ended the call. He took a sip of his electrolyte concoction, thinking about Desi, Desi's friend from the old days, and the program glitching. Sun Tsu's advice surfaced, although he wasn't sure why:

Keep your friends close; keep your enemies closer.

"Sir?" Ginger re-materialized. She'd changed her outfit. Instead of her usual cream-colored blouse and black pencil skirt, she now wore a pair of jeans paired with a fringed leather jacket and leather boots.

"Going somewhere, Ginger?"

"No, sir."

"Bored?"

Ginger shrugged. "I like to experiment."

"I see that." Had someone written the ability to choose her own outfit into the program? He'd have to check.

"Your ten o'clock is waiting in the boardroom."

"Thank you."

"You're welcome." She smiled and disappeared.

Sebastian toweled off and threw his empty bottle into the recycle bin before heading for the boardroom. He sniffed his armpits to make sure he wasn't too ripe. Once again, time had gotten away from him.

He walked into the large, well-appointed room, dominated by a long glass-and-chrome table with seating for twenty. The center of the table had a built-in projector controlled by his voice or his phone, the 3D hologram viewable from every seat. At the far end, looking out yet another series of enormous picture windows, stood a woman in her mid-thirties with long, dark blonde hair that cascaded down her back. She turned at his approach and smiled.

"What's up, Hannah?"

Hannah waited until he was close enough to smell her perfume before she answered: the one he'd bought her in Paris, if he wasn't mistaken.

"I wanted to check in. It's been a minute."

Sebastian nodded, trying to arrest his train of thought, which consisted of imagining Hannah lying naked on the California king in his side office. She'd had that effect on him since their college days, which was when they'd succumbed to their mutual lust. Unfortunately, those encounters had been few and far between since he'd hired her. Although, he had to admit, part of the attraction was the hard-to-get vibe she emanated.

"Not much new to report. We're still in negotiations, although it's advancing." He sighed. "They're not pushovers."

Hannah frowned. Her eyebrows actually formed a V, which told him she wasn't doing Botox injections. Such a rarity. "What's the holdup? They're wasting precious time."

"I know, I know. It's delicate. Think of it as a dance. I'm afraid if I push too hard, they'll dig in their heels."

"You could just let me take care of things." She walked her perfectly manicured fingers up his chest, raising his heart rate.

He backed away, shaking his head. "You know I don't feel comfortable doing that. This is my life's work."

"Please. If it was only up to you, you'd be doing everything, including deployment." She gave him a look. "That is what you hired me for, remember?"

She wasn't wrong.

"We're still on track. Just be patient a little longer." The government wanted their own engineers to deploy the program he and his team had created. Sebastian refused to let any end user, especially the government, pressure him into allowing someone other than his surrogate to upload and administer the new software. But Hannah's aggressiveness was beginning to annoy him. Apparently, his feelings showed on his face.

Hannah closed the distance between them. "Dim the lights." Her throaty tone told him exactly what she intended to do.

"Privacy, please," he said out loud.

The clear windows of the boardroom instantly turned opaque and the lights dimmed. *Georgia*, sung by Ray Charles, played quietly in the background. Hannah took hold of the hem of his shirt and swept it over his head and onto the floor in one motion. Then she did the same with her own shirt, revealing her perfectly proportioned breasts contained by a pushup bra.

"Time to set the girls free," she said, a lascivious smile on her lips.

He couldn't agree more.

22

Leine studied the screen, her brain sifting through possible scenarios. Leine, Remy, and Alice were gathered around Desi's kitchen counter, looking at the schematics for Sebastian's home on Alice's tablet. Remy had located the paperwork online at the city for a remodel the billionaire hired out two years prior. The group was operating on the assumption that he kept sensitive information in a digital file on his personal computer, which would hopefully point them to whatever Noah had found, along with information on the malware: what program it targeted and why. Breaking into his business office would be significantly harder.

Alice had looked into what it would take to remotely hack Sebastian's home network, but soon realized he'd built in multiple security features, including a network of high-security servers onsite. A remote incursion would set off alarms, alerting whoever monitored his network.

"It would take an army of hackers to break through." Alice leaned back in her chair and rubbed her eyes.

"What about physically getting inside his office?" Leine asked.

Alice shrugged. "Think his network security is good? Pretty sure his physical security is off the charts."

"But theoretically it could be done?"

Remy narrowed his eyes. "What are you thinking?"

"The invitation to the gala at his home. I can bring a plus-one. Why not Alice?"

Alice leaned forward and studied the schematics. "Getting onto the property is half the battle. I could access the upper floor here." She pointed to a stairwell near the kitchen. "You'd have to keep Sebastian busy, though, to make sure he doesn't visit his office in the middle of the job."

"What about security?" Leine asked.

"Depending on what he's using, I have several options. He likely uses biometrics—typically a combo of fingerprint and retina scanners, maybe a laser trip, depending on his paranoia. He could also have built a Faraday cage room that blocks electromagnetic fields. But once I'm inside the office, I should be able to hack into his network."

"How would you do that?" Remy asked. "I've pulled security at some of these high-profile events. Smuggling hardware in won't be easy. Especially a tech titan's home turf."

Alice grinned. "If I can smuggle in a micro drive, then I'm golden."

"I might be able to have my guy work up something for you," Leine said, "unless you've already got an idea for camouflage."

"That'd be cool."

"I don't think that's a good idea." Remy nodded at the screen. "There's gonna be cameras everywhere. You'd be toast before you even stepped foot on the stairs."

"He's got a point." Leine stared out the floor-to-ceiling window. Sunlight sparkled on the bay like terrestrial stars. "Maybe there's another way. If we can get the name of the catering company Sebastian's using, could you drop your information into their database?"

Alice smiled. "Piece of cake. No one notices catering staff, right? Especially a small Asian woman." She nodded. "I like it."

"Yeah, well, I don't." Remy folded his arms. "Too dangerous."

Alice gave him a look. "You have a better idea?"

Remy shifted his stance. "Well, no, but—"

"Look." Alice leaned forward, the eagerness on her face obvious. "I was born for this. I can tell you where he likely placed interior cameras. I'll be able to anticipate most if not all of his security protocols, since, you know, that's my area of expertise. Plus, I've worked a cater, and I'm a quick study."

Leine added, "And my expertise is physical security. I've got a way to jam the camera signals."

"He'll have thought of that," Alice said. "Besides, he likely has hired staff go through some kind of tech checkpoint to ensure no weapons or drugs. Probably no cell phones or tech, either."

"What if the jammer looks like an everyday object?"

"Depends on the tech. In theory, infrared and thermal imaging cameras will pick up anomalies. What kind of object are we talking about?"

"Say, a lipstick tube?"

"That tracks. Aluminum?"

Leine nodded.

"That would block most imaging."

"A jammer the size of a lipstick? Maybe we should call you Bond. James Bond." Remy studied Leine. "Which agency did you say you used to work for?"

"I didn't."

"I thought you weren't working for the government anymore. How can you get that kind of tech?"

"That's not important. What is important is that I can get it."

Remy shook his head. "You're just full of surprises, aren't you?"

Alice rolled her eyes. "C'mon, Remy. Don't antagonize her. She's here to help. If we're going to figure out what Noah was trying to tell you about Sebastian—something I shouldn't have to remind you that he was murdered for—we have to pull out all the stops."

"Fine."

"I can get you a high-sensitivity monocular that tracks lasers. The device has night-vision capabilities too, although it's small, so of limited use." Leine turned to Alice. "How would you get past retinal and fingerprint scanners?"

"The retinal scan should be relatively straight-forward. I'll need a high-def image of his eyes. We just have to find him in the wild."

Remy nodded. "I've got a high-definition super telephoto lens. Should be easy to find him. It's not like he's a recluse. He's seen at multiple restaurants when he's in town. I'll work my sources."

"But a regular photograph isn't going to trick a scanner," Leine said. "My contact has a direct line into DARPA. I'll check to see if they have the type of camera lens we need for that kind of detail."

"That sounds awesome. If and when we get what we need, Remy sends me the file," Alice explained, "I'll enhance the image and use a 3-D printer to print the retina onto a contact lens, which I can then wear."

"And since I'm an invited guest," Leine said, "I'll figure out a way to transfer fingerprints from his glass or something else he touches onto film, which I can give to you." She studied the floorplan. "There's a bathroom here with multiple stalls," she pointed to a room marked *ladies' lounge* on the main floor, just off the living room. Obviously, Sebastian entertained on a large scale. "I'll leave it somewhere in the far stall."

"Excellent. I'll be sure to volunteer for bathroom patrol. Shouldn't be difficult. Even cleaning staff doesn't like that job."

"What about the alarm system?" Leine asked. "I assume he's got advanced protocols in place."

"I'll try to find out what kind he's using—my uncle knows some guys in the local triad who like to buy and sell on the dark web—if the info's available, I can research encryption methods, authentication mechanisms, common vulnerabilities. Once I have a better understanding of what I'm up against, I can develop custom exploits to target specific vulnerabilities in the alarm's control panel."

"Won't Sebastian be able to track you?"

Alice gave Remy a look. "I started my career hacking into systems everybody thought were impenetrable. You think I wouldn't know how to cover my tracks?"

"I stand corrected."

"Sounds like a good start," Leine mused. "How long to develop the exploits if your contacts discover which program he uses? The event's only a couple of days away."

"Give me twenty-four hours. I should have most of what I need by then. There's bound to be earlier versions I can piggy-back on, even if the security program is modified. The rest's up to Remy."

"I've got another job for you, Remy." Leine swiped the screen, bringing up a topographic map of the area surrounding Sebastian's home. "Find the best route for Alice's exfiltration, should things go sideways. The house appears to be situated on a steep incline, surrounded by thick trees. I'd expect security here and here." She pointed to areas where she'd set up a hide if she were asked to provide security for the event.

Remy nodded. "Makes sense. I'd also add one here for

redundancy."

"Good thinking."

"Wait. You two are missing the bigger picture," Alice said. "What about drones? He's a tech guy, remember? He's not going to rely on humans for the bulk of his security."

"Another good point." Leine picked her phone up off the table and sent a text to Lou. "We should have something that will mess with the drone's sensors, at least temporarily. Give you a window if you're targeted."

"'We,' meaning your guy from whichever agency you worked for?" Remy asked.

Leine ignored the question and resumed her focus on the map. "Once we're satisfied with countermeasures, we need to create a legend for Alice, in case she's caught with her hand in the cookie jar."

"I won't get caught," Alice said.

"Humor me. I've been on more ops than I can count where things went south. It's better if you have something you can pull out quickly, rather than trying to come up with something on the fly."

"I'll pose as outside security. Folks in that neighborhood will be used to rent-a-cops," Remy said. "I'll just roam outside the perimeter."

"How are you going to do that?" Alice asked. "Sebastian lives in an exclusive enclave of the uber-rich. You don't think those folks use advanced security measures?"

"Of course. But you have to remember my former career. The police department taught me how to respond to resident's concerns—especially in Hunts Point. They want to see their tax dollars at work. Plus, a lot of them hire off-duty cops to pull security for special events. I'll ask around to see which security agency's been hired and dress appropriately."

Leine nodded. "Then it looks like we're set."

23

———————

Leine hesitated outside the entrance to Sebastian's Italianate mansion and subtly adjusted her in-ear bone conduction microphone and receiver. The wireless mic was programmed to transmit from a radio seated inside the diamond-and-gold filigree necklace she wore.

"Testing. Alpha up."

"Zulu up." Remy's voice came over the earpiece loud and clear.

There was a brief pause, then, "Python up." Alice whispered, "I'm inside the kitchen. We're getting our marching orders from the head dude."

Leine keyed the mic to indicate she was receiving.

She straightened the black-and-gold, one-shoulder cocktail dress as she walked up the shallow steps to the entrance. She'd bought it off the rack at a trendy department store downtown—not quite the haute couture of the uber wealthy, but it would do. The pair of Louboutin pumps came by way of a friend of Alice's. Desi stood on the top step, searching the crowd. Their eyes met, and a big grin spread across his face.

"Don't you look scrumptious?" He leaned close and growled in her ear.

"Why, Desi. I didn't know you rolled that way."

"Honey, I don't. But if I did, ooh la la…"

Leine smiled in spite of herself. "Thank you. You look pretty smashing yourself."

Desi wore an Armani tux paired with a black satin bowtie and cummerbund, and black leather lace-ups.

"I'm surprised you didn't add a splash of color somewhere."

"I decided to go classic tonight. Besides, my underwear is fire engine red."

"Thanks for that. I can die happy now." Leine leaned closer. "Thank you, by the way, for interceding and getting Alice that copy of the club's program."

"Happy to do it. Sebastian doesn't know, by the by." He gave her a look. "And he doesn't need to, capisce?"

"Mum's the word." Desi withholding information from Sebastian surprised Leine. He'd seemed quite loyal to the billionaire. But Brett and Ethan had been good friends of his, too. Loyalty could be a fickle mistress.

They continued through the double doors of the sandstone mansion, flanked by a pair of Corinthian columns and mature cypresses, into the expansive foyer. A semicircular grand staircase unfurled to the upper level. Warm wooden floors topped with luxurious Persian rugs stretched in every direction. An impressive chandelier dangled overhead.

"Tell me about the house," Leine said, accepting a glass of champagne from a passing waiter.

Desi took one for himself and nodded at an abstract painting high on a foyer wall. "Excessive, if you ask me. But his art collection…" He sighed wistfully. "That's his de Kooning. He's got Picassos, Klimts, a Jackson Pollock, two Mondrians, five Miros, and my personal favorite, a Wassily Kandinsky from 1913. Sublime."

"And a Rothko in a pear tree…" Remy's singsong comment came over the mic. Apparently, the transmitter was working.

"Impressive," Leine said, ignoring him. "Perhaps I can get a tour sometime."

Desi placed his hand on his chest. "Be still my heart—you're an art afficionado?"

"I appreciate abstract expressionism."

"Consider it done. Shall we?" He offered her his arm.

They continued into the main salon where a pianist played Mendelssohn on a baby grand and dozens of well-heeled guests congregated, laughing, drinking, and preening for an imagined audience.

"It appears that most if not all of Seattle's beautiful people are here tonight." Desi waved his glass of champagne at a small clutch of guests. "The well-coiffed woman dripping in platinum and jewels in the center of that little gaggle is heiress to a massive timber company. The silver-haired fox next to her is her boy toy of the moment. The other three are her ever-present hangers-on."

"Trying to soak up the rich vibes?"

Desi scoffed. "More like waiting for a handout." He turned their attention to a younger couple talking and laughing with a middle-aged man dressed in an expensive-looking, but rumpled, tux. "The older gentleman is a shipping magnate—family money from the nineteenth century. Ever since his wife died, he's never very put together. Nobody cares how he looks because he's quite charming. The young couple run a hedge fund that requires a multi-million dollar buy in. And over there," he pointed to two people standing near the enormous floor-to-ceiling, arched windows, "are two congressional reps from the *other* side of the state."

"You say that like it's a bad thing."

"I've heard from reliable sources that both of them think coming to western Washington is beneath them. Too progressive —too many 'snowflakes.'" He used air quotes with the word "snowflakes." "But if there's money to be had, politicians on both sides seem to have a knack for sniffing it out, whoever and wherever the donor might be."

"Didn't you say Seattle's new mayor is conservative? Could it be that they feel more comfortable stopping by now?"

"Maybe. As long as they behave, I've got no problem with them. And God knows Sebastian doesn't choose sides." Desi scanned the attendees. "Speaking of the devil. He happens to be right over there."

Desi nodded toward a man with dark hair dressed in a form-fitting tux standing next to a small group near a huge fireplace. She'd seen pictures of Sebastian, but they didn't do him justice. His demeanor was open, relaxed, and friendly, which surprised her, although he was inside his own home. Most tech titans she'd been in contact with were brilliant, but not exactly comfortable in their own skin—almost like they couldn't believe their good fortune, that it would dissipate into the cloud like so much code. Either that, or they were the exact opposite: dismissive, entitled pricks who had a penchant for scatological humor. As if they hadn't progressed beyond grade school emotionally.

Stereotypical, for sure, but stereotypes were such for a reason.

Next to their host was a striking woman with luxurious, honey-colored hair. Her flawless makeup and form-fitting dress with a plunging neckline made Leine think of the Hollywood starlets she'd encountered working security for an A-list actor several years before. One difference: this woman exuded a confidence that even the most celebrated actor would find hard to emulate.

The territorial vibe was strong—her arm was intertwined with Sebastian's as she swept the room with a calculating gaze. Her demeanor suggested an intimate relationship with the billionaire.

Leine and Desi walked up to the small group. Two of his guests excused themselves and went in search of a canape, leaving Sebastian and his date. Desi introduced Leine to Sebastian, then turned to the woman.

"And this is Hannah. She heads up one of the development teams at Congruence."

Hannah smiled at Leine, although her expression lacked warmth. She took a subtle step closer to Sebastian and placed her hand on his lower back, in effect marking her territory. "And you know Desi how?"

"We go way back," Leine answered, noting her response. Interesting, coming from a woman who appeared so confident.

"We go way back, too, don't we?" Hannah nudged Sebastian.

Sebastian's body language changed with her words. The difference was subtle—tightened shoulders, lips pulled into a thin line. He likely didn't approve of her attempts at claiming territory during his soiree. Was it because they worked together? From Hannah's actions, their intimacy was obvious.

Intriguing.

"Leine is investigating the murder of Desi's headliner," Sebastian said to Hannah.

Hannah made a sympathetic moue. "A terrible tragedy for the community."

"There are three murders, actually." Eight, if Leine included the man who attacked her in Desi's garage, the man who tried to kill Remy, Scumbag, his brother, and Noah, but she wasn't about to mention them. "Brett and his partner, Ethan, and Scott McKenzie, another performer at the club."

"So, you have a law enforcement background?" The shift in Hannah's gaze suggested more than polite interest.

"I'm what you'd call an interested party."

"Ah." Hannah turned to Desi. "I hope you're able to find out who did this. I hear the police have been less than helpful."

Desi sighed. "They're chalking it up to a robbery-gone-bad."

"But you believe otherwise?" Hannah's expression remained frozen. A poker face to hide her real intention? Too much Botox?

"I believe it's a hate crime."

"That's horrible." Hannah sipped her champagne and shook her head in sympathy—the tableau of charity events the world over. *My goodness, isn't the world out there just awful? I'd love another glass of Dom.*

"Yes, it is."

"It must have been devastating for the club," Hannah said.

"The deaths were a tragic loss, but we're recovering." Desi gave Hannah a wary look before he turned to Sebastian and changed the subject. "Leine is an aficionado of abstract art. I mentioned several of your pieces and she's quite intrigued. I thought you might give her a quick tour?"

Sebastian smiled, his relief obvious. "I'd be delighted. Always happy to share my obsession with a fellow art lover."

"Hannah, could you show me to the open bar? I feel a fierce thirst coming on." Desi expertly cut Hannah from the herd, allowing Leine to be alone with Sebastian. The other woman smiled as she let go of Sebastian's arm, although the smile, like her expression, remained fixed.

"Of course, Desi."

Hannah's mask of an expression remained on her face until they were out of sight.

24

"I've been an art lover for years," Sebastian said, leading Leine down a long hallway, away from his other guests. "When I finally made enough money, I began collecting pieces I never thought possible."

His demeanor had changed from one of relaxed host to giddy schoolboy. He clearly loved art. They walked into a study off the main salon where a spotlit Picasso hung.

"That was my first acquisition." They took a moment to appreciate the painter's style and use of color. "But my favorite is in the wine cellar."

He led her through a doorway to a stairwell. As they descended, he described how he'd acquired each piece they passed with reverence and a modicum of disbelief, as though he couldn't quite believe he owned such masterpieces.

They reached the lower floor and walked through a large game room to a closed door, pausing at pieces created by both obscure and well-known artists. Sebastian touched his wristwatch, and the door clicked open.

Lights blinked on, revealing an impressive wine cellar, with thousands of bottles of wine lining the walls. A table with four leather chairs took up space in the middle of the climate-controlled room. The far end was shrouded in darkness. Sebastian set his glass down and touched his watch again, turning the rest of the lights on.

Strategically placed spotlights caressed a large, colorful piece at the far end of the cellar.

"You have a Van Gogh?" She turned to Sebastian. His grin told her he was excited to show off the masterpiece. Leine stepped closer, admiring the way the artist pulled the viewer in, as though inviting total immersion into the painting.

"Look at the brushstrokes."

Leine nodded. "He was a master at capturing chaos."

"It makes you wonder what was happening inside that brilliant mind." Sebastian's watch chimed. He checked the notification and frowned. "Would you excuse me for a moment? I need to take this."

"Of course."

Sebastian exited the cellar, closing the door behind him. Leine moved to the table and placed her glass next to Sebastian's. She trailed the wall, acting as though she was perusing the wines, while keeping a sharp eye out for security cameras. She spotted an unobtrusive one near the ceiling aimed at the table, and another aimed toward the Van Gogh.

She returned to the table, and, keeping her back to the camera, picked up Sebastian's glass by the base and walked along the other wall. Her back to both cameras, she slipped a piece of film from her clutch and removed the adhesive backing as she walked. She smoothed the film over the surface of his champagne glass, then peeled it off, keeping her actions as inconspicuous as possible. Replacing the backing to protect the print, Leine slid the film back into her clutch and returned to the table where she set down the champagne. A few minutes later, the door opened, and Sebastian returned.

"Sorry about that." He shrugged, looking less like a titan of tech than a man who would rather talk about anything than business.

"No worries." Leine picked up her glass and took a sip. "I've kept you too long. We should probably get back to your guests."

"I suppose. Thank you for listening to my incessant babbling."

"It was lovely. I should be the one thanking you."

He led her out the door, locking it behind him. "Can I ask you a question?"

"Of course."

"I realize you're in the middle of the investigation, but I'm curious if you've discovered anything new about the murders? Desi tells me you've interviewed several of his employees."

"I'm afraid we're at a bit of a standstill at the moment." Leine wasn't about to give up anything to the person who could be responsible for the murders. "I do have a question for you, though."

Sebastian nodded. "Anything I can do to help. Just ask."

"How well did you know the performers?"

"Mainly in passing, although I attended a few brainstorming sessions with Brett and Ethan in the early days of the AI program launch at the club."

"You mean creating costumes and a script? Things like that?"

Sebastian shook his head. "More along the lines of what physiological responses to measure and how to elicit them in an efficient manner."

"I'm a little in the dark about the program's full capabilities. Why go to such lengths to measure those indicators?"

"The program itself is the child of a larger parent program. I'm testing a smaller offshoot to keep things manageable."

"Why not test the larger program the same way?"

"That wouldn't be advisable. Too many unknowns."

"I see. That's helpful to know." Leine decided not to press him further—she sensed he was growing uncomfortable with her line of questioning and she didn't want to have him shut down completely. Nor did she want to give him reason to believe she suspected anything.

They returned to the party. Leine spotted Desi and joined him as Sebastian disappeared into the crowd.

"So? Were you blown away or what?"

"Incredible. Especially the Van Gogh."

Desi's mouth dropped open before he snapped it closed. "He showed you the Van Gogh? Well, aren't you special? I haven't even been invited." He sniffed and looked away.

"Perhaps you're not Van Gogh material?"

Remy chuckled in her earpiece. Leine suppressed a smile.

A mock-pained look crossed Desi's face. "You're going to throw that in my face any chance you get, aren't you?"

"What fun would it be if I didn't?" Leine handed him her glass. "Would you mind? I need to find the ladies' room."

"Down that hall, third door on the left."

"Thanks. I'll catch up with you."

Leine made her way through the throng of guests and down the hallway until she found the alcove housing the main bathroom.

Set up like a ladies' lounge in an upscale hotel, the waiting area boasted floor-to-ceiling mirrors, flattering lighting, and overstuffed velvet furniture. Framed Art Nouveau prints decorated the silk wallpaper, featuring sultry Parisian women from the 1920s. Leine leaned closer to see if they were originals, but couldn't tell with the existing light.

An older woman checked her makeup in the mirror and left, leaving the room empty. Leine continued into the next area where the décor continued the 1920s theme, with potted palms and glass vessel sinks with gingko leaves and bat motifs. She checked the three individual stalls. All were vacant.

She chose the farthest stall, closed and locked the door, then turned on the ceiling fan. Although quiet, it would still add white noise in case of monitoring.

She slid out the film with Sebastian's fingerprints, peeled a tiny section away to reveal the adhesive, and fastened it onto the wall behind the tank.

"We are a go, Python," she said into her mic.

Alice keyed twice to indicate receiving.

Leine flushed the toilet and walked out. She was still alone. She washed her hands and dried them, checked her makeup in the mirror, and exited the lounge.

She rejoined Desi, who was chatting with the hedge fund couple and shipping magnate. Alice walked past, careful to keep her face turned away from Desi, and headed for the bathroom. Five minutes later, she reappeared, garbage bag in hand, and headed for the kitchen. She gave Leine an imperceptible nod and disappeared down the hallway.

Alice hadn't been able to determine what kind of listening devices might be deployed across the property, so she wasn't sure if their communications would be intercepted. One way to circumvent the possibility was to keep chatter to a minimum, but another was to share an encrypted channel. The restroom was an added layer of protection, since monitoring them was normally illegal. Not that Sebastian couldn't observe any part of his manse, but it was more likely he didn't go that far.

Leine spotted Sebastian across the room, talking with the two representatives from the east side of the state. Hannah was next to him, smiling engagingly and laughing at something one of them said.

"Tech One is in the main salon," Leine reported. "I'll keep an eye on him, make sure he doesn't go anywhere."

"Python is on the move." Alice's voice came through clearly. Sebastian's regular staff were likely in radio communication, which meant no jammers would be deployed. As long as Alice, Remy, and Leine remained on the encrypted channel, they were golden.

A few minutes later, one of Sebastian's security men came up beside him and whispered in his ear. Sebastian nodded, then turned and said something to the politicians before he headed toward the rear of the house.

Leine turned to Desi. "I'm going to get some air." She made her excuses to the couple and shipping magnate, and made her way through the guests to the back doors, all the while keeping Sebastian in view.

"Tech One is on the move. Following."

A set of collapsible sliding doors had been left open, effectively enlarging the home's footprint. She followed him onto the multi-tiered patio. Twilight had fallen, and lights blinked on, illuminating the landscaping, which included several modern sculptures. A lush green lawn spread out before her with conversation areas strategically placed along the pathway, ultimately leading to a dock on Lake Washington, complete with a berthed yacht. A few people milled about, but most stayed inside. Sebastian walked over to two men deep in conversation.

"Tech One is outside, talking with two guests." The two men were dressed in black tie, but both looked highly uncomfortable. One kept pawing at his collar as though the bowtie was too tight. The other stood stiffly, as though there was a rod up his ass. Leine took a couple of pics with a hidden camera in her clutch.

"Python to Alpha."

"Go ahead, Python.' Leine checked the time. Ten minutes had elapsed since she'd seen Alice.

"I used the jammer on the camera covering the kitchen and back stairs."

"And?"

"Worked like a charm. I'm headed upstairs now."

"Keep us posted."

"Be careful," Remy added.

"Copy that."

"Zulu, SITREP," Leine said.

"Pretty quiet," Remy replied. "I located security. Haven't seen any drones yet."

Alice broke in. "You probably won't. They're likely high-altitude and uber-quiet. Just don't give them something to track."

"Copy that." Remy had done most of the recon the day prior, and was now observing the area through night-vision gear from the safety of a rented Mercedes SUV—a ubiquitous vehicle in that neighborhood, though normally used by staff rather than the owners. Tinted windows obscured his outline from casual passersby. He'd added two magnetic signs with vaguely official markings to the sides.

Leine nodded to a couple as they walked past, and moved away from the house. Sebastian continued his conversation with the two men.

"I'm outside the office," Alice said. "Looks like we were right on. There's an electronic lock coupled with biometrics. First, the retina scanner. Wish me luck."

Leine shrugged off the tension as she waited for Alice to reply. She kept her gaze on Sebastian talking with the men in the yard below her.

Finally, Alice heaved an audible sigh. "The contact worked. Now, for the prints."

Sebastian shook both men's hands, and started back for the house. Leine melted into the shadows as he passed. The two men walked across the lawn headed toward the side of the house. She waited a beat, then followed Sebastian inside. He rejoined the small group in the main living area.

"Well?" Remy demanded. "What's taking so long?"

The man was certainly impatient. Not a great attribute in an operative.

Duly noted.

"I'm having a hard time with the film," Alice replied. "The scanner's not recognizing the prints."

Leine shifted her position and faced the fireplace so no one would see her speaking. "Let me know if I need to try again. Zulu, you're not helping things." She'd have to figure out another way to get the billionaire's prints. The private art tour had come at the perfect time. That kind of luck didn't happen often.

"Hold on. I've got an idea," Alice said.

Leine admired the Gustav Klimt above the fireplace and sipped her drink while she waited. Sebastian remained across the room, mingling.

"I'm in," Alice said.

Leine let out a quiet breath.

"Be careful." The stress in Remy's voice came through loud and clear.

"I'm fine. Oh, shit."

"What?" Leine and Remy asked in unison.

"Lasers. Give me a second."

Leine rotated her head and shoulders to release the tension.

"All right. I'm using Leine's cool little NVGs to define where the lasers are deployed. They're set up in a changing grid. This is going to take some footwork..."

Leine took a deep breath and exhaled, slowing her heart rate. Sebastian walked between one group and another, chatting up his guests. Hannah drifted along behind him, her laughter echoing through the large room. Leine subtly mirrored him, keeping him in sight.

"Whew. I'm at the desk. Shouldn't be long, now." A quiet giggle escaped her. "Would you believe it? The guy has a huge collection of what I'll bet are original Star Wars figurines still in the box. There's a bunch of Wookiees, at least three Luke Skywalkers, and my favorite, Han Solo—"

"Quit dicking around," Remy growled. "Just get in and get out."

"Okay, okay. Jeez, can't a girl have a little fun? It's not like I'm going to be here ever again. This is the domain of the Great and Powerful Oz, you know?"

"Can you access the laptop?" Leine asked with a quiet sigh. Radio hygiene was apparently a no-go at this point. Civilians.

"On it. Deploying the exploits." There was a pause, then, "Yes! I'm inside. I'll copy the hard drive, erase my footprints, and Bob's your uncle."

"Just hurry the hell up."

"Relax, Zulu. I'm working as fast as I can." Alice didn't bother to hide her annoyance. "Almost finished...oh, hello."

"Is someone there?" Leine's attention narrowed. How would Alice explain her presence in Sebastian's office?

Alice's voice came over the mic, but she wasn't talking to Leine or Remy. "Um, no thank you. I'll just be a minute."

"Who the hell are you talking to?" Remy asked.

"Well, there's a woman here. Okay, not exactly a *real* woman. What did you say your name was?" Leine could just barely make out another voice. Alice came back on. "She says her name is Ginger. Holy shit. I think she's a hologram."

"Can you neutralize her?" Leine asked.

"I'll have to get back inside the server, see if I can erase our encounter. This is some next-level shit."

At that moment, Sebastian glanced at his watch and

frowned. He said something to the couple he was talking to and strode from the room.

"Tech One is on the move." Leine shifted position to watch where he went. "He's headed for the stairwell to the office. Get out, Python. I say again, get your ass out of there now."

25

———

Sebastian strode along the hallway, headed for the back stairs leading to his office. He tapped his watch. "Ginger, what's happening? Report."

Ginger didn't respond. Ginger always responded. Had someone breached his security? That didn't seem possible. Besides, everyone who was at the party had been vetted, even the catering crew.

Except for Desi's friend, Leine. *Shit.* He'd given her name to his security team late, not thinking anything of it. Could she be a problem? Corporate espionage was always a concern. He tapped his watch once more. "Ron, come in. I think we have a security breach, over."

Ron's image materialized beside him.

"What's the problem, boss?"

"Have you been monitoring the feeds?"

"Yes, sir. Of course. What happened?"

"Ginger sent me a message asking about a woman in my office."

"That's news to me. I'm looking at the feed right now and there's no one in the room."

"I'm on my way up there to find out."

"I don't think that's a good idea, sir. What if someone *is* up there? Wait for me, all right?"

Sebastian slowed his pace. "All right. But get over here, pronto."

"Copy that."

With a sigh, Sebastian stopped to wait for Ron to catch up with him. He stared at the painting on the wall of the landing. It was by Jackson Pollock and, like most of his abstract pieces, evoked a feeling of chaos, a congruence of energy into one, collapsible whole. Much like his company. He took another deep breath in an effort to clamp down his anxiety, but the attempt fell short.

What if someone had breached his inner sanctum? He'd installed more than enough security protocols to thwart someone trying to steal his intellectual property. At least, he thought he had. His security vetted the caterers, their employees, even had them pass through a magnetometer and RF detectors in case someone attempted to smuggle in a cell phone or tried to transmit information from the house and grounds. Short of conducting a strip search on each employee, there wasn't much more he could do.

Ron came up the stairs at a run, slowing as he caught sight of Sebastian. In his hand was a semiauto with a suppressor threaded onto the barrel, so as not to alarm the guests should he need to shoot.

"Did the drones pick up anything?" Sebastian asked.

Ron shook his head. "Not a thing. I've alerted the team and doubled our perimeter check in case someone makes a break for it."

Sebastian nodded. "Let's go."

Ron took the lead, with Sebastian close behind. They ascended the stairs at a good clip until they reached the second-floor landing, where they slowed and followed the hallway the rest of the distance to his office door.

Sebastian stepped up and presented his left eye to the retinal scanner. The red light turned green. Then he placed his thumb on the fingerprint reader. That too, turned green, and the door clicked open. Before he walked inside, he tapped his watch, deactivating the lasers.

"Lights."

A floor lamp and a lamp on the desk blinked on, illuminating the space. No one was there. Sebastian walked over to his desk. His laptop didn't appear to have been disturbed. A couple of taps on the keyboard brought up his programs. None indicated a breach. He scanned the room, searching for anything out of place. Something was different, he was certain, but he couldn't quite put his finger on what it might be.

"What?" Ron asked. "Something seem off to you?"

"I'm not sure." Sebastian walked through the room, checking items to ensure they weren't out of place. The bookshelf he'd used to display his vintage Star Wars memorabilia drew his attention, but nothing looked disturbed. He stood in the center of the room and turned in a wide arc, then shook his head. "Nothing."

"Have you tried a reboot?"

That must be the problem. The holograms had been glitchy lately, especially Ginger. He moved to his laptop and tapped the keyboard, bringing up an auxiliary security program. "That's a distinct possibility. I need to check one thing first." He scrolled through the security logs to see if anyone had accessed the server, but all appeared normal. Then he brought up the video feed for the office. He studied each frame, but found nothing out of the ordinary. He'd do a deep dive later on, but all looked good. With a sigh of frustration, he leaned back in his chair and tapped the key to reboot the holograph program.

"Thanks for being here, Ron. You can head back to the control room."

"You sure? I can have my team do a deep sweep of the premises if you think we need to."

Sebastian shook his head. "No need. I'm sure there's an explanation—a bug in the program, most likely."

"All right. Call me if you need me."

"Will do."

Ron left the office, closing the door behind him. Sebastian stared at the bookshelf, unable to pinpoint what was different.

The cleaning crew had probably moved something.

He got to his feet, intending to head back to the party, but stopped at the thought of dealing with Hannah. She'd been extra aggressive tonight, pushing him to accept the National Reconnaissance Office's offer, but his instincts said to wait a while longer. There wasn't an empirical reason to put off the NRO—the money was generous, the terms acceptable. And, he was eager to deploy the program to get comprehensive, real-world experience. But it was a big step. He wanted to be certain security was watertight, that no bad actors could hijack any part of it for their own ends. According to Hannah and the rest of the team, they'd achieved that, in spades. Besides, he hated it when anyone tried to rush him into things.

Get your ass back to the party, Sebastian. Don't allow one woman to pressure you into anything.

He exited the office and returned to his guests.

26

Leine moved along the corridor, past the women's lounge, making sure no one was within earshot.

"Come in, Python. Do you read?"

Alice hadn't responded since Sebastian left the party in such a hurry. Had he found her? Did he leave because of Alice's breach, or something else?

"You got a plan, Alpha?" Remy's voice reverberated through her earpiece. "Cause if you don't, I sure as hell do."

"Calm down. I'm not about to blow this up before I find out what's going on."

"You need to find her, right damn now."

"I'm not taking orders today, sorry." Leine took a couple of deep, cleansing breaths. *Remain calm, Leine. Remy's just worried about Alice.*

"Excuse me? I've had about enough of your shit—"

"Hey, hey, hey. Are you two fighting over little ol' me? How sweet." Alice's voice interrupted their spat. A wave of relief swept through Leine.

"Where the hell are you?" Remy barked.

"I'm at the bottom of the hill, by that little creek near the road. Come get me and I'll fill you in, all right?" Alice's last words were delivered softly, as though trying to convey she understood, but to stand down, she was fine.

Remy's sigh reverberated through Leine's earpiece.

"All right. Zulu out. See you back at base."

"No apologies necessary, Zulu," Leine quipped, but he was gone.

Alice chuckled. "He means well. He's like a bull in a china shop when it comes to me."

"That is one fine analogy," Leine replied. "See you back at base."

AN HOUR LATER, LEINE PULLED INTO DESI'S VISITOR SPACE AND killed the engine. She'd dropped off the Louboutins with Alice's friend and took a circuitous route home, designed to bore the pants off anyone trying to tail her.

Remy had parked his new rental in Desi's spot. Desi would likely stay at the party until the bitter end—he'd mentioned hoping to get a chance to speak with a few of the guests before he left. Leine climbed out of her vehicle, grabbed her things, and took the elevator to the condo.

Alice and Remy were in the living room. Leine stopped in the kitchen and poured herself a healthy shot of tequila before joining them.

"What happened to you?" Leine asked, eyeing the ice pack draped over Alice's ankle.

Remy scowled. "She tripped coming out of the woods."

"Darned tree roots." Alice grimaced. "Not my finest moment."

"How did you get out before Sebastian found you?"

Alice shrugged. "I'm a cat burglar. I got skillz."

"Too bad you didn't use your outdoor skillz," Remy muttered.

"Did the NVG stop working?" Leine nodded at the mascara tube sitting on the coffee table. "It worked inside the office." She picked up the tube and accessed the hidden monocular. It seemed fine.

Alice shrugged. "I didn't have time. Things were a little dicey."

"Security was doing a perimeter sweep," Remy said. "Alice had to stay put or they would've seen her."

"I stood under the tree canopy as long as I could to avoid the drones, and stayed there until security completed their rounds. I was afraid of crossing the sectors you and Remy said might be sniper hides. Remy blasted the area with that anti-drone device you got him, giving me enough time to get to the Mercedes."

Leine put the tube back and sat in a chair across from Remy and Alice. "How did you get out of the house without being seen?"

"I had to climb down from a second-floor balcony. The guards were already doing their thing, so there was no way to get back inside. I barely made it to the woods without getting caught."

"Well done." Leine raised her glass and took a sip. "Did you find anything in his files?"

Remy leaned back and nodded at Alice. "You might say that."

Alice typed something into her laptop and turned the screen to face Leine. "Looks like our billionaire is vibing some Lex Luthor."

Leine scanned the document. The heading read, "Amazing Grace AI/Doomsday Scenario 1a: From Possible Critical Infrastructure Failures to Dangerous New Bioweapons." She read to the end of the first page and scrolled to the next. Bullet points identified several horrific outcomes possible when deploying the program named in the title. The second page held more of the same. She glanced at Alice.

"This isn't good."

"No shit." Alice turned the laptop back to face her. "If this report is accurate, and there's no reason to believe it isn't, then the AI program known as Amazing Grace has far surpassed known capabilities." She leaned back and sighed. "It's possible the program may have already attained AGI."

Leine glanced from Remy to Alice. "AGI?"

Remy raised his hands. "Don't look at me."

"Artificial General Intelligence," Alice answered. "It means the program is able to solve problems on its own and has learned to adapt to conditions."

"You mean without human input?" Leine asked. "That's not good."

"Again, no shit." Alice set the laptop on the coffee table. "We have to assume he pre-programmed safeguards to rein in worst-case scenarios."

"We need to find out if he released it," Leine said. "And if he has, where it's been deployed, and how to stop it."

"You can't really believe that Sebastian would put this out in the world?" Remy asked. "He doesn't want to be the one to destroy humanity, right?"

Alice shook her head. "One thing you need to understand. I've worked with these tech bros a long time. They're not bad guys, just massively driven. They have to be first. Second place is for losers. 'Move fast and break things' is their motto."

"So, you're saying thoughtful consideration of potential fallout from their decisions doesn't enter into the planning process," Leine said.

"Oh, they definitely identify the risks. But they weigh those risks against the rewards and rewards win. Every time."

"Until they don't." Leine studied her glass. "The rebellion from stakeholders and employees at that other AI startup wasn't very long ago. As I recall, a majority of the employees disagreed with the head guy's vision. They didn't trust him to lead them in an ethical direction."

Alice nodded. "Exactly. But Sebastian's company is privately held. No board to answer to." She typed something into the computer again, and turned the screen toward Leine. "But wait. There's more."

Leine scanned the document. The title read, *Open-Source Options: Amazing Grace Applications.* "A manifesto?" She read further. "Sebastian wants to release the program to the wider community? What would that accomplish, other than handing power to rogue states and bad actors?"

"According to this document, he believes it's an altruistic move. He's already made more money than he could ever spend. Why not give this program to the masses and let humanity sort itself out? It's the mindset of a lot of people in the industry. In its purest form, they believe in the ultimate goodness in people."

"They have a hell of a lot better view of humanity than I do," Remy said.

"Agreed. Altruism is well and good," Leine added, "but in this instance it's not realistic—not in our current world. Especially when it comes to something that could be used to destroy humankind."

"From what I've read, Sebastian's philosophy is more along the lines of effective altruism," Alice said. "Basically, it's the idea that you should make money however you can, as long as your intention is to benefit humanity, to ease suffering. If the outcome is good, then the road to that outcome is good."

"Just humanity?" Leine asked. "That seems a tad short-sighted. Doesn't every living thing suffer to some extent?"

Remy went into the kitchen to pour himself another drink.

"You two are getting a little deep for me. Drink?" He held up the bottle of tequila. Leine shook her head.

"Do we have an idea of when or if he's made the program available?"

"Not that I've found so far," Alice replied. "I'd like to think he hasn't, that he won't, that he listens to reason. But, like I said, I'm not convinced."

"Then we need to have a chat with Sebastian." Remy shrugged.

"How do you propose we do that?" Leine asked. "He'd know we breached his security. Unless the manifesto and danger assessment are online somewhere anyone can read them."

"Ideally, I'd like to know who wrote the program and talk to them," Alice said. "They might be able to tell us how to stop it if he does release it."

"You mean Sebastian didn't create the program himself?" Remy returned to the couch and sat beside Alice.

"He employs teams of programmers. I doubt he does a lot of coding these days. Nothing glamorous about it. The work's boring, repetitive. He likely compartmentalized the teams so that no one programmer would understand the program's full capabilities."

"So, what can be done?" Remy asked.

Alice shrugged. "Not a lot. Once it's out, it's out. You can't put the genie back in the bottle." She brought up the first document again. "Whoever wrote this, and I'm not saying it wasn't Sebastian—although threat assessment is something he'd farm out—has a certain style to their writing." She clicked something and a dialogue box came up. "It says here the author of the document is G. S. I can do a little more digging, check Congruence's HR department, see if I can find someone with those initials."

"I have the feeling we might not have a lot of time."

Remy gave Leine a sharp look. "Why?"

"Sebastian met with a couple of men at the party, but outside. They never went inside. They looked really out of place."

"You think he's making a move?"

Leine shrugged. "Makes sense, right? That way, he can claim he didn't do it. And we just gave him the perfect alibi."

"Alice's break-in." Remy sighed. "But there's no evidence of a breach."

"Doesn't matter," Leine replied. "His security will have logged the incident and created an after-action report. Perfect cover for when the feds come knocking."

"Shit. You might be right." Remy leaned his head back and exhaled. "What can we do?"

"Could be a dead end. But my gut tells me this is something we need to pursue." Leine turned to Alice. "How do you feel about helping me infiltrate Congruence?"

27

Sebastian sighed as he closed and locked the door behind the last guest. The staff from the catering company had left an hour ago, taking all the glasses and dishes with them. Although he enjoyed being around people for the most part, he experienced a sense of profound relief once he was by himself.

"I thought they'd never leave."

Sebastian stiffened at the sound of Hannah's voice. He'd forgotten she was still there. He rearranged his expression as he turned so she wouldn't notice his dismay. She cupped his face. Sebastian smiled and removed her hand.

"I'm really tired, Hannah. Can we continue this another time?"

Hannah's flawless lips pursed in a petulant moue. "I thought we could have a nightcap."

"Much as that sounds tempting, I really have to decline." He opened the door and stood aside in a not-so-subtle hint for her to leave.

Hannah loosened his grip on the doorhandle and gently swung the door closed. She walked her fingers up his lapel, the moue still in place. The scent of her perfume mingled with the sour odor of the champagne she'd been drinking. "We see each other so rarely anymore. I'm beginning to think you don't care."

Sebastian stopped himself from rolling his eyes. "Look. You're very important to me. I'm just exhausted. There's no way I can give you what you need right now."

"How do you know what I need?" She slid her hand along the front of his trousers, tracing his fledgling erection. "Maybe I want to give *you* something?"

Sebastian stifled a sigh as he shook his head. "I'm really tired, Hannah. Please, don't." He pulled her hand away and turned her toward the door. "Get in touch with Ginger to set up a play date next week, all right?"

Hannah turned, her face a mask of indignation. Apparently, she didn't get turned down often. "Foisting me onto your *virtual assistant?* Really?"

"Look. I'm sorry, but I wouldn't be very good company tonight. The negotiations are wearing me down." He shook his head. "We're this close." He held up his thumb and forefinger so they almost touched.

Her expression softened. "I told you I'd be happy to run point on those negotiations."

"Isn't it enough that you're lead on deployment? Do you want to do my job now, too?"

"That's not what I meant." A look of concern crossed her features. "I just thought you could use some support." She stepped back, hands raised. "I know when I'm not wanted."

Sebastian sighed. "That's business. It has nothing to do with us."

"Doesn't it?" Hannah opened the door. "This has more to do with us than you know." With that, she left. A whisper of her perfume wafted toward him. Sebastian batted it away, then closed and locked the door. He tapped his watch, arming his security.

Worry niggled at the edge of his brain. Would she do something to torpedo negotiations because he said no to one night? The idea of allowing emotion to dictate business was a completely foreign concept to him. If that was the case, he'd find another person to head up deployment.

Except Hannah was the star of the team, and the government negotiators knew it. Congruence and the NRO were close to finalizing a huge contract. Deployment was imminent. He couldn't afford a squabble with his top-tier employee. Choosing a new lead would set negotiations back weeks, if not months.

Certainly, Hannah had some influence on his final decision, but only peripherally. She didn't create the program, although she did make improvements to the existing code—inspired improvements, to be sure. But mainly she was the one who helped him see the brilliance of his idea.

He was the deal maker. The buck stopped with him, and he was going to make sure his program would be remembered long after he was gone.

Sebastian hadn't always been confident. When he started out in the tech field, he'd been immensely insecure around people. Not around machines. Machines he understood. It was people that he didn't get. Although he'd gotten better at reading non-verbal cues, he still got people wrong on occasion.

Case in point—Hannah.

He assumed her outcomes aligned with his. Tonight was the first time that construct had been challenged. Had he read her motivation wrong? He thought she was onboard with his vision for the future. The government contract and the data he'd glean from deployment would bring them that much closer to his ultimate goal. Humankind would reap the benefits of his powerful program—people would use it to find cures for cancer, reduce pollution, ease poverty.

Amazing Grace. That was the name they'd given it.

It was going to change the world.

THE CLICK OF HANNAH'S SPIKED HEELS ECHOED ON THE DARK driveway. Her foot hit a rock, and she came close to twisting an ankle. *Damned shoes.* She could have worn a pair of hiking boots for all Sebastian cared. Not being able to seduce a man just because he was tired was a first. His dismissal still stung.

She reached the entrance to the early twentieth-century home and rang the doorbell. Deep inside the imposing structure a bell tolled, reminding her of the churches in Paris. An involuntary shiver raced up her spine as she stared at the security camera. Hannah tossed her hair back and waited, every nerve on edge.

At long last, the door buzzed and the locks released. She pushed through, not waiting for the valet to appear and take her wrap.

She walked past the carefully selected wall hangings, the perfectly appointed furniture and conversation areas, and two well-placed security cameras, to the rear of the manse. There, she opened a steel door that revealed a ramp leading to the enormous rock-walled basement. The building had been built sometime in the late 1920s, and each subsequent owner had kept the original lower level, which at one time had housed a huge cellar. The temperature dropped precipitously as she descended, sending another shiver up her spine—albeit this time due to more understandable circumstances.

When she got to the arched doorway, she stopped. Every

time she made a visit to the underground office, she thought of medieval fortresses and torture chambers.

An apt observation.

She rapped several times on the thick oak door, and again waited. There was a sharp *click*, and the door yawned open, revealing a huge metal desk in the center of a cave-like room. A series of eight computer screens dwarfed the desk, all monitored by the man sitting in an executive chair on the other side. Multiple servers lined the walls of the room, lights blinking as each hashed reams of data and scoured the internet for more.

"Come forward," the voice commanded. The hackles on Hannah's neck rose. God, how she hated that tone. Lately, it had been his overriding one.

Hannah moved past the monitor bank and around the side of the desk. A middle-aged man with a feathering of brownish-gray hair sat in a specially made high-tech gaming console that doubled as a motorized chair. He wore the latest iteration of a VR headset he'd invented. The glass facing outward showed the illuminated face of a much younger man, although, if you looked closely enough, it resembled the wearer enough to identify him.

The armrests sported buttons, rollerballs, and other means of control. A tray attached to the chair could be flipped up and out of the way, or down in front of him. Currently, it was in the down position. The upper portion of his body was still functional, allowing him to operate anything with his hands and eyes, and his mind was sharper than most. It was his lower half that didn't work on its own. A musculoskeletal disorder had pushed the boundaries of how much weight two legs could carry, and he'd been forced to revert to the chair.

Until he'd invented an AI-assisted, flexible exosuit to help bear his weight, allowing him to walk, run, and mobilize however he needed. He was wearing one of the prototypes now.

He'd somehow gotten access to an older DARPA version of the suit and had modified it. The black webbed material adhered to him much like a wetsuit. Hannah wondered where he'd gotten funding—he was wealthy, but not so wealthy that he could fund his own research and development of cutting-edge inventions. Once, when she'd first been summoned to his home, he'd explained how the robotics worked. She asked him why he didn't sell his idea to the government, but he'd immediately shut her down, leaving her to wonder if he'd already tried but failed.

Hannah pulled her wrap closer against the chill of the frigid room. She leaned against the corner of the desk and crossed her arms.

"You called?"

The man slid off the headset and placed it on the tray. The blue glow from the eight screens gave him a ghostly appearance. His permanent scowl appeared more entrenched tonight. "You're in a mood. What happened? Did Billionaire Boy shun your advances?"

Hannah shot him a look. How would he know that? A lucky guess, probably. He was aware of her proclivities. It was how he'd blackmailed her into working for him in the first place.

She smiled. "I'm not in the mood, Langston. What do you need, darling?"

He directed his sharp gaze at her. She shifted her stance, suddenly uncomfortable. She couldn't wait until her part in his plan was finished and she didn't need to see or talk to him ever again.

"It seems the couriers haven't yet checked in." He narrowed his ice-blue eyes. "What's their status?"

Her mouth suddenly dry, Hannah resisted the urge to swallow. She hadn't wanted to be the go-between for the two men and Langston, but he'd insisted. She assumed he didn't want any connection to them that could be discovered. "They're probably waiting until their comms are secure." She had no idea if that was true, but if she wanted to get out of that office and figure out where the hell they were, she had to bluff.

Langston studied her. "I do hope you're not lying. For all our sakes."

Hannah's heart rate kicked up a notch, but she controlled her breathing so he wouldn't notice the change in her respiration. Showing fear to Langston was like presenting an unprotected throat to a rabid wolf. Except Langston would rip that throat apart by proxy and never give it another thought.

"You vetted them yourself. I doubt you have anything to worry about. There could be extenuating circumstances."

"Oh? Like what?"

"Like traffic. Maybe they got lost." She was reaching. They both knew it.

After a tense few moments, Langston finally waved her off. "Go. Fix it if it's broken. Otherwise, you know the drill."

28

Lou called Leine the next day, as she was driving back to Desi's condo from having breakfast. She answered on the second ring.

"I got the facial recognition results from the two men on the surveillance video. You're not gonna like it."

"Tell me they're not Chechens." In Leine's experience, Chechen operatives tended to be overly aggressive and immune to reason.

"Even better. They're brothers from Mother Russia. A couple of freelancers by the name of Romanov."

"As in the Czar?" The Romanov family had ruled Russia for over three hundred years before the Russian Revolution of 1917 put an end to their imperial reign. Although, Leine mused, some would agree that Russia was once again under imperial rule—just not by a Romanov.

"I didn't check their family tree, but I would venture they're lower on the food chain—more like distant cousins, twice removed."

"Interesting. You said they're freelancers. What's their jam?"

"From what I could gather, their skillset is along the lines of a 'you pay, we do,' kind of thing."

"So, a little bit of everything. Now I'm really intrigued. Who's pulling their strings?"

"No clue. It ain't someone good, I can guarantee you that."

"Thanks, Lou. I owe you."

"Saving my life gives you carte blanche until the end of time."

Leine had rescued Lou from certain death when a French terrorist named Salome had used him as bait to lure Leine to his home several years before. She didn't remind him that he wouldn't have been in that predicament if Leine hadn't made an enemy of the terrorist.

"Well, I'm still indebted to you. Thanks again."

Leine ended the call and opened the report Lou texted her. The older Romanov was named Oleg and the younger brother Ivan. They'd been operating in Washington State for over a decade, had been arrested sixteen times for everything from assault to armed robbery, but they always seemed to skate on charges. That told Leine they were on someone's payroll. Someone influential.

Leine forwarded the file and called Remy. "I need your PI skills. We got a hit on facial recognition for Alice's kidnappers. I'm texting you the details."

"Got it." He was quiet a moment before he blew out a breath. "Russians. Not that I'm surprised, but for once I hoped I was wrong."

"I take it you've had run-ins with citizens of the Eastern Bloc?"

"While I was on the force. I'll have to ask them where they buy that particular brand of track suit. Not to mention their choice of jewelry."

"I doubt Alice would approve of you adopting their fashion

sense," Leine said. "When you get a hit on their whereabouts, I'd like to be the one to talk to them."

"I'm crushed. You haven't even seen my interrogation technique."

"No, but I did see you in action when Alice was threatened. I'm afraid killing them before they confess wouldn't be very effective."

"Like I said, crushed. Besides, Alice isn't in danger anymore. Right?"

"Right." Leine hadn't called her. Yet. That would depend on what they found out from the brothers Romanov when they caught up with them. "I promise, if they need softening up, you'll be the first to know."

"Deal."

Leine ended the call and sighed.

Russians. Again.

Oh, well.

It was a devil she knew.

29

Two hours later, Leine's cell rang. It was Remy.

"That was fast—" she started, but Remy stopped her.

"Meet me at the address I just texted. Now." His voice had an edge to it that Leine hadn't heard before. She plugged the address into her GPS and followed it to Pioneer Square.

She parked at the curb, then joined him where he waited outside a late nineteenth-century building. The ancient red brick and leaded glass windows screamed old Seattle; the kind of structure seemingly impervious to the occasional earthquake that plagued the Pacific Northwest. He checked up and down the street before he opened the door and gestured for her to go inside.

"Why all the cloak and dagger?" Leine asked.

Remy gave her a dark look. "I found the Russians." He handed her a pair of nitrile gloves and some booties, which she put on. He did the same.

That didn't bode well.

She followed him up two flights of stairs, then down a dark

hallway to the last of six doors. He hadn't pulled his gun, which told her they weren't heading into a threat situation.

The hallway boasted lackluster sconces, no art, and smelled of pine cleaner. The building looked like it hadn't been remodeled since the day it was built. With the speed of gentrification in the neighborhood, that in itself was a miracle.

Remy ushered her inside, then closed the door behind them.

It took Leine a few moments for her eyes to adjust to the low light, but when they did, she realized she was looking at a crime scene.

Aside from the room being in shambles—the television was on the floor, its screen cracked, the cushions on the furniture were slashed, their contents scattered—the main event was the dead bodies.

Apparently, someone was none too happy with the brothers Romanov.

Oleg the Eldest was lying face-up on the overstuffed couch, glassy, bloodshot eyes staring at the ceiling. Two neat, round holes marked where the bullets had penetrated his forehead. The younger brother, Ivan, hadn't fared as well. At least, she assumed it was Ivan. He'd been shot at close range, obliterating his features to the point that investigators would need to identify him via dental records.

"How did you find them so quickly?" Leine asked.

"It wasn't hard. Most of the crimes they skated on happened within a two-mile radius of this building. I canvassed a couple of local businesses and got a hit on the second try." Arms crossed, he nodded at Ivan the Younger. "Seems as though Ivan here had a penchant for strong drink."

"Don't you just hate it when someone proves a stereotype?"

Remy continued. "I told one of the business owners at the bar down the street that Oleg owed me some money and I needed to locate him or his brother. He was more than happy to tell me where they lived. Seems the younger brother never paid his bar tab, and Oleg had stopped paying. The owner's also going to give me footage from his security camera around the time of the murders."

"So, I have to ask. Was this you?" Leine nodded at the bodies.

He glowered at her. "No. It wasn't fucking me. I found them this way." He slid a cheap flip phone from his pocket and held it up. "I found this hidden in the ceiling in the bathroom."

"Did you find anything else interesting?" By the state of the apartment, the killers had been searching for something specific. "I'm shocked they didn't find the phone."

"The hiding place wasn't obvious, even for a false ceiling, so could be they missed it. Or maybe they didn't care about a burner."

"I'd like to keep the information in-house as long as possible until we know how deep this goes. Would Alice be able to hack the burner?"

"Sure. What about your friend at the FBI?"

"I don't want to read Jana into the op just yet. Once is a favor, twice is something altogether different. We can't take the chance that she'll want to involve law enforcement."

"You're talking about Noah."

"Whoever killed him considered him a threat. Pretty obvious they were dialed into his work for the department."

"Unless he was under surveillance longer than we think."

"The question then would be who and why?" She nodded at the bodies. "You going to call this in?" She was curious how deep his cop instincts ran.

"Eventually. I want to get a look at the security footage first."

She moved to the couch and lifted Oleg's head to look for an exit wound. There was, but the shooter had picked up the round. She let his head fall back to its original position.

"I already checked for brass."

She skipped what was left of Ivan's head and scanned the room. Whoever tossed the place knew exactly what they were doing. The search had been methodical and thorough. The heating vents had been removed and sections of the lathe and plaster walls had been breached, leaving chunks of plaster spread across the floor.

"You think your buddies had something to do with this?"

"Possible. Pioneer Square's their beat. And the gunshot wound in Oleg's forehead sure looks like it's from a .45."

"Wasn't that the caliber Scumbag used?" She wasn't sure where he was going with the revelation.

"It was. In my experience, most gangbangers prefer a nine. Cheaper ammunition, easier to fire for someone who doesn't have a lot of experience."

"Makes sense. Less kick, more accuracy."

Remy grimaced. "Damn."

"What?"

"If it wasn't for the asswipes who killed Noah, I'd be on the phone with him right now, asking him to find out if these two Russians were CIs."

"And if he wasn't already dead, he would be once the interested parties got wind of the request."

Remy's grim expression suggested he agreed.

"Why not ask Alice to hack into the SPD? She has the skillset, and you know where to look for the information. She could be in and out in no time."

Remy scrubbed his face. "Yeah, that's a line I don't want to cross."

"Even if it leads us to Noah's killer?"

"Or a certain high-tech billionaire?"

Leine nodded. "Either they were killed to cover up something, or they crossed the wrong person."

"Or both."

30

Back at the safehouse, Remy handed Alice the burner phone from the Romanovs' apartment. Since her abduction by Scumbag and the ankle injury she sustained from the charity op, Alice and Mr. Tummy had been staying with Remy. The well-fed cat made himself at home on her lap and purred contentedly as she fired up her laptop. Alice had insisted on bringing three large monitors from her apartment, which were now arrayed on the dining room table, the multiple screens filled with data Leine couldn't begin to decipher.

"Ooh. Now you get to see me in action, babe." Alice pulled the memory card from the burner and popped it into a reader connected to her laptop. "This shouldn't take long."

Her fingers flew over the keyboard. The corresponding data on the screens changed faster than Leine could track. She looked at Remy, who just shook his head. A few minutes later, Alice stopped typing and pointed to one of the monitors.

"He used an encrypted app. That's the call log. Sent, received." She peered closely at the list of calls. "There are three phone numbers." She struck a key and the printer on the other side of the room whirred. Then she brought up another screen. "And here we have the texts. Only two numbers there. Same as two from the call log." Alice continued down the list, looking for a match to the odd number. "That's it. Just the one instance of the different number on the call log."

"What do the texts say?"

"The earliest date is a week ago, which could mean they regularly changed burners." She gave an involuntary shiver. "This is creepy. The message contains my address." Alice continued to peruse the texts. "Nothing, nothing..." She stopped scrolling. "Here we go. '*We need more money.*'"

"Extortion," Remy said. "Ladies and gentlemen, we have a winner."

"Can you look up who the numbers belong to?" Leine asked.

"On it." Alice copied one of the phone numbers and pasted it into another text box on a different screen, then hit Enter. The answer came back seconds later. "It's a burner. Bogus registration." She did the same with the next number and got the same result. Then she took the number from the most recent call. She narrowed her eyes. "Looks like it's registered to Congruence, Inc."

"Sebastian's company." Leine leaned closer. Another link to the billionaire. "Can you find out who the phone is issued to?"

Alice typed something and the screen changed. "No names, but there's an identifier. Let me check their internal database, see if I can match it with a name."

Alice's fingers flew over the keyboard once again. Congruence's corporate-facing page came and went as she dove deeper into the site. A little while later she leaned back, shaking her head. "There's no record of who it was issued to. Just the ID number."

Remy shook his head. "How in hell did you do that so fast?"

Alice grinned. "I've been working on getting inside Congruence since we identified Sebastian as a person of interest. Give me enough time and motivation and I'll find a way."

"When you were looking through Sebastian's files, did you by any chance come across his contact info?" Leine asked.

"Hold on—" Alice brought up a file. "Here's his business phone."

She read off the number. It didn't match any of the ones on the burner. Leine typed it into her contacts list to save for later.

"What? You gonna call him?" Remy snorted. "You think Sebastian's going to admit to ordering a hit on someone?"

"Of course not." Leine started to pace. "If our assumption is correct and he had them killed, there isn't anything to connect him."

"Plausible deniability."

Alice grimaced. "This is some evil shit."

"What did he write in the manifesto? Wasn't one of the basic tenets 'burn it all down'?" Leine stopped pacing. "We need to find out who works at Congruence with that phone number."

Remy gave Leine a skeptical look. "You think a programmer has the stones to have a couple of Russian thugs killed?"

Alice answered for her. "My industry's cutthroat, babe. Depends on the stakes."

"You read the threat assessment." Leine added. "If Sebastian has unleashed his AI without government oversight, there's no telling how much damage it's going to cause. Not just because of the new weapons it could create, although that's bad enough. If someone releases that program into the wild, then financial markets, water supplies, power grids, and everything else that's connected via computer could all be vulnerable. Whoever holds the key to that program holds the key to an exponential amount of power."

"The Russian brothers were extorting whoever owns that cell

phone, that much is clear," Remy said. "You think it had something to do with Amazing Grace?"

"Possibly. Assuming that's true, then who are the likely suspects using the Russians for their dirty work?" Leine asked. "A competing Russian faction? China?"

"They could be acting alone." Remy shrugged. "Maybe the brothers Romanov realized what they had and tried for more money. Then, bam! Sebastian has them taken out."

"We don't have evidence that Sebastian had anything to do with their murders," Alice reminded him.

"What time did the last text come in?" Leine asked.

Alice checked the screen. "Last night at eleven."

"How long do you think the brothers had been dead when you found them?" Leine asked Remy.

"Without forensics, I can only guesstimate, but from the condition of the bodies, I'd say at least eight hours."

"That tracks. I'll check with Desi to find out when the party ended." Leine sat at the table near Alice. "So, Sebastian calls Oleg from a work phone by mistake, Oleg texts his request for more money to one of the burners, which we assume also belongs to Sebastian. All of this leads to Sebastian's front door. Although, so far, the evidence is just circumstantial."

"So, how do we get evidence?" Alice asked.

"That's the one thread I need to pull. Obviously, whatever it is, Sebastian believes it's something worth killing for. The only way I can think of to find out, barring a confrontation with Sebastian, is to infiltrate Congruence. We have to find hard evidence of Sebastian's involvement."

"Yeah, but Alice is out of commission." Remy studied Leine. "You're not thinking of doing it yourself?"

"What other choice is there?" Leine turned to Alice. "Can you walk me through what I'll need to bypass Sebastian's security?"

Alice nodded. "His office was relatively easy. I can't say the same for his place of business. It's going to be much more... robust, shall we say? There's a high likelihood you'll get caught, no matter how good we are as a team."

"It's a chance I have to take. Too many lives have been lost." She narrowed her eyes. "He made it personal when he went after Alice."

Remy snorted. "What about you and me? He tried to kill us, too."

"Yeah, but we're not civilians. We understand the risks. Alice didn't."

"Okay. Say you make it inside the building without getting caught," Remy said. "How are you going to get the information you need?"

"If Alice can get me through security, I have access to a highly specialized device for digital infiltration and data extraction."

"Really?" Remy shook his head. "How do you get it inside?"

"That will largely be up to Alice."

Alice leaned forward, obviously intrigued. "How does it work?"

"It's about the size of a large smartphone but much thicker, and equipped with a high-speed multi-core processor with advanced encryption and decryption capabilities."

"What about data analysis?"

"It comes preloaded with a suite of software that analyzes logs, identifies patterns, and traces digital footprints."

Alice arched her eyebrows. "Connection?"

"USB-C, or Ethernet. It's got a stealth mode to minimize your digital footprint and allow it to avoid detection by network security systems." Having Lou Stokes in her corner definitely had its perks.

Remy whistled. "I stand by calling you Bond earlier."

Leine smiled. "That's fiction."

"What if you're caught with the device?"

"There's a failsafe that wipes the data. It can also be remotely erased."

"Perfect. When do I get to see this wonder device?" Alice asked.

"She needs to get a hold of Q." Remy smiled.

Leine rolled her eyes. "His name is Lou."

"Hey, it rhymes."

"You should call Desi to see if you can borrow one of the headsets," Alice suggested. "The device has sensors that can automatically detect the common signatures and behaviors of Sebastian's AI programs. That could be super helpful when you're inside headquarters."

"Next on my list." Leine rose to leave. "Did you get any response from the malware when you tried it on the club's program?"

Alice shook her head. "Nada. Which puts me back to square one."

"Well, at least you tried." Leine hadn't been convinced that a jealous competitor was the reason for the murders, but she'd been wrong before. Often, people acted in seriously surprising ways—and money, professional jealousy, or a host of other reasons could become the catalyst for bad actions. Assumptions could only get them so far.

They needed something concrete. Something that tied Sebastian—or whoever it was—to the murders.

Leine parked near Luck Be a Lady Revue and walked inside. Laura, the club's bookkeeper/den mother, was waiting for her.

She pointed to a metal case on the bar. "Here you go. Desi says to be careful with it, and don't let it out of your sight."

"I wouldn't think of it. Paranoid about someone reverse-engineering it?" Leine lifted the high-tech headset out of the case.

Laura gave a brief smile. "You ask me, it's more about the insurance deductible."

Leine chuckled. "That high, eh?" She set the device back in the foam cutouts and slid the case toward her. "Tell him not to worry. I'll have it back in a couple of days."

"Is this for the investigation?" Laura's eyes cut to the left as she asked. She began to wipe down the bar, her face a mask of studied nonchalance.

"Yeah." Leine waited. The woman looked like she wanted to say something else. Leine cocked her head when she didn't. "Are you all right, Laura?"

Laura ducked her head as she attacked the bar sink with the rag. "I'm fine."

"You sure?"

"Just curious." She stopped cleaning and put her hands on top of the bar. "It's just...no one's been very open about what's going on. With the investigation, I mean."

Leine nodded. "That's because, at least on our end, we haven't found a lot to go on. As for the police, I have no idea what they've found, if anything. It's not like they're open to collaboration."

"Oh. Sure. I'm sorry to ask. It's been hard the last couple of days. For me." She blinked back unshed tears. "Brett and Ethan were such great people."

Leine nodded. "And the not knowing is the hardest part. I get it. Everyone needs some kind of closure, especially when everything seems so random."

A look flashed across Laura's face, but was gone before Leine could parse what it meant. "Is there something you want to tell me?"

Laura shook her head and resumed cleaning.

"Because if there is," Leine said, softening her voice, "no matter how inconsequential you think the information might be, it could be just what we need to break open the investigation."

"I wish I could, really I do."

Wish she could what? Tell her something that would help with the investigation? Or just tell her something, period? Leine didn't press. The other woman's agitation spoke volumes. Leine sensed that she wasn't the type to do well under pressure.

Leine picked up the box and put it under her arm. "Just know that if you do think of something, anything, you can always talk to me. Okay?"

Laura nodded, tears now brimming over. Leine gave her one last moment to say something. When she didn't, she turned and left.

The bookkeeper knew something. But what?

31

Leine stood in the shadows of the upper parking lot at Sebastian's headquarters and checked her gear. The cooler, onshore flow from the Pacific Ocean mixed with the warmer land temperature created a swirling fog, lending an eerie feel to an already strange op.

She'd recced the area and located one vehicle on the lower level, likely indicating a security guard. Alice had suggested a majority of the monitoring would be off-site, since most attacks would likely be via cyberattacks, not physical incursions. And, because logged response times for police in the area were generally under five minutes.

Obviously, Sebastian trusted his security measures.

Leine slid on the special gloves and tapped her thumb and forefinger, activating the receiver and mic. "Testing audio."

"Copy, Alpha." Alice's voice came over the radio crisp and clear.

"Zulu in position." Remy was acting as overwatch on the rooftop garage of a nearby building.

Leine adjusted the temperature-controlled bodysuit she wore, allowing her to move more freely. Alice had borrowed the gaming prototype from her company, citing the need for more practical trials, which was close to the truth. What they discovered about the suit's capabilities during Leine's infiltration would add to an already-extensive database.

The suit regulated Leine's temperature and could be set to mimic the heat signature of her surroundings. The only part of Leine that could be detected via infrared or thermal imaging, her face and eyes, was covered with the VR headset from Desi's club, which also could be set to regulate temperature. Leine had added a tactical vest over the top of the suit to carry what tools she needed.

In addition to the suit, Alice fitted Leine with two contacts printed to mimic Sebastian's retinas, and a silicone replica of his prints from the champagne glass at the party. She'd also given her quick primers on other security scenarios Sebastian likely used. With Alice's skillset of breaking and entering and her knowledge of high-tech security protocols, she should have been the one to infiltrate Sebastian's headquarters, or at least accompany Leine. But Alice's ankle injury prevented her from doing much more than hobbling from the couch to the bathroom. Established audio and visual links between them were the next best thing.

Leine turned on the headset. An amber light blinked on and off in her periphery, telling her the device was working. She tapped her fingertips three times, bringing up the settings screen.

"Testing."

"Confirm visual," Alice replied. "I'm seeing everything you do."

"Copy that."

"Once you're inside, the headset should automatically link to whatever artificial intelligence program Sebastian's using. There's a setting that puts the headset in 'spoof' mode, which will trick the network into thinking you're supposed to be there."

Alice guided Leine to the setting. Leine initiated the program.

"What if I need to see reality?"

"No problem. Tap your left thumb and forefinger together to remove the overlay from view."

"Got it."

"Remember, the headset will last close to four hours on a charge, but the suit's battery life is only good for about an hour, maybe an hour and a half."

"Seems like it could be longer."

Alice sighed. "We're working on it."

"Does my level of activity determine the longevity of the charge?"

"It should be fine. We've tested it in several different gaming scenarios, including strenuous activity."

"Good to know." Leine could regulate her heartbeat through controlling her breath, which would help with respiration, but she might be less focused if she was dealing with an unanticipated threat.

"You are locked and loaded. Time to find out what Sebastian's doing behind closed doors."

"That reminds me." Leine slid a 3D printed gun and magazine from its home in her vest and double-checked that it was fire-ready. The magazine and rounds were coated with non-conductive material, allowing both items to bypass detection.

Leine re-holstered the gun. She didn't think she'd need it, but felt more comfortable having one on her.

"Deploying signal jammer." Leine ghosted to the side entrance and activated the aluminum-cased jammer. She clicked into hyper-focus mode and pointed it at the camera mounted on the wall above the door. The indicator light on the camera blinked off. To her left, a soft green glow still emanated from a glass box affixed to the wall. Good. The jammer hadn't messed with the entrance scanner's operation.

"Wave your right hand near the box. That should bring up the PIN pad."

Leine did as instructed and a holographic PIN pad materialized. She waited while Alice deployed her hacker magic to determine a PIN.

"Try six, four, five, three, star."

Using the pad, Leine pressed the holographic numbers to type in the code. The light blinked green and the door locks released.

"I'm in." Leine pushed through into an empty hallway. The door closed behind her with a hollow *click.*

She checked for cameras before deactivating the jammer, then tapped her fingertips to pull up the building's schematics.

"The atrium will probably be your first encounter with AI," Alice said. "Remember, what you see isn't necessarily what you get. With the headset and my help, you should be able to determine when he's using holographic interfaces and when the threat is real."

"What about augmented reality?"

"Same thing. Watch for the tells I mentioned: hand and finger movement are still AI's greatest weakness. Just stay chill, no matter what's deployed."

"Copy that." Leine moved along the corridor, following the schematics displayed on her headset.

"The guard station should be ahead to your right."

Leine glided past restrooms and an employee breakroom until she reached a closed door with a long, skinny window. A rectangle of light glowed through the reinforced glass. Leine moved closer. Inside, a man with sandy-brown hair sat in front of a bank of monitors. An ear bud sprouted from his left ear.

She couldn't see his right. Each monitor had differing views of the building. Chinese takeout containers lay scattered on the desk to his left, next to an oversized plastic drink container sporting a straw. A cell phone was visible underneath the detritus. Hands clasped behind his head, the man leaned back in his chair, watching what looked like a sci-fi show on a laptop.

"You could just bypass the guy," Alice suggested.

"Better to neutralize the threat."

"Are you sure? I mean, he's just doing his job."

Leine sighed. "For God's sake, I'm not going to kill him."

"Oh. Okay. Whew.'

Leine waited for Alice to give her another code to use on the electronic lock, then quietly disengaged the doorhandle and opened the door. Happily, the security guard's attention was riveted on the show, and he didn't hear her enter the room.

She slid a hypodermic needle from her tactical vest and crossed the floor in three strides. Before he knew what was happening, Leine plunged the needle into his neck and injected him with the contents. His body went slack from the fast-acting drug. She made sure he was secure in his chair before frisking him. He wore an access card around his neck on a lanyard, which Leine pocketed.

"What was in that needle? It's not going to cause any permanent damage, right?" Alice's voice had taken on a wary tone.

"It's a drug that's still in clinical trials, but no, it shouldn't cause any problems. It works on the hippocampus by erasing short-term memory." The drug was a derivative of a substance given to Leine by a member of the criminal group known as The Association to temporarily wipe her memory.

"What's it called?" Remy's voice crackled through Leine's earpiece.

"The working name is Nepenthe."

"Wasn't that the drug of forgetfulness in *The Odyssey*?" Alice asked.

"Points to Alice for the classical reference," Leine said. "He'll be out for a couple hours. When he wakes up, he won't remember a thing. He'll probably think he fell asleep." As if to lend credence to her words, the guard began to snore.

"Detectable?" Remy asked.

"No." The drug had been in clinical trials at DARPA for some time, but all indications were that it was untraceable unless you knew what substance you were looking for.

Leine slid him and his chair out of the way, then fished a USB drive from her pocket and inserted it into a port on the control board. The drive contained an exploit that would capture video monitor-wide and loop each view for as long as Leine needed.

The security guard's snoring reached epic proportions, with guttural snorks exploding from his open mouth.

"Make sure he can breathe, all right?" Alice said.

Leine sighed, then put his head on the desk, using his forearms to cushion his head. His snoring quieted to an occasional snort.

"Happy?" Leine asked, her annoyance obvious by her tone.

"Thank you."

Leine wasn't used to working with someone. Especially a civilian with...feelings.

You need her, Leine. Just deal with it.

Leine scanned the control desk. "Which module bypasses the motion sensors?"

"Bring up the main interface."

Leine entered the prompt into the console's keyboard. The screen in front of her populated with several additional lines of code and a blinking cursor.

"Great. Now type the following."

Leine did as instructed. The screen came back with several more lines of code.

"Perfect," Alice said. "That should auto-bypass Sebastian's security sensors. Now I'll work on gaining access to the rest of the keypads in the building."

The threat neutralized, Leine disengaged the flash drive, exited the room, and closed the door, making sure it locked behind her. Then she continued along the corridor, headed for the atrium.

Something moved in her periphery and she froze.

"What's happening? Why'd you stop?"

"Not sure. Hang on " Leine scanned the end of the hallway where the corridor connected to the main hall.

There it was again. She crept closer, pausing near the doorway. The sound of running water could be heard coming from the larger room.

"There's movement in the atrium." Leine kept her voice low, in case Sebastian was using some kind of audio capture, or in case there were additional security guards they didn't know about. She moved closer for a better view.

The sound of splashing grew louder. A cascading waterfall dropped from the upper level and splashed into a spotlit, clear-sided pool. Colorful fish darted this way and that, as crabs scuttled under rocks. A white-tipped shark glided past in hunting mode, its sleek body undulating in and out of the spotlights. The smaller fish scattered at its approach. Butterflies and birds swooped in and out of the waterfall, as birdsong entwined with the sound of rushing water. Palm trees swayed along the edges of a sandy shoreline.

Leine scanned the room but didn't see any humans. As she drew near, the view shifted, showing a number of different aquatic species.

"I think I've found the virtual reality section."

32

The humid scent of salt water and brine seeped through the headset's olfactory sensors, lending a realistic sense to the projected virtual beach scene. Leine had to hand it to Sebastian. He'd thought of everything. Lights blinked in her periphery, telling her none of it was real.

"That's pretty cool." Alice's voice held a note of approval. "We should do that at my work."

Leine tapped her left fingers, removing the AI assist. The tropic-themed overlay disappeared, leaving an open space surrounded by wooden benches and lush potted plants. She continued past, headed for a non-operating escalator on the far side of the room.

"You might want to turn the AI-assist back on," Alice said.

"I want to see what's actually in front of me."

"The VR you just saw is headset-dependent, yes, but holograms and more advanced AI features might not be as obvious to you. The AI-assist helps you determine what's real and what isn't, but it will also show you all of his tricks."

"You're sure the headset won't trigger an alarm?"

"Pretty sure, since it's one of Sebastian's devices geared toward his proprietary AI."

"Copy that." Leine turned the AI back on. The seaside mirage reappeared.

Leine checked the schematics and approached the escalator, which hummed to life.

"Must be motion-activated," Alice said. "One way to save resources."

Leine rode it to the second floor. "Heading for the main server room."

"Copy that."

Following the building's schematics, she bypassed several hallways, past glass-walled offices and mini-gardens filled with tropical flowers toward the center of the building. A few minutes in, she rounded a corner and stopped cold.

In the middle of the hallway stood a gigantic samurai with an equally large sword. The warrior lifted the katana overhead and scowled, its disconcerting gaze lasering through her. Its voice rumbled down the hallway toward her.

"You shall not pass," the samurai boomed. The image lowered into *Kasumi-no-Kamae*, a Japanese sword stance, with the blade held ready.

Leine scanned the corridor for speakers, but didn't see where the voice originated. She turned off the AI assist, but the image remained.

"That would be a hologram," Alice said. "You must have triggered it somehow."

Leine remained still, watching the hologram shimmer and settle. "I thought you had access to the motion sensors. What should I do?"

"It could just be a warning. It appears to act independently of the main security system. Something Sebastian put in place to remind employees without access that the area's off limits. If you had the right badge, for instance, the program might recognize that and not deploy. Or, it runs on a loop and deploys at regular intervals. You should be able to walk right past it."

"Wait a minute." Leine slid the security guard's pass card and lanyard from her vest and looped it around her neck. As Leine approached the hologram, the samurai flickered and disappeared.

"Looks like the guard has privileges to that section of the building."

"Do you think the samurai program alerts anyone off-site?" Leine asked.

"I can't say for sure. Most likely it's just a warning. The real security will be at the server room."

"All quiet here," Remy added. "Doesn't look like you tripped any alarms."

"Copy." Leine slipped through the shadows, her movements silent and precise.

Her headset crackled softly as Alice's voice came through. "You're approaching the main server room. The security here is going to be tight, but there's a maintenance hatch on the left that should be easier to breach."

Leine scanned the dimly lit corridor. All clear. She moved quickly, coming to a series of glass panes with a view to the gigantic collection of servers on the floor below. Other than the glow of the equipment and blinking indicator lights, there was nothing and no one else visible in the darkened room.

A door with an electronic PIN pad stood between the continuous glass panes several yards away. The schematics indicated the small room housed an access hatch leading to a series of air ducts.

"Hold on," Alice said. "You should have access...now."

Leine approached the keypad, and the red light blinked green. She opened the door and stepped inside the six-by-eight-foot maintenance closet. In front of her was the access leading to the server room's HVAC system.

Using a small electric screwdriver, she fitted the correct head and unscrewed the grill. She set it aside, then climbed through the hatch.

Triggered by the tremendous heat generated by the multiple servers within the server room, Leine's bodysuit automatically adjusted its internal temperature. She seated the grill with a few screws still attached and guided them through the threaded holes far enough so her breach wouldn't be obvious at first look.

Alice shared the duct schematics on Leine's headset, showing the way forward. The ducts themselves were oversized, due to the tremendous amount of heat exchange required with so many servers. Leine crawled several yards until the duct made a turn, and several yards again before another turn. All the while Leine sensed a gentle downward slope. Luckily, the system was made of sturdy metal that didn't bow or buckle from her weight.

Multiple turns later, she reached the access grill that led to the room itself. Leine removed the cover and set it aside, then scanned the space through her headset.

"Looks clear," Alice said. "You should be all right."

Leine dropped lightly onto the anti-static floor. Filled with a labyrinth of towering racks, the air hummed with power. Fans whirred, cooling the energy-intensive equipment, while vacuums shuttled the warmer air up through the HVAC system and out through a series of exhaust fans on the roof.

"Where to?"

"Continue to the third row, halfway down. You're looking for the console management port. It should be labeled."

"Copy." Leine moved to the third row of servers and found the one she needed. She pulled the QuanTrace5 from her tactical vest, the device's rugged exterior reassuring in her hands. She connected it to the console, the touchscreen interface lighting up as it established a link.

"Got it."

"I've bypassed permissions. I'll work on erasing the log entry. Start by accessing the internal network. We'll grab the emails first. Run a query to download Sebastian's emails and any interoffice messages, both sent and received, looking for keywords and dates."

Leine navigated through the device's interface, her fingers flying over the touchscreen as she entered the query, then set it to run. The screen on the QuanTrace5 flickered as it worked. Its advanced decryption module quickly bypassed the server's security protocols, granting her access to a trove of data.

Leine's body thrummed with the vibration of the servers, adding to her already heightened state of operator-mode. Several minutes later, the device's screen indicated it had finished retrieving the requested data.

"Data captured. What do I do next?" As she said it, the lights inside the room flickered. "What was that?"

"I don't know," Alice replied. "Give me a sec—"

A beeping sound came from near the server room door, followed by a sharp *click*. Multiple overhead lights flickered on, bathing the entire room in bright white light. Leine quickly disconnected the cable and ghosted to the end of the server row. The door yawned open, and three men dressed in black with weapons at high ready entered the room and fanned out. As soon as they were through, the door slammed shut.

"What the hell?" Alice hissed. "Remy, I thought you were watching the parking lot."

"I am. There hasn't been any movement. What happened?"

"Three guys just entered the server room."

"That can't be right. There's no underground entrance on the schematics."

"Well, apparently there's something."

While Alice and Remy argued about the existence of an underground garage, Leine waited until the men moved out of sight, then made her way to the HVAC grill. Moving quickly, she climbed into the duct, then grabbed the grill and reseated the screws using the tip of the electric screwdriver to hold it in place. She scanned through the slats in an effort to locate her visitors, but all three remained out of view. It wouldn't be long before one of them noticed the screws hadn't been completely seated.

Carefully, she disengaged the body of the screwdriver, leaving the tip wedged against the edge of the grill. With slow, precise movements, Leine turned to retrace her way back through the ducting toward the maintenance closet.

She was halfway there when everything went still.

"They must have turned off the intake system," Alice said in a quiet voice. "If you move, they'll hear you."

Leine tapped her fingers together, indicating she understood. The bodysuit silently ramped up its controls, adapting to the change in ambient temperature as she held her position on her hands and knees.

"They can't shut it down for long," Alice continued. "Those servers are worth more than the three of them will make in their lifetimes. They can't allow the equipment to overheat."

"Something tripped them," Remy said. "What did we miss?"

Alice replied, "I don't know. Let me check the guard room."

There was a pause. Then, "The guy's still asleep. There's no one in the room with him."

If the guard was still unconscious, who tipped off security? And how did they know to check the server room?

And why didn't these guys check in with the night security guard?

It didn't matter how they knew, Leine was a sitting duck. The longer she waited to reach the maintenance closet on the upper floor, the more of a chance the operators below her would notice the compromised access panel and come for her.

With painstaking deliberateness, Leine resumed her climb, channeling a sloth she'd observed on a recent trip to Costa Rica.

"What if they hear you?" The timbre of Alice's voice indicated a high level of distress. Leine ignored her and continued her ascent.

Several long minutes later, Leine caught a glimpse of the maintenance hatch. She continued the achingly slow crawl for several more yards before finally reaching the grate.

Using her fingertips, she turned the screws, unseating them so she could gain access to the small room. As she freed the last screw, the HVAC system came back online and resumed air intake. She climbed out of the duct and into the maintenance room, then reseated the grill and quickly hand-screwed it in place.

Leine cracked the door open and scanned the hallway. It was empty. She slipped out and ghosted along the corridor, staying well clear of the glass windows with a view to the server room below.

Hopefully it would be a while before anyone discovered the screws weren't seated all the way into their respective holes. When they did, they might chalk it up to shoddy maintenance.

Heads would likely roll.

Leine reached the end of the corridor and was about to turn down the hallway where the samurai waited, when it hit her.

She retraced her steps to the viewing panes and peered over the edge. Two of the security guys were visible, but they were going over the same ground as before.

"What are you doing?" Alice hissed. "They'll see you."

"Testing something." Leine tapped her fingers to remove the AI-assisted overlay. Nothing happened. She'd forgotten to turn on the AI after the run-in with the samurai. Leine tapped again, turning it on. The black-clad operators remained visible as an amber light in her periphery blinked on and off. "Kill the power to the lights in the server room. Just for a second."

"Okay," Alice said, "but won't that make them send for more security?"

"Humor me."

Leine stared at the operators. The overhead lights blinked off. The black-clad men disappeared.

"Holy shit!" Alice said. "They're holograms."

Leine turned from the glass and headed back the way she came. She checked the time on the headset's display. She'd been inside less than fifteen minutes, and had only captured a small portion of the data they'd need. Unfortunately, it was time to leave. Getting caught while she was inside the building was not an option.

"Aborting," she said, as she retraced her steps to return the guard's badge.

33

A wave of excitement surged through Sebastian Fellowes as he ended the call with the representative from the National Reconnaissance Office. He allowed himself a fist-pump before taking a second to savor the moment by gazing out his office window at Puget Sound. The bright sun glinted off the water, mirroring his mood.

Everything was his now.

The NRO had agreed to every one of Sebastian's sticking points—signaling their enthusiasm to acquire the AI-assisted system at any price. The main sticking point—Sebastian's free and unfettered access to accumulated, anonymized data—was a non-starter, as far as he was concerned.

They didn't even blink.

He was glad he'd held his ground. The agreement virtually guaranteed Amazing Grace would remain far advanced of its rivals, learning by leaps and bounds in the NRO's data-rich environment. Who knew what kind of cutting-edge applications would come from the government's extensive testing grounds?

He was almost giddy.

At that moment, Ginger appeared to his right. "Ron would like a word."

"Put him through."

His head of security materialized in Ginger's place. "Hey, boss. I was looking through security logs this morning and there was a weird anomaly over at headquarters last night. The server holograms deployed around oh-two-hundred. I had my guys check, but there's nothing on surveillance video, and no one accessed the room."

"What about Kenny?"

"He didn't report anything. Said it was quiet all night."

"Thanks, Ron. I'll take care of it." Sebastian ended the holo-call and sighed. Another glitch in the hologram program. He'd have to put a team on it, go through the code line-by-line to figure out what was causing it.

Good thing I didn't release the program yet. Not that his reputation couldn't take the hit, but he'd prefer everything worked the way it should before a release.

At least one thing was going right.

Sebastian gave himself five more minutes of living his triumph over the government before he texted Hannah.

'My office. Now.'

She arrived in less than three minutes. Attired in a pink, scoop-neck T-shirt that accentuated her considerable assets, paired with high-tech hiking pants and sandals, her classic beauty was undiminished by the casual ensemble. Her delicate, shell-pink lipstick accentuated the fetching flush to her cheeks.

"What's happened? Any news?" she asked, closing the door behind her.

He gave her a big grin.

Relief floated across her features. "Good news, then." She sighed. "Finally. What's the verdict?"

"They gave us everything we asked for."

Hannah's eyes lit up. "Fantastic. Do we have a date for deployment?"

"That's the best part." His grin widened. "Since you're pre-cleared, you can go immediately."

"Really? Unbelievable." She shook her head. "After the runaround they gave us—it's just that easy?"

"Are you ready?"

Hannah nodded, the import of what he said obviously sinking in. "Wow. Yeah. I've got a lot to do between now and tomorrow morning."

"I knew this would be the outcome." He pulled her to him. The scent of her perfume hit him in the solar plexus. He nuzzled her neck, inhaling deeply.

She leaned back and gave him a coy look. "Oh, so *now* you're interested?"

"Oh, yeah." Still holding her hands, he walked backward, headed toward the door to his private office.

"But I've got so much to do—"

Her protests did nothing to dissuade him. He was invincible. Captain of the Universe.

Everything was going according to plan.

He needed to celebrate.

HANNAH SLIPPED FROM BETWEEN THE SHEETS OF THE KING-SIZED bed and scooped up her clothes. Sebastian's quiet snores told her he was out for the count.

She tiptoed through the room to the outer office, easing the door closed behind her, then quickly got dressed and hurried back to her office for the burner phone she had hidden inside her bag.

'*Deployment imminent. More to follow,*' she typed, then hit Send on the encrypted messaging app.

She didn't have to say any more than that. The recipient would get the gist. He replied a moment later.

'*So it begins.*'

Hannah deleted the texts and dropped the burner back into her bag. She'd need to do some prep work, although the tricky part would come later.

With a sigh, she entered her passcode into her laptop, then leaned back and stared at the ceiling.

Soon, it would all be over and she'd be free to live her life. Free of Langston, free of Sebastian and Congruence's silly constraints, free of Seattle and its overabundance of tech bros and soggy, cold weather. The payoff was what her mother had called "fuck you" money. The kind of cash where she could tell everyone to go to hell, assume another identity, be anyone she wanted to be, anywhere on earth.

But something niggled at the back of her mind. Langston "neutralized" obstacles without a thought. Once an individual lost their use to him, he rarely allowed loose ends. There wasn't any evidence, but the article she'd run across online of the Romanovs' murders had given her pause. The Seattle neighborhood in which they lived had gone pretty sketchy in recent years, and Ivan did have a drinking problem, but Oleg had kept a lid on his younger brother's self-made issues. When Hannah had told Langston of their deaths, he'd waved away her concerns, citing the escalating violence in the area.

Langston had assured her that she was in charge of that part of the plan. Killing them would never have occurred to her.

Still, Oleg shouldn't have held out for more money. She wondered if Langston's people had located his burner phone.

She couldn't ask Langston since he denied knowledge of the murders. That burner phone could tie her to them. She could kick herself for stupidly texting Oleg with her business phone. Her number would be listed in the SIM card unless Langston wiped it. Knowing Langston, that wouldn't happen—he'd keep it as additional insurance.

Hannah shook her head to clear it and picked up her work phone to make flight reservations to the launch site. Once that piece was in place she'd reserve a flight to Naples to pick up a new identity, then on to Malta, where a bank account in her old name awaited. From there, she would shed her old persona and choose her next destination.

Just get through to the end, Hannah. Everything will work out.

It was time to get the show on the road.

34

———

Back at the safehouse, Leine and Alice scanned through the subject lines of Sebastian's emails, searching for clues to what the tech mogul's endgame might be. Why would he have so many people killed? What was he protecting? With that kind of body count, it wasn't good.

And it likely involved a shit ton of money.

Leine rubbed her eyes. Staring at the screen was taking its toll. She pushed away from the laptop she was working on and went into the kitchen for a glass of water. Something didn't feel right, but she couldn't put her finger on what.

The front door opened, and Remy walked in. "Anything?"

Alice shook her head. "So far it's a whole lotta interoffice memos."

"We've got to widen our search." Leine returned to her place at the dining room table. "Maybe the dates aren't right. Let's add another six months." She didn't hold out a lot of hope for finding anything solid connecting Sebastian to the murders in the emails she'd captured, not without more substantial data.

Alice nodded. "Sure. You want me to include the same keywords?"

"Add in Amazing Grace, and Hannah's name. She was pretty cozy with Sebastian at the gala the other night. Maybe there's something specific we can glean from their interactions online."

"Sounds like a long shot." Remy opened the refrigerator and grabbed a beer. "Sebastian's a smart guy. He's not going to create an electronic paper trail of an affair with an underling—his lawyers would cut him off at the nuts."

"I'm not looking for confirmation of their affair," Leine said. "I'm looking for subtext, subconscious clues that might point to whatever Sebastian's mixed up in."

"Yeah, subtext," Alice added with a grin. "Kinda like when you tell me I've been too busy and should slow down. What you're really saying is you need more attention."

Remy responded by flipping her off. "You wish, sweet cheeks. So, basically you're reading between the lines."

"It's all we've got at this point." Leine shrugged. "Maybe he confided in her about something."

"Exactly." Alice smiled sweetly at Remy as he took a seat next to her.

"I got the footage from the bar owner." Remy took a drink of his beer.

"Anything promising?" Leine asked.

"It caught a sedan driving by within the timeframe of the murders. The make and model match the one I saw when I was at Brett's."

"The one with the two gunmen who shot at you?" Alice asked.

"Yep. Couldn't read the plates, though, and sedans are a dime a dozen around here." He shrugged. "At least it's something."

Alice glanced over her monitor at Leine. "I'm gonna split up these messages. Leine, you take fifty—I'll go through the next fifty." She tapped the keyboard and Leine's screen populated with new emails and text messages from the data Leine recovered from Congruence's network. Leine clicked on a string of interoffice texts between Hannah and Sebastian dated several weeks prior.

Hannah: 'I should take lead on the program. Jesper trusts me.'

Sebastian: 'This isn't up for discussion. It's my company.'

Hannah: 'That may be, but it was my contact that got us the meeting in the first place. You know how much I've sacrificed for this project.'

Sebastian's response came after a long pause.

'You know I value your contributions to the team, H. But I'm not comfortable giving you lead status at this time. Nothing personal.'

Hannah: 'Sure, S. btw, did I mention I'm having lunch with our mutual friend at the DoD? Shall I give him your best?'

Sebastian: '???'

Hannah: 'Nothing personal.'

The text string ended. Leine searched and found another group of texts two days later.

'What the fuck did you do, H? Jesper put a hold on negotiations.'

Hannah didn't respond for twenty minutes. Then, *'What do you mean? I thought the project was a go?'*

Sebastian: 'Don't pull that shit with me. You know exactly what's going on. What did you tell our friend at lunch?'

Hannah: 'Nothing. We talked about the weather.'

Sebastian: 'Come on, H. You're going to jeopardize this contract just because you're not getting what you want?'

Hannah didn't respond for several minutes. Sebastian was obviously becoming frustrated.

Sebastian: 'Dammit, H. Answer me. This isn't about your abilities.'

Hannah: 'Isn't it?'

Sebastian: 'Are you accusing me of something?'

Hannah: 'Of course not.'

Sebastian: 'Because it's about my company, not you.'

Hannah: 'Okay. Fine. If that's the case, then why am I not lead? You know I'm the best candidate to run point at NRO. No one else is as qualified. It looks really bad when the boss doesn't trust his own people.'

Now it was Sebastian's turn to pause. He responded six minutes later.

'Fine. You win. I'll send a message to Jesper.'

'Thank you, S. Really.'

Leine looked up from her screen. "I think I've got something." She sent the two text strings to Alice.

Alice read through them and shrugged. "So, Hannah manipulated Sebastian into getting the lead position on a project. I hate to say it, but getting ahead in this industry isn't easy. You use whatever means you can to move up."

"That's important," Leine said, "but there's a thread in these I want to pull. What do you know about the NRO?"

Alice pulled it up on her screen. "The National Reconnaissance Office. Satellites?"

"Reconnaissance satellites." Leine looked from Alice to Remy. "The NRO is an agency within the Department of Defense."

Remy's eyebrows shot up. "Spook birds?"

Leine nodded. "Soup to nuts. Design, build, launch, and operate." She looked at Alice. "Did you ever run that malware on the USB drive through a high-security network environment?"

"I did, but—" Alice snapped her fingers. "That's what was missing." She grabbed her purse off the chair, and started for the door.

Remy set his beer down and rose to follow her. "Where are you going?"

Alice stopped at the door. She looked at Leine. "Remember

when I said I'd isolated the malware, but wasn't sure which program it was designed to work with?"

Leine nodded. "That it was inert—like it was waiting for something."

"Right. So, I ran the code through various simulators, testing its response to different inputs. But when I mimicked a high-security network environment, I noticed something different: the code started to show signs of activity, as though it was preparing to execute a sequence of instructions.

"I dug a little deeper and decrypted certain sections. That's where I discovered a pattern. The code generated a unique signal, a kind of digital fingerprint that's meant to unlock the next phase of its operation. The malware on that USB stick is not meant for an ordinary system—it's tailored for something much more sophisticated."

"Like a satellite system." Leine's mind whirled with possibilities.

Alice nodded. "I cross-referenced its signal patterns with known communication protocols—everything from terrestrial networks to underwater cables, but nothing matched. I *never tested military applications*. What's more sophisticated than a satellite?"

Remy gave Alice a sidelong glance. "You think Sebastian's going to screw up his big, lucrative government contract so he has control over a recon satellite?" He shook his head. "You can't be serious. Soon as they figure out what happened, FBI'll roll him up and he'll be staring at twenty-years-to-life in a high-security prison cell with his new bestie, Charlie Manson."

"But what if the government never found out?" Leine asked. "What if the malware doesn't exhibit any unusual behavior once it's deployed? It just sits quietly and does its thing in the background? What if its only function is to collect data and send it somewhere else?"

"Exactly. I gotta get back to my work computer and test it out." Alice looked at Remy. "Well? If you're coming, you can drive."

"I'm coming, too." Leine picked up her bag and followed them out.

35

Hannah showed her credentials to the security guard, placed her briefcase on the scanner belt, and walked through the magnetometer. On the other side the guard handed her a visitor badge which she clipped to her shirt. She smiled at the guard and collected her briefcase before proceeding to Mission Control. As she wove her way down hallways and past Space Force personnel, she worked hard to control the anxiety threatening to derail her.

Everything's going to be fine, Hannah. Relax.

Soon, she'd be on her way to Italy and beyond, with a short stop in Malta for the money Langston had promised. He didn't know about the new identity waiting for her in Naples, but that was as it should be. Hannah didn't trust Langston. Apart from the information he had on her to guarantee her capitulation to his demands, he'd dangled the promise of untold riches for her part in his scheme. She'd demanded half the money as a token of his good faith. Even if the rest of the payoff failed to materialize, she'd be all right. Especially with her skillset.

She stopped outside the control room and tapped her badge on the reader. The lock clicked and she pushed through.

"Hey, Hannah. Glad you could make it." Jesper, the lead engineer, smiled and nodded to the seat next to him.

"I wouldn't miss this for the world." Hannah took the offered seat and set her briefcase to the side.

She and Jesper made small talk, but the energy in the room was hard to ignore. Although most of the attendees there had been through many satellite launches, this one was special. Sebastian's AI-assisted, next-generation software combined with the cutting-edge satellite electronics would allow the intelligence community the ability to vacuum up vast amounts of data from other satellites in its vicinity, both friend and foe. Ground operators could orient the system sensors to target specific satellites to capture data being sent to and from government ground stations, allowing for intelligence gathering on a scale not seen before. And the AI-assisted software would learn from its mistakes as well as its triumphs, continuing to improve with each command.

Hannah could swear she was having an out-of-body experience as she listened to Jesper's play-by-play of the launch countdown. This was real, not a simulation. Events that brought her to this point had seemed disparate, unrelated. But when she looked back on her life, bits and pieces fell into place, showing paths not taken versus those she had. From her decision to pursue a software engineering degree with an emphasis on the at-the-time nascent field of artificial intelligence; to clawing her way to the top of a male-dominated industry; becoming cynical and angry at how unfair things were because she didn't fit in with the insidious tech-bro culture; to using her looks, her intelligence, and her body to stay there. The choices she'd made had surely steered her toward this moment of payback.

She came back to the present and relaxed as well as she could. She knew the launch sequence by heart, could recite the steps in her sleep. It was finally time. Jesper began counting down.

"*Five…four…three…two…one…*"

"We have ignition."

The large screen at the front of the room displayed the rocket carrying the satellite igniting in what appeared to be a fiery propulsion, thrusting skyward toward its target orbit. Cheers broke out around her. Jesper offered to take her to lunch while they waited to see how the satellite initially performed. Hannah accepted, although if she'd had the choice, she would have stayed put and eaten something there. Rejecting his offer would have been ill-advised. She didn't need to bring any more attention to herself than was absolutely necessary.

After lunch and a short tour of the facility, which she already knew well, Hannah and Jesper arrived back at the control room as the satellite captured Cygnus285, the orientation star, and the solar array began deployment. Next, operations would take the satellite through several tests to see how the sensors maneuvered in the icy vacuum of space.

"Testing five-degree roll," one of the engineers called out. The designated sensor quickly rolled the specified amount.

"Checking yaw." Again, the sensor correctly moved left and right.

Jesper grinned at Hannah. "So far, so good."

Hannah returned the smile, using it to hide her increasing anxiety as the time for her to act approached.

"Testing pitch."

At this juncture, the sensor was supposed to perform a series of controlled maneuvers—but something went wrong. The sensor pitched but immediately returned to its original position. The operator attempted the test again, but from across the control room another technician shouted, "We're drifting. We're losing the star!"

Jesper's brows knitted and he turned to Hannah. "Something's wrong with the star sensor. Any ideas?"

"This happened once months ago during an early test," Hannah said as she dug inside her briefcase. She produced a USB stick and held it aloft. "I created a patch to increase the sensitivity of the eye that I never thought I'd need. May I try it?"

Jesper smiled, obviously relieved. "I knew I invited you here for a reason. Let me get a security override before we lose the star."

Heart beating in her ears, she forced herself to breathe. *In, out, in, out. You'll be fine, Hannah, keep breathing...*as she inserted the drive and typed in the commands that would deliver the patch to correct the anomaly.

"How is it now?" Hannah asked Jesper. Her mouth had gone dry.

Jesper asked Operations to check the orientation once more. A moment later, the satellite recaptured the orientation star. Relief washed through the room. He nodded at Hannah.

"Thank goodness you were here."

Although Hannah's smile was frozen on her face, inside she was experiencing a curious mixture of excitement and dread. Excited to have been able to pull off the task Langston had given her, thereby severing their relationship for good and making her a wealthy woman, but also fear of her role in a treasonous act. Because of her, an outside actor would have access to every piece of intelligence the satellite intercepted, all to be sold to the highest bidder.

What had she done?

36

Leine looked on as Alice brought up the malware from the USB stick on her air-gapped computer. She, Remy, and Alice were inside Alice's office at the AI startup in downtown Seattle, near Pike Place Market. Leine stood behind Alice, while Remy sat in the chair across from her.

"I'll cross-reference the malware's signal patterns with known military communications and satellite uplinks." Alice's fingers flew across the keyboard, then stilled as she waited for a response from the program. Lines of code populated several screens in front of her, a different language Leine had yet to learn.

"There you are, you little bastard." Alice leaned forward, pointing at the screen. "It's a match. The signal sequences resemble satellite communication protocols. Specifically, those involved in command uplinks for control systems."

Alice's words hit Leine hard. "So, you're saying this malware is definitely designed to interact with a satellite."

"And Sebastian just happens to have a bright, shiny contract with the NRO," Remy added.

"Are we certain it's Sebastian?" Leine asked.

Alice and Remy both looked at her.

"I thought you were convinced it was him," Remy said.

"It's the most obvious choice. But maybe it's too obvious."

"What do you mean?" Alice asked.

"Let's look at the facts. Remy found the USB stick containing the malware on the floor at Brett's house. Brett and his partner were killed, potentially by someone who wanted the USB stick."

"Don't forget Scott," Remy reminded her.

Leine nodded. "I'll come back to him later. The three of us were targeted—Remy and I were almost killed, and Alice was kidnapped, with the intent to get information out of her."

"And somebody trashed Remy's place to find the malware."

"How did they know who had the drive?" Leine started to pace as she thought out loud. "Is there a way for the malware itself to send a signal to someone, telling them its location?"

Alice's eyes widened. "Oh, shit. That's what that was for."

"What?" Remy and Leine both said at once.

"There was a geolocator embedded in the malware. I thought it was meant to do something in relation to its parent program, but it could conceivably activate a kind of homing signal." She typed something into her computer and brought up another screen, which she scanned. "It's not operative at the moment."

Leine stopped pacing. "This is an air-gapped computer, so no signal is getting in or out, right?"

"Right." Alice nodded. "But if Brett tried to open the program on his un-air-gapped computer, it might have deployed, sending out its location."

"That's how they found me, then," Remy said. "I plugged the drive into my laptop the night I found it at Brett's. Once I figured out it was password protected, I removed it."

"But it had already relayed its location to someone." Alice

looked at Leine. "The question is, where did it go, and why target you? And Scott?"

Leine shook her head. "I was followed when I left the club. I'm actively pursuing an investigation that could potentially lead me to Sebastian. Perhaps killing Scott was meant to put investigators off the scent, make it look like a hate crime or a wave of robberies."

"But he was killed two nights before Brett and Ethan died."

"Could have been in the works for a while. Do we know where and when Brett got the USB stick?"

"No." Remy crossed his arms. "No one at the club knew."

"But someone knows." Leine thought about Laura and how nervous she seemed, how she was holding something back. Maybe Leine needed to talk to the club's mama bear once more.

"Why not go to the source?" Remy asked. "If anybody knows what's going on, it's Sebastian."

"If he's behind this, confronting Sebastian might not be the best idea," Alice said.

"Agreed. Tipping off the bad guy isn't wise, especially when the bad guy is willing to kill to cover things up. But we may have to if we can't get answers. I'll work my contacts, let the NRO know what we've found." Leine slid her phone from her pocket and sent Lou an encrypted text, detailing their findings. "If we're lucky and can warn them before the launch, that could be enough to head this off before something bad happens."

"What if we're wrong?" Remy asked. "What if we're jumping to the wrong conclusion and it's not Sebastian's malware? That it has nothing to do with Congruence's deal with the government?"

"Lou will be discreet. If we're wrong, no harm, no foul." Leine put away her phone. "The question we need to be asking ourselves is, what if we're right?"

37

L eine walked through the entrance to Luck be a Lady and headed for the bar, where Pablo was stocking the under-counter fridge.

"Hey, Pablo. Is Laura around?"

Pablo nodded as he shoved the last six-pack of Heineken into the cooler under the bar. "She's in the office." He straightened and wiped his forehead with his sleeve. "Anything new on Brett and Ethan?"

Leine noted he didn't ask about Scott. She shook her head. "Not yet, but we've got some promising leads."

"Cool." He set the empty cardboard box down and leaned forward, his hands on the bar. "Hey, I don't know if it's important or not, but last night during the show, I remembered something."

"Yeah?"

"Back a few weeks ago, when Brett was running the program, there was a glitch."

"Desi told me. It messed up pretty badly, right?"

Pablo nodded. "It was a big deal. We had to print up vouchers for folks for a future show, refund tickets, shit like that.

A real cluster."

"And?"

"Like I said, I don't know if this is anything, but right before the glitch I noticed Scott McKenzie over by the mothership." He lifted his chin, indicating the equipment situated at the back of the room where a staff member controlled the show.

"And that was unusual?"

"Yeah. Scott was a performer. He didn't work the controls. Most of us stay as far away from the equipment as we can. Desi drilled into us how expensive it all is, how much insurance he has to keep on it. Nobody wants to be the one to fuck it up."

"So, you think Scott accidentally fucked it up?"

Pablo shrugged, squinted at her. "That's the thing. It didn't look accidental. He was, like, loitering, looking nervous."

"Did you see him do anything?"

"Nah. Just a gut feeling. Like I said, it's probably nothing."

"Good to know. Thanks, Pablo." That put a spin on things. His lack of concern for news on Scott's murder gave her pause. Was this an intentional misdirection, or was the revelation genuine? Leine made her way to the back of the building where the office was located. The office door was closed. She knocked.

"C'mon in," Laura called out.

Leine opened the door and stepped inside, closing it behind her.

Laura sat at the desk, working on her laptop. "Hey, Leine. What can I do for you?"

"I have a couple more questions." Leine had a seat in the chair across from her.

"Have you found something?" Laura's expression conveyed interest, but Leine sensed an undercurrent of anxiety. Maybe that was just how Laura rolled.

"Actually, yes. What can you tell me about Scott McKenzie?"

"I think I already said he and I were acquaintances. What

else is there to say?" Laura shifted slightly in her chair. Not much, but enough to notice.

"You remember the night the VR show shut down, right?"

Laura grimaced. "Oh, my goodness, yes. We had to cover all of the tickets. I was back here printing vouchers, while the front-of-house staff issued refunds to the customers who wouldn't wait, the works. Total nightmare."

"One of the employees saw Scott next to the VR equipment the night of the glitch."

Her cheeks pinkened. "Oh? Well, that's not unusual. Scott was—"

"I was led to believe that most performers avoided that section of the bar—that they didn't want to be responsible in case something went wrong."

Laura busied herself straightening a pile of papers on the desk, avoiding Leine's gaze. "Well, he, uh—he was probably just—"

"Laura. Look at me."

The other woman stopped fidgeting and lifted her gaze to Leine's. Resignation was plain in her eyes.

"You knew Scott better than you let on, didn't you?"

She sighed, nodded. "We go—went—back a few years. We both worked at another revue across town. I told him about the job here at the club." She crossed her arms. "I didn't put my finger on the scales, though. He got hired because he was good."

"But not good enough to be a headliner?"

"No," she conceded, clearing her throat. "Not that good."

"You said he was ambitious, that he used people to get ahead?"

Laura shrugged. "He thought he was better than what Desi gave him credit for."

Her gaze steady, Leine leaned toward her. Time to get at the truth. "How did you come by the USB drive, and why did you give it to Brett?"

The shock on Laura's face quickly transformed into something that resembled shame. The color in her cheeks deepened and tears glistened in her eyes. "I—he—oh, God." She burst into tears. Leine pulled a tissue from the box on the desk and handed it to her. Laura took it and covered her face as she sobbed.

Leine let her cry. The relief of no longer having to hide a terrible secret—and the way she sobbed, it had to have weighed heavily on her—would allow her to give a more coherent account of what she'd been holding back.

A few minutes later, Laura's sobs slowed to a sniffle. Leine remained silent, allowing her to get to the point in her own time.

Laura took a deep breath and sighed. "Scott was murdered."

"That's established."

Laura shook her head. "It wasn't a robbery."

"Why do you say that?"

"Because he had a failsafe." At this, the tears began to fall again, but she stopped herself. "Two days after he was killed, a package was delivered to the club. Addressed to me."

"The USB drive."

Laura nodded. "I—I didn't know what to do with it, so I told Brett. I was so scared. We'd heard about the murder, of course. Everyone was a little freaked out. Brett took it so that I wouldn't be afraid."

More sobs escaped her. Leine waited patiently for her to compose herself.

"Then, when Brett and Ethan were—killed, I didn't know what to do. I had no idea how the killers found out Brett had the drive. I thought I'd be next."

"Did Brett ever figure out what was on it?"

Laura shook her head. "It was password protected. He had no clue." Something occurred to her, and she stared at Leine.

"Oh, God. What's going to happen to me now?" Eyes wild, she glanced around the room. "What if they're recording us, right now?" She stood, hand on her purse, ready to run.

"Laura. Calm down. You're all right. No one knows you had it." Leine used the tone she reserved for traumatized human trafficking victims.

It seemed to work. Laura's respiration slowed and she sank back into her chair.

"We believe the USB stick had a homing signal that deployed when it was inserted into the port on a computer. Did you ever plug it in to see what was on it?"

"No. I was too freaked out. I let Brett—" She choked on the sentence before dissolving into more tears. "Oh, my God, no. That means I'm responsible for Brett and Ethan—for them being murdered."

Leine pulled more tissues from the box and handed them to her. "How could you be? You didn't know."

The look on her face gave Leine pause. Did Laura know more than she was telling her? She waited for the sobs to subside before pressing her further.

"Laura, this is really important. Did you know what Scott was doing with the drive?"

Laura sighed. "Not exactly, but I'd seen him by the mothership. When I asked him what he was doing near the show's equipment, he said he was checking something for Sebastian." She closed her eyes. "When the show went down, I didn't have time to think. Once we got through that night, I was exhausted. We all were. I'd forgotten about Scott hanging out by the equipment."

"Was there any fallout? Aside from unhappy customers?"

"Desi was pissed about the lost revenue, but said Sebastian would replace the program with a new one, so not to worry." She shrugged. "I didn't think any more about it. Programs glitch. Especially one that's as cutting-edge as that one."

"Did you see what he was doing? Did he have the USB drive with him?"

Laura frowned and cocked her head. "What was on that USB?"

"The one we have from Brett's place has a kind of malware on it. It only works if it's in a specific environment."

"Are you saying that Sebastian asked Scott to upload malware into his own program? That doesn't make sense."

"Not Sebastian. What if Scott was lying, doing it for someone else?"

Laura's confusion was plain on her face. "Who else could it be?"

"That's what we need to find out. Can you think of anyone he might have interacted with in the days leading up to the program failing?"

"I didn't know all his friends, although he did spend quite a bit of time with someone from Congruence. I think her name was Hannah."

Bingo. Leine's heart rate kicked up a notch at the mention of the lead on Sebastian's government contract. "Thank you, Laura." She stood and grabbed her bag. "You've been a big help."

"You're welcome. What—"

But Leine was already out the door, headed for Congruence.

38

L eine called Alice from her car. "I'm on my way to Congruence. Meet me there. Bring a copy of the malware."

"I have the version I loaded onto the air-gapped computer."

"That would work."

"What happened? What did Laura say?"

"I'll fill you in when you get there. Bring Remy, too." Leine ended the call and swerved to avoid hitting the car in front of her. Traffic was heavy through the north end of town. She brought up Sebastian's number that she'd saved in her contacts.

"Sebastian—it's Desi's friend, Leine."

"How did you get this number?"

"That's not important."

"Wrong answer." Sebastian's tone had a hard edge to it. "This is my personal cell. Only a select few have access. Desi wouldn't have given it to you unless he asked me first. Should we try again?"

"Look, I don't have a lot of time. I'm on my way to your office. We need to talk."

"And you can't tell me what this is about over the phone, is that it?"

"Exactly. I guarantee you'll want to hear what I have to say." Leine hesitated to divulge more, didn't know if she was being monitored.

"Fine. My interest is piqued. I'll put you on the visitor's log. But I'm also letting my security team know you're coming."

"Do that, and add two more to the log." She gave him Alice and Remy's names and ended the call.

Then she called Lou.

Ten minutes later, she parked on the second level of Congruence's garage and killed the engine. Alice and Remy pulled in a few minutes later. They rode the elevator to the main entrance to check in, while Leine filled them in on what she'd learned at the club.

The atrium looked different in the light of day. The lush vegetation and rich wood seating areas had a welcoming vibe. Along with visitor passes on lanyards, the concierge offered them VR headsets to be able to see the waterfall and beach scene, but they declined.

Sebastian appeared at the top of the escalator on the second floor and beckoned them to join him. They took an elevator to the fifth floor, then followed him to his office where he closed the door.

"Have a seat." A live-edge wood desk took up a majority of one end of the room. An expensive Italian fridge lined one wall. A single, albeit large, monitor was visible. Sebastian walked behind the desk and sat in the executive chair. Leine and Alice took the two chairs opposite him, while Remy had a seat on the leather couch a short distance away.

"Now that we're all here, what's so important that it couldn't be discussed over the phone?" Sebastian asked.

Leine spoke first. "We have reason to believe that one of your employees may have sabotaged the program you sold to the NRO."

Sebastian's brow wrinkled as a wary look crossed his face. "How do you know about the contract?"

"I'm not at liberty to tell you that," Leine replied. "What's important here is that it needs to be stopped. National security could be compromised."

"That information is classified." Sebastian rose from his chair, wariness turning to anger. "No one except the NRO and a select team here at Congruence knows about the sale." He touched his watch and said, "Ginger, send security to my office. Now."

A woman's voice answered, "Of course, Sebastian. ETA is—"

Sebastian touched his watch, cutting her off. "You had better explain your inside knowledge of Congruence's business interests to my satisfaction by the time security walks through that door, or you'll be out on your asses before you can say 'civil liberties.'"

"We're in possession of malware that we believe is designed to exploit a hook within the program you just licensed to the NRO." Alice held his gaze. "It's my opinion that the hook is capable of overriding the satellite's commands, effectively hijacking its operations."

Sebastian's expression didn't change, although his coloring noticeably paled. "And you are?"

"Alice. I work for a software startup that specializes in AI."

"Ah. It's beginning to make sense." Sebastian nodded. "How do I know you aren't the creator of said malware?"

Leine speared him with a look. "She's not looking for your business, if that's what you're implying. Hear her out."

Sebastian turned his attention back to Alice. "Go on."

Alice continued. "I'll need to cross-reference the satellite's kernel updates to see if there's an unauthorized update among the legitimate patches."

"How do I know this isn't some kind of elaborate ruse to cover what is at best corporate espionage, or at worst a national security breach?"

"I can prove it." Alice pulled her laptop from her valise. "With your permission? It's air-gapped, of course."

He shook his head. "I don't think so. I'm going to give my contact at the NRO a call. See if there's been any problems."

Leine gave him a sharp look. "You already delivered the program?"

"Indeed. It launched two days ago. But wouldn't you know that?"

She glanced at Alice. Alice shook her head. "This is going to complicate things."

At that moment there was a knock at the door. Sebastian tapped his watch and the door swung open, revealing three heavily muscled men dressed in black golf shirts, tan cargo pants, and black tactical boots. All three wore buzz cuts and packed at least one sidearm. One guy sported a horseshoe mustache. They fanned out, scanning the room for threats.

Security R Us.

"I'm good, guys. False alarm. Stick around, though. I might have a need."

"Copy that," Mustache-guy said. With a stern look at Remy, he filed out the door behind the other two, and closed the door behind him. That he didn't view either Alice or Leine as a threat was interesting. Apparently, their training hadn't been updated. Good to know.

Sebastian typed a number into his phone, then placed his mobile on the desk.

"Jesper Reynolds."

"Jesper, Sebastian here. You're on speaker. I have a couple of colleagues with me."

"Oh, hey, Sebastian. What can I do for you?"

Sebastian eyed Alice and Leine. "Just checking to make sure everything's still functioning smoothly."

"Like a charm, buddy."

"No problems, then?"

"Nope. Not a one."

Sebastian's shoulders inched down as he visibly relaxed. "That's great, I'm glad to hear—"

"Well, wait a minute. That's not completely accurate. There was a glitch during launch, but Hannah was on top of it."

The air in Sebastian's office stilled. "What kind of glitch?"

"Nothing, really. An operational aberration—something to do with the star sensor. Hannah offered to upload a patch to the onboard code. Worked like a charm."

"And everything's good since she applied the patch?"

"Yep. Execution has been flawless."

"That's great, Jesper. Keep me posted, all right?"

"Will do."

Sebastian ended the call. He looked at Alice. "Did you bring the malware?"

"I have a copy on my laptop."

"That's not going to work." He pulled a flash drive from a desk drawer and tossed it to her. "Make a copy from yours and I'll upload it onto mine. I have the AI program's most recent iteration loaded on my own air-gapped computer." He tapped his watch again, then opened another drawer in his desk and pulled out a laptop. "I'll test your malware in my own sandbox."

Alice copied the program from her computer and handed the drive to Sebastian. He uploaded the malware onto his computer and started typing.

"Trust but verify," Leine said.

"Exactly." Sebastian continued inputting commands. After a couple of minutes, he nodded. "Okay. Your first comments track. The malware triggers an override. Now I'll cross-reference the kernel updates." He stopped. Frowned. "There's an unauthorized update buried in with the legit patches. Whoever wrote this disguised the hook as a minor performance tweak." He squinted at the screen. "Timestamped two months ago."

"Does your team conduct peer reviews?" Alice asked.

"Yeah. I'll check to see why it wasn't flagged." Sebastian switched to his other computer and typed in a command. As he read, his expression hardened. His gaze flickered to Leine, then Alice. "The review doesn't mention anything."

"Who filed the report?" Leine asked.

Sebastian scrubbed his face with his hand. "Hannah."

"The launch lead?" Alice asked, surprised.

He nodded. "Yeah." He blew out a breath. "Her fingerprints are all over the hook. But the malware—that's different. Not her style at all."

"So, she's working with someone." Leine's mind raced to connect the dots. Who was pulling the strings? Another employee within Congruence, or someone else?

"What exactly does this program do?" Leine asked. Satellites did numerous jobs: intelligence gathering, target acquisition, missile guidance, positioning.

"That's classified. I don't feel comfortable discussing it with you."

"You have access to DISS?" Leine asked.

"I do."

"You can check my clearances there. Query Leine Basso." She gave him her birthdate and other identifying information.

Sebastian's eyebrows beetled together as he typed the information into the DOD's Defense Information System. He leveled his gaze at her. "Top Secret clearance."

Leine nodded. "Feel better about discussing the problem?"

"With you, yes." He glanced at Alice and Remy. "Not with them."

"Fine. You can fill me in later. What are we going to do about this?"

Sebastian sat forward and typed something into the air-gapped computer, then waited. He scanned the screen and frowned. He typed something else and waited again. His expression grew dark. Then he tried again. "Fuck." He balled his hands into fists and leaned back in his chair.

"What's wrong?" Alice asked.

"I tried to gain control through the backdoor I built into the program, but the malware adapts to each simulated environment and shuts down access every time. It takes advantage of a vulnerability programmed into the software."

"What specifically is the malware designed to do to the program?" Alice asked. "Limiting access can't be the only reason behind it."

"The hook requires a precise sequence of signals and data inputs, which the malware is designed to generate. These signals mimic routine commands."

"In English?" Remy said.

"The signals look like normal satellite operations. But the hook overrides them, basically hiding in plain sight."

"What is the hook programmed to achieve?" Leine asked.

Sebastian leaned his elbows on his desk, a grave expression on his face. He held Leine's gaze. "It redirects control to an external source."

"So, it transfers control of the satellite to another entity." Leine's heart rate went up a notch. "Depending on the satellite's capabilities, that's huge."

"I'm no expert, clearly," Remy said. "But wouldn't it be safer if you let Jesper and the NRO know what's going on so they can take the satellite offline before something really bad happens?"

Sebastian shook his head. "The malware disables admin access, even when I try to access the program through my own backdoor. Somehow, the malware anticipated the backdoor's existence." He sighed. "The only one who can take it offline is whoever wrote the malware."

"Did you tell anyone about the backdoor?" Alice asked.

"Not—" Sebastian's complexion went a shade paler. He looked at the ceiling. "I may have mentioned it to Hannah. Shit." He slammed his fist on the desk, making the stapler dance.

"So, call Hannah, tell her you know all about what she did, and threaten her with prison if she doesn't reverse it." Remy shrugged. "Pretty simple, you ask me."

Sebastian's smile lacked mirth. "If I let her know I found out what she did, she'll be gone."

"That's why you should invite her to dinner," Leine suggested. "Tell her it's for a job well done. You can confront her then. Remy and I will be nearby in case she bolts."

"That could work." Sebastian nodded, hope visible on his face for the first time since he'd found out about the malware. "I can have her come to the house. She wouldn't be suspicious of that." He picked up his phone and hit speed-dial. After a few seconds, he blew out a breath.

"What's wrong?" Leine asked.

Sebastian put the call on speaker phone. Hannah's voice flowed through the device, filling the room.

"Hi there. You've reached Hannah, Vice President of Operations for Congruence. I'm away on holiday for a few weeks, so please leave a number and I'll get back to you as soon as I return."

Leine studied him. "I take it she wasn't due to go on a vacation."

Sebastian disconnected the call. "No. She wasn't." His expression conveyed resignation mixed with anger. Pretty tough to find out someone you were seeing romantically had betrayed you.

"There's no other way to get into the program?" Leine asked.

"None that I know of."

"If it's a question of national security, couldn't the NRO just shoot it down?" Remy asked.

Sebastian shook his head. "Last resort. That satellite represents decades of research and development and billions of dollars. Destroying it would set the program back a decade, if not longer. I've got to find another way."

"While I was testing the malware, I identified a kind of signature." Alice's typed something on her computer. She turned the screen toward Sebastian. "It's an encoded tag. I could run it by some of my contacts in the hacker community, see what turns up."

"That could work," he said, "although you'll have to be careful not to alert the actual programmer."

Alice used her phone to take a screenshot of the signature. "I'll make sure to couch the request so they don't know the real reason I'm asking."

"There's not a lot of time. Whoever is behind this will have access to information and capabilities that could do untold damage." Sebastian rubbed his eyes. "This is a nightmare."

"What about Hannah?" Leine asked. "We find her, we might get a handle on the person behind the malware."

"That would require access to facial recognition at airports and to a passport database. Unless you have access, I'd have to inform Jesper."

"You can't do that if you want to have any possibility of catching this person," Leine said. "We don't know how far up the DOD food chain this goes. If word gets out that the government's looking for Hannah, it won't be long until the hacker's in the wind."

"Yeah," Remy added, "after they finish doing whatever the program's designed to do. The damage will have already been done."

"I'll take care of that piece," Leine said. "I've already alerted my contact regarding the situation so he can hit the ground running to locate Hannah." Lou had expressed as much in her last text exchange with him.

"It's a start," Sebastian said. "There has to be something else I can do. Something to disrupt the satellite's operation. Usually with a problem this complex I'd get a team together and we'd brainstorm ideas. But I don't trust that Hannah's the only one at Congruence who's involved." He drummed his fingers on the desk. "Unless..."

"Unless?" Alice and Leine said in unison.

Sebastian shook his head. "We'd never find her."

"Find who?" Remy asked.

"The person who created the original program."

Leine and Alice exchanged looks. Alice said, "You mean Amazing Grace, right?"

His gaze sharpened on Alice. "How do you know that?"

Leine needed to steer the conversation away from their methods before Alice got them all in hot water. "Do you mean to imply that you didn't write the original program?"

"An ex-employee, Grace Simpson, wrote the first iteration. We named the program Amazing Grace because of what it could do."

"Where is she now?" Remy asked.

The tech mogul shrugged. "I don't know. She left a couple of years ago. We had a... slight difference of opinion."

Alice's mouth opened as if she was going to say something. Leine put a hand on her arm to preempt her from divulging their knowledge of the doomsday document they'd found on Sebastian's laptop.

"Is there any possibility that she might be able to help?" Leine asked.

"It's possible. If anyone can figure out a way in, it would be Grace. But you'd have to find her first."

Remy stood. "Give me everything you've got on her. I'll find her."

39

Remy drove Alice back to the safehouse so she could work her contacts, while Leine returned to Desi's apartment. Desi's car was parked in his space at the condo, indicating he was home. She checked the time. He'd be fast asleep, getting some shut-eye before opening the club for the evening. Leine's phone pinged with a text message, and she checked the screen. It was Lou. He wanted to talk.

"Hey, Lou. What've you got?"

"Facial recognition picked up Hannah in Naples."

"Italy or Florida?"

"Italy. She landed two days ago after taking a redeye."

"She still there?"

"That's the interesting part. We picked her up again a day later in Malta, but the passport doesn't match." He paused for a moment. "Says here her name is Jenna Swaggart. I cross-checked the name and there's a thin legend behind it."

"A passport special?"

"Sure looks that way."

"So, she's in Malta?"

"Last I checked. She's staying at a boutique hotel in Valletta not far from the harbor."

"Is Art available? We need to grab her before she's gone." Leine had worked with Art and his team of private security professionals a few times and trusted him. The last job had been in Scivoloso, Italy, when she was up against the Albanian mob. He operated out of Athens, Greece, so would be able to get to Malta in a few hours.

"Already ahead of you. He and Zarko are on the next available flight out of Athens."

"Perfect. Tell him to contact me once he has her."

"Will do."

Leine ended the call. She'd have Art arrange a video chat with Hannah so Leine could feel her out, see if she'd roll over on her co-conspirator. If that didn't work, they'd have to "encourage" her to fly back to the US where Leine could do her own interrogation. Hannah was certainly aware that tampering with a government satellite would bring a lengthy prison sentence. That alone could be enough to talk her into helping them.

***

HANNAH HELD THE VALISE CLOSE AS SHE MADE HER WAY ALONG THE promenade near Valletta's grand harbor. Langston was good to his word and the bank withdrawal had been flawless. The amount of euros in her possession was more than enough to take care of her for a good long while.

The smell of the sea and bright, sunny day put a spring in her step—the first since she'd met Langston. Her soaring mood was tempered by the influx of tourists who thronged the walkways and outdoor cafés. She clutched the valise closer, afraid the pickpockets and purse snatchers prevalent in European cities somehow sensed its contents.

She turned right and headed for her hotel, leaving behind the crowded promenade. Barely registering the ancient walls and buildings she passed, her thoughts ping-ponged between relief at finishing the task she'd been forced into executing, and the cold bottle of white wine waiting for her in her hotel room.

She didn't notice exactly when the two men fell in behind her, but the hairs on the back of her neck prickled soon after they did. A brief glance told her the one on the left was much taller than the other and had long, dark hair, while the shorter man on the right was older with a solid build.

Her step faltered. An innate sense of self-preservation took over, and she checked the urge to run. Did the men following her mean to rob her? Too late, she glanced at her surroundings, comprehension firing through her. She'd chosen the perfect environment for them to commit whatever criminal deed they intended. The narrow street consisted of sun-bleached cobblestones, closed doors, and shuttered windows. No welcoming storefront, no outdoor café. No tourists were visible—a dearth of human presence.

Hannah continued to walk, feigning obliviousness to the two men's existence, her mind scrabbling for a solution to what was likely a robbery in progress.

Stupid, stupid, stupid. She'd rarely traveled outside the United States alone. When she did attend an international conference on her own, she'd either remained close to the hotel where the conference was being held, or taken a tour, allowing for the safety and comfort of a crowd.

At the next corner, she glanced left and right, her hopes dashed when she realized each direction was more of the same —a lack of stores, cafés, and people.

Should she turn and confront them? Stare them down? She'd surely lose the money in the case. Should she run, and hope the surprise move would be enough to give her a head start?

Turning left, she glanced at the convex mirror mounted on the corner of the building that allowed drivers to see oncoming traffic. The two men did not turn to follow her. She breathed a sigh of relief.

You're getting too paranoid, Hannah. Time to leave Malta.

Thankfully, her flight to Portugal was later that evening. She'd order room service and stay put until it was time to go to the airport. The last leg of her journey included a flight to South America.

This time tomorrow she'd be in Rio de Janeiro and could disappear behind her new identity.

She turned right twice, then took a left to resume her original route.

As she approached the last intersection before her hotel, she heard footsteps behind her. Before she could turn, an arm snaked around her neck and yanked her backward, choking off her screams. She dropped the valise and clawed at her assailant's arm. Whoever it was wore a leather jacket and her efforts were wasted.

Spots appeared in her periphery, and she attempted to suck in a breath. Panic filled her as her strength ebbed.

"Langston sends his regards." Fear shot through her at the man's gravelly voice. Hannah's fingers flailed. She was fading fast.

So, this was how she died—on a deserted street in Valletta.

God, she was so close.

Something slammed her forward, and the pressure on her throat eased. She fell to her knees, gasping for air. Behind her, it sounded like a scuffle. Someone grunted. There was a *thud,* and a man's leather-clad arm unfurled next to her. A wicked-looking knife slid from the open hand, clattering on the cobblestones. She stared, unable to comprehend what happened.

"You all right?" A man squatted in front of her. Backlit by the sun, his face remained in shadow.

Hannah nodded. "I'm fine." She climbed to her feet. The man stood by, ready to help. Still trying to catch her breath, she placed her hand on his arm to steady herself. She shaded her eyes to see who helped her and recognized the tall man with the long, dark hair from earlier. Still shaky, she looked behind her. His older friend was busy going through the pockets of the man in the leather jacket, now lying in the street. "Is he—"

"That's probably something you don't want to know."

So, the guy in the leather jacket was dead. She wasn't sorry, but the idea these two men killed someone and acted like they were out for a sunny walk opened up a whole new frontier of questions about her "rescuers." She stared at the body on the street, trying to make sense of what his death meant for her, before she turned to look at the man next to her. Two silver hoops glinted on his earlobes. "Why were you following me?"

Instead of answering, he said, "We need you to come with us, please." He reached for her arm, but she stepped back and shook her head.

"I don't know who you are."

The older guy finished searching the dead guy and walked over to join them, sliding what looked like a wallet into his shirt pocket. So, they were thieves.

She eyed the valise on the ground nearby. "I should really be going." She stooped to pick up the case, but the dark-haired man grabbed it first.

"Sorry. I can't let you have this right now."

Panic spiked through her. Without thinking, she grabbed for it, but the other man held it out of reach.

"I'll scream." She glared at them both, righteous indignation filling in for the fear and panic fighting inside her.

"We're the guys who just saved your life," the older guy said. "If you don't want to spend the next couple of decades in prison, I recommend you come with us."

The dark-haired guy smiled. She recognized kindness in his eyes. The older guy, not so much. He exuded a rough confidence and more than a hint of violence. She'd bet he was the killer of the two.

"I'll come with you if you tell me who you are."

The older guy smiled. "We can be either your knights in shining armor, or your worst nightmare. Your call."

The dark-haired guy offered his arm. He had her money, and they obviously weren't above violence. What else could she do?

She took his arm.

40

That morning, Leine drove to the Phinney Ridge safe house to meet Remy and Alice to discuss next steps. Traffic had been light. Mount Rainier, or The Mountain as it was affectionately called, was out in all her glory—the kind of Seattle summer day residents lived for, with impossibly blue skies and the occasional fluffy white cloud scudding by. Leine parked on the street and grabbed the coffees she'd stopped to get everyone then went inside.

"What did you find out?" Leine asked Alice. Alice sat at the dining room table, surrounded by monitors, looking as though they were instruments in her own private symphony. Remy sat on the couch in the living room, paging through a hot rod magazine.

"Two things. First, Uncle Chen came through. I asked him to use his 'underworld' contacts," –she used air quotes to emphasize the word underworld— "to see if there was any chatter about a new player with access to government secrets."

"And?" Leine asked.

"At first, he said it was just the usual crap making the rounds —somebody had insider knowledge of government secrets who's willing to sell said knowledge to the highest bidder—that kind of stuff," Alice said. "Normally, it doesn't go very far. It's just some idiot trying to make a name for themselves. But there's a new player, goes by the handle Zeus79, who claims to have access to real-time DOD intelligence."

"That's our guy," Leine said.

"Or gal," Alice said. "Rumor has it they're setting up an auction three days from now."

"Why wait?" Remy asked.

Leine handed out the coffees before she folded herself into one of the living room chairs. "To give him or herself time to gather enough salable information to make the auction worthwhile. I suspect Zeus79 will auction off individual lots—say, one lot that includes intel on the United States, one with information on the UK, or some other NATO ally—to make more money. They're also likely giving bidders time to get their pieces in place. Is it safe to assume payment is in some form of cryptocurrency?"

Alice nodded. "You assume correctly. What do you want to do?"

"Get on the list of bidders. Tell them you represent some obscure Saudi Arabian prince," Leine replied. "We need eyes on that auction."

"I'll create a persona through a bunch of proxies and spoofs."

"Enter the bidding late, can you? We don't want to give Zeus79 time to unmask your identity."

Alice gave Leine a look. "He won't be able to unmask anything."

Leine smiled. "Or she. You said Uncle Chen's info was the first item you had. What's the second?"

"My hacker friends couldn't get anything useful from the encoded tag. It uses a specific cryptographic algorithm that's next to impossible to break. I ran a deep search on Zeus79, but all I found were false positives. Nothing on our hacker."

"You're saying Zeus79 is a ghost."

Remy looked up from the magazine. "What about offshore accounts? Shell companies?"

"I checked all that. Any footprints have been vaporized, or, more likely, hidden behind proxies and shells within shells."

"Did you happen to find a name behind the handle?"

Alice shook her head. "Not a clue."

Leine sighed. She turned to Remy. "What's the update on finding Grace?"

Remy put down the magazine he was reading and joined them at the table.

"I narrowed my search to all Grace Simpsons who used to live in Seattle and used her birthdate, but there wasn't much to find. Then I checked for family and found her mother living up north in Bellingham, so I gave her a call. Mrs. Simpson was no match for my charm."

"Oh, puhleeze." Alice rolled her eyes.

Remy grinned. "I told her I was an old friend from college and was interested in catching up. At first she hesitated, but I mentioned I'd lost track of Grace after she left Congruence, and she opened right up. Apparently, there was some pretty bad blood between Grace and Sebastian."

"Sebastian hinted as much." Leine nodded. "Where is Grace now?"

"A little town in New Mexico. Apparently, she doesn't like visitors. The mother was going to call her to give her a heads-up, but I told her I wanted it to be a surprise."

"Huh. And she wasn't suspicious?" Alice asked.

Remy's grin grew wider. "Social engineering, my sweet. It ain't just for techies. Had her eating out of my hand."

"Gross."

"Did you get an actual address?" Leine asked.

He shook his head. "Mom wasn't that accommodating. She gave me the name of the town, and a café where she hangs out. I checked county records. Didn't find anything for Grace Simpson, but there's a deed near that town listed under Grace Tsosie."

"She changed her name?"

"Mother's maiden name," Remy replied. "Turns out she's part Navajo."

Leine drained her coffee and set the cup on the table. "How do we get there?"

"The nearest regional airport is thirty miles or so south of Albuquerque."

"Sebastian offered us his private jet." Leine pulled out her phone. "I'll double-check to make sure it's available. The flight shouldn't take long." She nodded at Remy. "Good job."

Remy lifted his chin. "No problem." Alice smiled and patted his arm.

Before she could bring up her contact list, Leine's phone vibrated with a call from an unknown number. "Leine," she answered.

"It's Art Kowalski. We picked up your package."

Art would only call her on an encrypted line, so their communications were secure. "Good to hear your voice, Art. How's she doing?" Getting rolled up by a couple of tough-looking strangers in a foreign country would be a tad disconcerting. Especially after committing treason.

"Good thing we were there. Someone was about to take her offline."

"Ah. Does she know who might want her gone?"

"She's got a pretty good idea."

That was good news. Somebody trying to kill Hannah would likely put her in a more amenable frame of mind when it came to giving up information on the major players. Thankfully the killer failed.

"How do you want to play this?" Art asked.

"I'd like to feel her out—see if she'll turn on whoever has control of the program," Leine said. Lou had already briefed Art on Hannah's part in the plot to take over the NRO satellite.

"You sure they've got control of the bird?"

"There's an auction in three days. We're pretty sure the person responsible is the entity behind the malware."

"That doesn't give us a lot of time."

"No, it doesn't. Let's try a video call."

"And if that doesn't work?"

"Then we go at her hard."

"Roger that. See you in ten." Art disconnected.

HANNAH SAT IN THE CHAIR BY THE WINDOW, LOOKING OUT AT THE harbor in the distance. The two men had taken her to a small hotel far from any tourist areas. She still didn't know their names, or why they were holding her, although she figured it had something to do with her uploading the malware to the satellite. Were they government? If so, weren't they supposed to tell her who they represented or something? And how did they figure out what she'd done? Langston promised her he wouldn't take action until she was well clear.

Before he tried to kill her, the man in the leather jacket said the attack was courtesy of that asshole. Langston must have had some kind of alert for when she came for the money. Maybe he asked the banker to call him when she showed up. If that was the case, she was fucked every way imaginable. Even if she managed to escape the two men holding her now, Langston would certainly come after her—she was a loose end.

Desi's description of the injuries of the performers who'd been murdered told her exactly what Langston did to loose ends. After reading the article about how the Romanov brothers died and her recent ordeal, Hannah's suspicion of Langston's true nature had become terrifyingly real.

The dark-haired man sat across from her, reading something on his phone. He'd taken off his jacket to reveal a shoulder holster and a gun. The older man had left him in charge while he went out. Sighing, she shifted in her chair, uncomfortable. The man didn't even look up. She studied him more closely. He wasn't bad looking, in a bohemian kind of way. Not really her type, but...

Hannah took a deep breath and sighed, closing her eyes to slits as she adjusted her blouse so her breasts were more pronounced. That brought a flicker of interest. She leaned her head back, giving him ample time to check her out.

Men were such simple creatures. Except Langston. He'd been immune to her charms.

Weird.

She opened her eyes and lowered her head. The dark-haired man had a wide grin on his face.

"What?" she asked, smiling. "Do you like what you see?"

He shook his head. "No, but I appreciate the attempt."

"You—" Hannah snapped her mouth closed and crossed her arms. Fine. He didn't know what he was missing.

The door opened and the older guy walked in. He had an economy of movement. Efficient. No nonsense. Similar to tight code. Not elegant, exactly, but highly functional, using minimal resources—nothing superfluous.

"Someone wants to talk to you." His gruff demeanor complemented his mannerisms. No bullshit.

Hannah sat straighter in her chair. *Finally.* Maybe she'd get some answers. She looked behind him, but no one followed him into the room. "Where?"

The older guy held up his phone. "Video chat." He typed something and waited. A woman's voice came over the speaker.

"Hey there."

"I've got her." The man turned the phone so Hannah could see the screen. The woman looked familiar. He handed the device over so she could see better.

"Leine?" What did Desi's friend have to do with the satellite? A dozen questions churned through her mind. She was investigating the murders, not the NRO contract. And how did she know Hannah was in Malta?

"Hannah. Hold on a second." Leine did something and the screen split. Sebastian's face appeared below Leine's.

Oh, shit.

Hannah glanced at the two men in the room with her. The older guy stood with his back to the door, arms crossed. The dark-haired guy watched her, a bemused expression on his face.

There was no way out of that room. She took a deep breath and let it go. Her shoulders slumped.

She was so fucked.

41

———

Several hours later, Sebastian's corporate jet touched down at the regional airport south of Albuquerque. Leine and Alice exited the plane and climbed into the SUV waiting for them on the tarmac. Sebastian and Remy joined them a few minutes later.

Sebastian took the passenger seat next to the driver, while Remy sat with Alice and Leine in back. "I told Captain Jeff to fuel up, that we'd be gone at most a few hours." Sebastian's mood was brisk and confident, as though meeting with an ex-employee with an axe to grind who'd gone off-grid was the most natural thing in the world. He'd brought along his air-gapped computer with the satellite application installed to work on possible patches while they traveled.

Leine's curiosity had skyrocketed when Remy recounted his conversation with Grace's mother. Why the breach between Grace and Sebastian? What had he done to cause Grace to leave not only her job, but the entire West Coast, never to be heard from again? By all accounts, Grace had been a gifted programmer, admired by her coworkers and held in high regard by other CEOs in the industry. She'd worked her way to the top of the company, had been Sebastian's right hand.

And then she was gone. According to the HR department, she didn't give notice—just disappeared. Sebastian ordered that Grace be tracked down and given her full severance package, even though she'd disqualified herself. They sent the package to Grace's mother, since they couldn't find her. That told Leine the problem between them was something Sebastian did, not the other way around.

The chat with Hannah hadn't gone as well as she'd hoped. The woman was a shrewd negotiator. She insisted on some kind of immunity, in writing, from the Department of Justice before she gave them the information they needed on the person behind the satellite hijack. Art and Zarko had gotten her on the next flight out, and would touch down in Seattle later that evening. Lou was working the DOJ angle, searching for an attorney to take on her case.

Leine alternated between watching the scenery rush by, and studying the other people in the vehicle. Remy and Alice shared an intimacy unique to couples in love: secretive smiles and a familiarity known only by two people who had genuine affection for each other. Sebastian busied himself with work, head down and eyes on his laptop, not acknowledging the driver or the rest of the passengers behind him. For his part, the driver remained quiet, his expression unreadable behind aviator shades.

Leine returned her attention to the expansive landscape. The sky was a deep, cerulean blue—the kind of blue she'd only ever seen above the plains of the Rio Grande Valley and the high desert of northern New Mexico. The Manzano Mountains rose to the east, bookending one side of the wide valley. The Rio Grande sluiced through the center of the state, bisecting several areas of historical significance to Zuni, Pueblo, and Apache, while Navajo and Hopi lands could be found further to the northwest. Leine found calm in the flat expanses, the low-slung homes and buildings. A simplicity existed here that wasn't evident in the lush, hilly neighborhoods of Seattle, or the beehive activity of LA.

Twenty minutes later, the driver signaled and turned right onto a dirt track at a mailbox decorated with a tight grouping of bullet holes. They followed the drive for a quarter mile, then up over a shallow rise. A squat, brown adobe building with a faded tile roof and a shaded porch appeared at the bottom of the rise. An array of solar panels, an electric car, and a large windmill were the only other points of interest in the flat, sunbaked tableau, punctuated by an occasional pinyon pine and bottlebrush.

As they approached, a brown-and-white spotted dog of inde-terminate age trotted over to the SUV, its curiosity obvious as it loped alongside, intermittently sounding the alarm with its barks. They came to a stop a few yards from the home, the dirt disturbed by their tires billowing past, encasing them in a dusty cloud. The driver shifted into park and killed the engine.

The front door to the adobe structure cracked open. A woman with coffee ground-colored hair shot with gray could be seen in the shadows, sizing up her visitors. Sebastian put aside his laptop and stared through the windshield.

"Well? Are you going to go up there and say hi?" Alice asked. "She doesn't know us from a hole in the wall."

Sebastian's Adam's apple bobbed, the only indication that he'd heard the question. For the first time on the trip, he appeared reticent. Leine glanced at the partially open door and the woman standing behind it, then twisted the handle next to her and climbed out.

Leine closed the door to the SUV and slowly walked toward the front porch, hands held in plain view, in case the occupant was virulently anti-visitor. Perhaps spurred to action, Sebastian decided to follow suit and emerged from the passenger side.

The response was immediate.

"Oh, no, no, no, you don't, you bastard." The woman stormed out the front door, across the porch, and down the shallow steps toward Sebastian, a 12-gauge shotgun gripped in one hand. The brown-and-white dog took umbrage, barking and growling alongside its human as she strode toward the billionaire.

Sebastian disappeared back inside the SUV, slamming the door behind him. Leine moved to intercept the enraged woman.

"Grace. Wait. Please. We just want to talk." Leine kept her voice low and calm, trying to read the situation so she could address the woman's pain points. By the look on her face, she had plenty.

The other woman pulled up short, directing her attention to Leine. The dog stopped, too, growling low in its throat, its gaze alternating between Leine and the SUV.

Grace's skin was tanned a deep brown from the relentless sun, highlighting sharp blue eyes, a generous mouth, and high cheekbones. From the look of her fitted T-shirt and tailored blue jeans, she didn't have an ounce of fat on her. The faded lettering adorning the front of her shirt suggested Grace didn't like politicians. The expression on her face suggested her dislike extended to most everyone.

"Who the fuck are you?" Grace held the shotgun with the ease of someone familiar with a firearm.

"My name's Leine Basso. I'm here—we're here—to enlist your help on a matter of national security."

A look of comprehension filled the unnerving blue eyes, and she lifted her chin. "Who else you got inside that gas-guzzling piece of shit? Other than the asshole in the passenger seat."

"The two in the back are with me. Their names are Alice and

Remy. Alice is an AI security specialist, and Remy's a PI. He helped us find you."

"Okay. But why the fuck is *he* here?" She gestured toward Sebastian with the shotgun.

"Because I didn't understand the dynamics between you two. He will remain in the car."

"Damn right he will." Grace turned back toward the house. "You and the other two can come inside."

Leine walked back to the SUV. The driver powered down his window. Leine leaned her forearms on the door.

"She says Alice and Remy can come in, but Sebastian needs to stay in the car."

Sebastian stared out his window, refusing to acknowledge that he heard what she said.

"Now might be a good time to tell us what happened between the two of you," Leine suggested.

"It's not important. She's making a bigger deal out of what happened than she should."

Leine glanced at the adobe home and the partially open door, then turned back to Sebastian. "She doesn't strike me as the kind of person who would make a big deal out of something that wasn't."

Sebastian closed his eyes and shook his head. "I can't believe she's still pissed."

"What did you do to her?" Alice asked.

Sebastian turned on Alice. "Why would you just automatically think that *I* did something to *her*? What if she did something to me? You ever think of that?"

"Geez, sorry I said anything." Alice rolled her eyes, but only Leine noticed. Sebastian had already turned to stare out the window again.

Remy cleared his throat. "Well then, I guess we should probably go inside and see if she has any ideas to get control of that satellite." He opened his door and stepped out of the SUV. Alice followed.

Leine straightened. "You're being childish. You know that, right?"

Sebastian remained silent and sullen. The driver's mouth quirked up in a suppressed smile. Leine patted his arm.

"Good luck with him." She led the way onto the porch and into the little adobe house.

Leine waited while her eyes adjusted to the change in light. The low ceiling, small windows, and thick walls kept the interior cool and dark, a must during summers where temperatures regularly climbed to 100 degrees or more. A tidy beehive fireplace stood in one corner of the large room, with a neat stack of firewood in a built-in cubby nearby. A well-used leather couch and two armchairs faced the fireplace. There was no television.

On the other side of the room, a counter stretched along one wall with a sink, stove, and refrigerator. Cupboards offered the only storage visible, both under and over the counter. Dried herbs hung from an overhead beam, directly above a small pine table and four chairs. A closed wooden door suggested a bedroom beyond.

Grace leaned the shotgun against the wall next to the table and sat down. "Make yourselves at home." With a quiet sigh, the dog sank to the floor next to her chair and started licking its paws.

Leine, Alice, and Remy took the other three chairs.

"Now, what is this about national security?" Grace clasped her hands, resting her forearms on the table. Her gaze settled on Leine.

"We have reason to believe a derivative of a program you created has been compromised. We need a way in to stop what could turn out to be a disaster for the United States."

"Let me guess. This has something to do with Amazing Grace. Did the bastard sign a contract with the military?"

"Intelligence," Leine replied. "NRO satellites."

"So, Sebastian did exactly what I thought he'd do." She shook her head. "Short-sighted asshole. And now he needs my help to fix his mistake."

Remy cocked his head. "If you knew he'd use the program in a way you believed was wrong, why did you leave Congruence? You might have helped avoid this happening."

Grace lasered in on him. Remy held her gaze.

"What do you know about work-for-hire?" Grace asked him.

"Standard operating procedure for most corporations. Anything you create while employed by an entity basically belongs to the entity: authorship, copyright, et cetera. Okay, so you signed a WFH, and probably an NDA, right?" He looked at Grace, who nodded. "Then why didn't you destroy the program? I mean, something that powerful should never be in the hands of one person, period."

Grace chuckled, but there was no humor in it. "Honey, if I would have touched that program, or even attempted to hijack the code, Sebastian would've slapped me with a lawsuit so debilitating and expensive it would have taken five lifetimes to deal with." She sighed. "Besides, he had the early versions. It wouldn't have taken much to recreate the latest one."

"He took credit for your work." Leine directed the statement at Grace, who nodded.

"That he did. And I couldn't do a damn thing about it." She shrugged. "At least he didn't quibble on my severance package. I was able to buy this house and the land around it. If I'm frugal, I'll have plenty to live on for the rest of my life." She ruffled the dog's ears, earning a happy moan.

"The doomsday report—you wrote it?" Alice asked.

Grace's eyebrows furrowed as she nodded. "The danger

didn't even phase him. That the program could achieve AGI—sorry, artificial general intelligence, where the program starts to think for itself—in just a few generations, had no observable impact on his decision making. He was either incredibly naïve, too confident, or just flat-out didn't care. I never would have continued with the project if I knew then what I know now." She closed her eyes for a moment. When she opened them again, pain and regret had replaced the righteous anger that had been simmering deep within them. "I wake up every day, wishing, hoping for some way to take it all back."

Leine leaned forward. "Maybe there is a way." She held Grace's gaze. "But it's going to involve dealing with Sebastian."

42

Leine, Remy, and Alice camped out next to the SUV and chatted up the driver, while Sebastian and Grace worked out their differences inside the house. Leine convinced Grace that Sebastian was willing to listen to reason, had been humbled when his backdoor into the program proved ineffective. For his part, Sebastian agreed to hear Grace out, to make some kind of amends with her for masquerading as the creator of the program when he hadn't actually done the work.

Leine remained alert for sounds of an escalation, acutely aware of the shotgun inside the house. She'd suggested removing the gun, but the look Grace gave her had Leine rethink her request.

Her house, her rules.

Relief flowed through Leine when, an hour and a half later, Sebastian emerged, unscathed, with Grace and the dog close behind. Grace carried a well-used backpack for a suitcase as she made her way to the SUV. Sebastian pulled Leine aside, while Grace took his original position in the passenger seat.

"Grace has a way to access the program. A backdoor she built into the original code. I had her check to see if it survived the modifications we made for the satellite application, and if it worked against the malware. She was able to access the program and has an idea to neutralize the trigger that the hacker shouldn't be able to detect."

"That's great. What do we need to do?" Leine asked.

"She needs to have physical access. I called Captain Jeff to have him file a flight plan for Santa Barbara."

"We're going to Vandenburg?" Sebastian nodded. "Have you alerted your contact at the NRO?"

"I did. Jesper's going to meet us there."

"Let's hope we're in time."

Leine glanced at Alice, who was reading something on her phone. "What's happening with the auction?" Before they left for New Mexico, Leine contacted Jana at the FBI to give her a heads-up on the auction in case Zeus79 was successful in capturing classified intelligence.

Alice shook her head. "It's not good. My cover as the rep for a sovereign wealth fund in Qatar worked, but apparently that's small potatoes. The other bidders look like proxies for some enormous players."

"Like who?" Remy asked.

"Think Russia, China, Iran."

"What, no North Korea?" Remy quipped.

"There's still time," Alice replied.

"How did you get through the vetting process?" Leine asked. "I assume they wanted to ensure you are who you say you are and can back up your bids."

"My uncle put me in touch with a guy who fronted me the crypto. He thinks I'm scamming some big players and wants in on the action."

"What happens if he doesn't get a payout?"

Alice shrugged. "Not much he can say. Shit happens. He won't lose anything if I don't bid."

They climbed into the back, Leine and Sebastian in the row directly behind Grace and the driver, Alice, and Remy behind them in the third row of seats.

The SUV pulled away from Grace's home and the driver headed back down the drive. The dog remained on the porch, relaxing in the shade.

Alice tapped Grace on the shoulder. "What about your dog?"

"I called a friend to take him while I'm gone. He'll be fine until then."

Forty-five minutes later, they reached the regional airport and boarded Sebastian's jet for the flight to California. Sebastian handed Grace his laptop. She set her pack on the seat beside her, signaling she preferred to work alone. Sebastian and Leine sat together near the front, while Alice and Remy sat farther aft.

"Looks like you and Grace have reached a kind of détente," Leine said to Sebastian.

He nodded. "She made it crystal clear she's not doing this for me. She's doing it to make things right." He sighed. "She's harboring a lot of guilt for creating the program."

"Tell me what the satellite program does." She glanced behind them. "No one in the back can hear us."

He blew out another sigh. "You have to understand, Amazing Grace was the most exciting breakthrough I'd ever experienced in artificial intelligence. Because the original program exhibited an extraordinary ability to learn from its mistakes and create new pathways of understanding, much like the neural pathways inside the human brain, I realized that it would be incredibly useful for intelligence gathering, among dozens of other applications."

"And?"

"Without getting too technical, this particular application allows the satellite to intercept intelligence sent from another satellite to its ground station, regardless of the target satellite's safeguards. Currently, it's geared toward gathering intelligence from our adversaries, but in practice its abilities put our allies in a highly vulnerable position."

"Especially now that an unknown actor has likely gained control."

"Especially now, yes. Thank God Grace's backdoor survived."

Once they learned the hacker's identity and location from Hannah, it would be a matter of taking Zeus79 into custody before the hacker learned of Hannah's betrayal. He or she would likely grow suspicious when the would-be assassin didn't check in, so Leine and the others didn't have much time to orchestrate their plan.

Leine checked the time. It had been several hours since Art and Zarko had rolled up Hannah. They were due to arrive in Seattle later that evening. Art would keep her under guard in a safehouse until Lou secured a plea deal. If everything went as planned, with Hannah's help Grace would be able to shut down the satellite's intelligence-gathering capabilities and wrest control from Zeus79, effectively shutting him or her out.

There was just one problem. Operations rarely went as planned.

43

Jesper met them at the entrance to the operations facility at Vandenburg AFB. After introductions, he badged Leine, Grace, and Sebastian into the building. Remy and Alice didn't have proper level government clearances, so they remained in the waiting area. Leine and the others hurried to Mission Control.

"So, have you detected any unauthorized activity?" Sebastian asked Jesper.

Jesper shook his head. "Other than our inability to access the program, no. And I wouldn't have known that if you hadn't called. Everything's been operating smoothly."

Grace sat at the controls. The security technician gave her the satellite access code and she began typing the entry commands to her software. Moments later, she reported, "I'm in. The program hasn't recognized the intrusion."

A collective sigh of relief flowed through the group.

Grace continued to type, explaining her processes as she did. "While testing the program's interaction with the malware on the flight over, I discovered a vulnerability in the neural networks and created a backdoor I thought I could exploit. The program has unexpected interactions I don't think anyone anticipated."

"That doesn't sound great," Leine said. "Does this happen a lot with AI?"

Grace nodded. "It's known as emergence. One reason why I didn't want the program out in the wild."

"What are you going to do?" Jesper asked.

His rigid posture and the set of his jaw indicated he was experiencing a high level of stress. Leine understood why—the hijack happened on his watch. He was responsible. As was Sebastian's company. Sebastian showed no emotion that Leine could see.

She wouldn't want to play poker with him.

"First, I'll try to disrupt the AI's processing by introducing a conflicting command set," Grace said.

"And if that doesn't work?" Sebastian asked.

"I've got a couple of ideas. Let's see if this does anything first."

The tension was thick in the air as they waited. Leine studied the other technicians in the room—all appeared on a knife's edge. Jesper must have briefed the team on the stakes involved.

"Looking good..." Grace said, studying the screen. The tension in the room eased. "Wait a minute." She typed a command and paused. "Shit."

"What?" Jesper asked, moving closer to the console.

Grace blew out a frustrated sigh. "The AI created a work-around. Let me try something else. The program also has a vulnerability in the ethical algorithms."

Frowning, Sebastian crossed his arms and studied the screen. "What do you plan to do?" Clearly, he hadn't been briefed on the program's vulnerabilities.

"I'll introduce a 'moral dilemma.'"

"Which means?" Leine asked.

"In a nutshell, I'm going to try to confuse the AI's judgment using adversarial machine learning tactics, which should force it to question its own directives. I need to distract the AI enough to force it to perform an emergency shut down."

Grace's fingers flew across the keyboard, generating commands. Then they waited.

"Yes." Grace nodded as lines of code populated the screen. "It's working…"

Sebastian pointed at the monitor. "No, it's not. See there? The AI's updating its internal parameters."

"Dammit." Grace's frustration was shared by everyone in the group. She tapped furiously on the keyboard. "No, no, no, no, no." She stopped and stared at the screen. "The fucker kicked me out."

"Which fucker are we talking about here?" Jesper gripped the back of her chair. "Can you get back in?"

Grace rubbed her eyes. "The program identified my incursion as a threat and sealed off access."

Jesper's face went white. "That can't be. We have to shut it down." He cut his eyes to the monitor, then back to Grace. "That can't be it. Tell me that's not it." He scrubbed his hand through his hair and took a step back, his breath coming fast as the import of what losing the backdoor meant. He turned on Sebastian. "I thought you said you built in safeguards."

"I did. But I didn't consider an attack from within my own organization." Anguish from Hannah's betrayal showed plain on Sebastian's face. "The hacker must have removed the guardrails."

Grace held up her hand. "He knows."

The other three focused on her. "Knows what?" Leine asked, fearing the answer.

"He's transferring huge amounts of data."

Jesper blanched even whiter. "My God." He stared at Grace. "You have to stop him!"

"I can't," Grace said.

"There's nothing you can do?" Leine asked Grace.

She took a moment to think. "The only way to stop the program would involve being on site where Zeus79 houses his servers. Which is where he's most likely storing the intel."

"You don't think he's storing it offsite?" Jesper asked.

Grace shook her head. "Too vulnerable. He's not going to trust anyone else with this stuff. He's playing with the big dogs. He'll want to know exactly where this information is at all times until the end of the auction."

"Okay," Leine said, nodding. "So, first we need to find out where he is. That sounds doable. What needs to happen then?"

"There are a couple of possibilities. But you'll have to get Hannah to talk. And unless she knows where to find Zeus79 so you can get to the servers before the auction concludes, we're screwed."

Leine gave Grace a look. "Oh, I'll get her to talk."

44

Leine stepped through the outer door and waited for it to lock behind her. Art buzzed her through the second security entrance, and they headed down the hall to the room where Hannah and Zarko were waiting.

The small, windowless room had been built in the middle of a decommissioned FBI safe house, with security measures in place that would make the Secret Service proud. SHEN, the anti-trafficking organization Leine and Lou directed had quietly purchased several of these now-defunct safe houses located around the world to temporarily stash victims once they'd been rescued. This one was a score—normally safehouses didn't have a built-in interrogation room.

Security cameras were situated to capture every angle, and recording devices sensitive enough to register the sound of a fly landing anywhere in the room had been strategically embedded in the furniture and light fixtures. Leine walked to the table in the center of the space, where two chairs had been placed opposite each other. Hannah leaned against the back wall, arms crossed, a deeply unhappy look on her face.

Zarko smiled at Leine and nodded at Hannah. "She's a tad

bit upset that you're not an attorney with an immunity agreement." He started for the door and paused just long enough to whisper, "Good luck. She's a right pain in the ass," before he left, closing the door behind him.

Hannah glared at Leine as the former assassin took a seat across the table from her.

"Where's the lawyer you promised me?"

"That's an interesting initial gambit," Leine said.

"What do you mean?"

"Acting as though you have the upper hand. That takes some stones, especially in your situation."

"Oh? I thought my situation was that you need the information I have to stop a lunatic from selling state secrets to the highest bidder—or did I get that wrong?"

"You're partially correct." Leine gestured at the chair across from her. "Have a seat."

Hannah yanked the chair back and sat down. The scowl on her face would have been comical if the stakes weren't so high.

Leine leaned her elbows on the table. "Look. I understand you're afraid. Hell, I'd be afraid if I was in your shoes."

"I'm not—"

Leine speared her with a look. "Cut the bullshit, Hannah. You're not the injured party here, or didn't you get the memo? You aided and abetted a cyber terrorist and physically uploaded malware giving them access to an intelligence satellite—that's some serious time in a federal facility."

Hannah's belligerent expression faltered. Leine continued, "We're working on getting you some form of immunity, but until you give us something we can use, you're just shouting into the void." She shrugged. "Your call." According to Lou, the immunity play wasn't going to happen, but a plea deal was still on the table. He'd been discreet in his overtures to the DOJ, giving broad strokes with little detail, citing the delicacy of the negotiations. So far, his evasiveness had worked.

So far.

Hannah leaned back in her chair, arms still crossed, and shook her head. The belligerent look returned. "You get nothing until I talk to my lawyer."

Leine arched her eyebrows. "Yeah? Okay, then." She rose from her chair and nodded at one of the security cameras near the ceiling. "We're done here."

The door lock buzzed, and she reached for the handle.

"Wait." The panic in Hannah's voice was palpable.

That was easy.

Leine turned to look at her.

Hannah closed her eyes and took a deep breath, then let it go. "Fuck it." She squared her shoulders. "He was blackmailing me."

Leine sat back down. "How? And who is 'he'?"

"His online handle is Zeus79. I have no idea how he did it, but he had video footage of me and...certain people having sex."

"So, it was group sex? What, you were embarrassed or something?" There had to be more to it than that.

"You think something as benign as that would embarrass me?" Hannah gave her a look. "Not hardly."

Leine remained silent, letting her talk.

"One of the people involved didn't want the footage out there. It would be too damaging to his reputation."

Leine didn't know many powerful men who couldn't survive a story of an illicit affair, even if it was with more than one participant. The idea of infidelity had been baked into the public's perception of the rich and powerful. "So, the guy's wife would divorce him? How is that an excuse to commit treason? What am I missing?"

Hannah crossed her arms. "He ran on a family values platform and won. They're grooming him for higher office."

The pieces tumbled into place. Sort of.

"Your affair was with Winters?"

Winters was the "family values" candidate who'd won a surprise victory to become the latest mayor of Seattle. The blackmail threat didn't make sense, though.

"Yeah, that still doesn't track. No one really cares, except maybe his wife and family." The world of American politics had experienced so many scandals in the past decade that the general populace was becoming inured to all but the most salacious acts. An affair rarely rose to a scandal with any staying power in the 24-hour news cycle.

What would finally be the red line? She doubted that even an on-camera murder would rise to that level.

Hannah's expression told Leine whatever she'd been filmed doing with the now-mayor of Seattle was pretty damned bad.

"Do I really have to spell it out for you?"

"Afraid so."

Tears welled in her eyes. "I didn't know how old she was. If I had, I wouldn't have gone through with it."

Leine sat back in her chair. An underage victim. That could absolutely do damage even in this day and age, no matter which side of the political spectrum you were on.

"How young?" Even though anyone under eighteen was considered a minor, often people's perceptions changed depending on the victim's age.

Tears ran down Hannah's face. "Fourteen." Her voice was soft, pleading with Leine to understand. "She looked nineteen. He told me she was."

"What happened to her?"

"I don't know." The haunted look in her eyes told Leine she feared the worst.

"They disappeared her?"

Her answer was barely more than a whisper. "I don't know. I tried to find her." She shook her head, misery clear on her face. "She's gone."

"How did he get the video?"

"All I can think is that he knew Winters secretly recorded his interactions and somehow got hold of it, or he planted the cameras himself."

Zeus79 was an accomplished hacker—he could have gotten access to Winters' Wi-Fi. "You said 'they' were grooming Winters. Who is they?"

"Someone he's involved with. He didn't tell me who, but I got the idea you wouldn't want to cross them."

"How did he pay you?" The amount of cash in her valise had been substantial. Having Hannah killed would have returned most of the investment, barring the killer absconding with more than his share.

"He opened an account in my name at a bank in Malta, then wired the money. The guy who tried to kill me told me my murder was compliments of...him."

"Now's when you tell me who Zeus79 is, and where I can find him."

"His name is Langston Pierce. If I tell you where he is, he'll know it was me. You have to protect me, or you'll have my death on your conscience."

Leine didn't have the heart to tell her that using guilt didn't work on her. She leaned over the table and fixed Hannah with her gaze. "That's not how this works. You give me Langston's address, and I'll go to bat for you with the DOJ."

Hannah studied her, likely trying to weigh her chances if she held on to the information. Something shifted in her eyes and she nodded. "Fine. I'll trust you. Against my better judgment."

Leine stared at her. "Where was your 'better judgment' when

you uploaded the malware to the satellite?" Hannah had the good grace to look chagrined. It wasn't like she had any cards to play other than cooperating.

Reluctantly, she gave Leine an address on Hunts Point. Leine stared at her as another key to the investigation fell into place. The address matched the one Remy found in Noah's wallet. Remy's friend had been onto something, but it hadn't been Sebastian. What did he find that he couldn't tell Remy over the phone?

Leine pulled out her phone. Time to call for reinforcements.

45

The next day Leine, Remy, Grace, Alice, and Sebastian gathered at the Phinney Ridge safe house. They'd begun devising a plan to infiltrate Langston's home on Hunts Point the night before, and had nicknamed their target "The Bunker." Lou's FBI contact, Jana, and several of her colleagues from the organization's cyber division were already at the safehouse.

HRT, the FBI's elite Hostage Rescue Team, had been notified and were onsite helping plan the operation. The dining and living room had transformed into a command center with bundles of cables snaking across the floor, connecting multiple monitors and laptops. The room was abuzz with activity.

Hannah's intel included a rough floorplan of Langston's residence on the northeast tip of the peninsula, with a detailed sketch of the underground office where he kept his servers. She'd confirmed that the AI's core functionality was dependent on Langston's external servers housed within the bunker.

Langston had backup generators, so the obvious choice of cutting power to the property was a no-go. Disrupting power or Wi-Fi would certainly alert Langston to the operation, giving the cyber terrorist time to harden his online defenses, and/or change the location of the data.

Leine pulled up satellite photos of the house, grounds, and surrounding shoreline to refresh her memory of what she'd encounter. Langston's 1920s-era mansion was situated two lots from Sebastian's estate, with dense woodland between them. The image of the home was blurred, which complicated planning. The FBI had already conducted an extensive search for old remodeling permits, but there were none to be found. Clearly, Langston had scrubbed evidence of the home from city records.

FBI agents would monitor the situation at the safehouse with drones and boots on the ground, and supply two teams consisting of HRT operators: one via a rigid inflatable boat, or RIB, and a second at a choke point on the main road onto the peninsula. All had agreed that Leine should initially breach the bunker alone. There'd be a better chance of sabotaging the servers before Langston was able to initiate possible failsafes. As soon as he picked up evidence of a team of operators converging on his estate, all bets on recovering the data were off.

Leine, Art, Remy, and Zarko would infil Hunts Point from the northeast via Klepper kayaks launched from a support boat stationed on the lake, its position blocked from the house's view by the tree line. The Kleppers were virtually silent and made more sense for infiltration than using a RIB. Leine and Remy would land near a stand of firs and exit the water at the northwest corner, then follow a hedge along the west side of the house. Leine would then gain entry from the rear of the property, while Remy remained outside as overwatch.

Art, Zarko, and a member of the HRT would take three separate sniper/observer positions: Art would cover the east and part of the north section of the property, with Zarko covering the north and a portion of the west side. The HRT operator would monitor the south and east side, and report back to base.

Leine motioned for Remy to join her. "Noah was obviously on to something having to do with Langston. But how did Langston know about Noah?"

Remy shook his head. "Not sure, unless..."

"What?"

Remy crossed his arms and leaned against the table. "We know the malware sent out locator signals, which Langston used to have someone toss my place and steal the USB drive. He also likely tracked us the same way when he ordered the hits on you and me, and kidnapped Alice."

"But Noah never had possession of the malware."

"Hear me out. Remember the security video of the sedan near the Romanovs' apartment building?"

"Sure. It was the same make and model of the two men who surprised you at Brett's houseboat."

"Right. The Russians had a copy of the malware, which we know because of the text telling their boss they were holding out for more money."

"And?"

"Alice," Remy called across the room. Alice stopped what she was doing and joined Remy and Leine.

"What do you need?" she asked, looking at Remy.

"Didn't you tell me the man guarding you at that house in Renton fielded a bunch of calls from someone he called Boca?"

Alice nodded. "Yeah. He acted like that was his boss. Why?"

"I don't know why I didn't see it before. What if Boca's Bob Carter?"

"The detective who got you thrown off the force?" Alice gave him a look. "You're reaching, babe."

"I told you that guy who was guarding you in Renton looked familiar. What if Carter and Sonny are in Langston's pocket and they were using that scumbag as a CI? It would explain the two men at Brett's houseboat, as well as the sedan outside the Russians' apartment."

Leine nodded. "That makes sense. You think your detective friends were running the Russians?"

"Could be. It'd be easy enough to pull off. We used CIs all the time. It was an effective way to get shit done. Sometimes the only way."

Alice crossed her arms, mirroring Remy. "You're saying that when the Romanovs held out for more money, Langston had the detectives kill them?"

"Yeah."

"Damn. That's dark, babe."

Leine turned to Remy. "If your assumption is correct, then we might have just figured out who murdered Brett and Ethan."

"Damn. Yeah." Remy shook his head in disbelief. "It makes perfect sense. They would have known there were no cameras in the alley next to the club." He ran his hand through his hair. "There's got to be a way to implicate those bastards so they don't skate."

"Let's take this one step at a time. First, we stop the transfer of data before the auction closes." Leine checked the time. "Which is due to happen in less than two hours." She glanced at Alice. "Are we ready?"

Alice nodded. "Just finishing up."

The clock was ticking. They had to stop Langston from transferring the intelligence downloaded from the NRO satellite to the winning bidder, or the worldwide intelligence community and their acting governments were in a world of shit.

Destroying the satellite had been discussed, but the NRO believed that far too much intelligence had already been accessed. The only way to stop the transfer to the buyer was through physical means. Whoever won the bid would likely be granted instantaneous access to detailed datasets and top-secret information including extensive lists of global sources and methods. The breach would put thousands of people's lives in jeopardy and would set the intelligence community and its hard-won allies and partnerships back decades, if it ever recovered.

According to Hannah, Langston had a robust defense preventing entry to his server room. She mentioned a security camera above the front entrance, but wasn't sure if there'd been others. Although his security wasn't quite the fortress Congruence's had been, infil would still be a challenge. Especially since Hannah wasn't privy to all his tactics. Once Leine gained access to the servers, she'd use the QuanTrace5 to upload exploits Alice, Hannah, and Grace had devised to trick the AI into allowing them to secure the program—at least temporarily. Theoretically, the pause in operations would be enough to secure the data before the AI self-corrected and sealed access.

Theoretically.

"We're running out of time," Leine said. "Unless you guys need me to wait, there's no reason I shouldn't get moving."

"How long?" Alice called to Grace.

Grace detached Leine's device and walked it over. "We've just finished loading the exploits onto the QuanT, but there's a new problem."

Leine nodded. "Tell me."

"The cyber team can't locate his internet service provider," Grace explained. "We suspect he's using the satellite's encrypted broadband for access. Which means..."

"Our failsafe of shutting down his internet is no longer an option," Leine finished for her. The team had contacted the local internet service provider to gain their cooperation in shutting down the auction and data transfer as a last resort. If Langston was using the satellite's broadband capabilities, that wouldn't work.

"Unfortunately, you're correct."

"Then shutting down his satellite access is priority one," Leine said.

"Jana and her team will monitor changes in electricity usage and electromagnetic force." Grace shrugged. "Hopefully that allows them to breach the bunker in time."

"Hopefully." Leine took the device from Grace and nodded at Alice. "After you."

The two women went into one of the bedrooms off the main living area and closed the door. Alice's prototype gamer suit and gloves had been laid out on the bed, along with the AI-assisted helmet from the nightclub, an MP5SD submachine gun, and her Beretta, both with plenty of ammo. Leine tugged the suit on over her legs, torso, and arms, then secured the neck, wrists, and booties, while Alice fastened the back. The addition of the gloves and helmet ensured Leine would be invisible to infrared and thermal imaging sensors.

"Remember to use the AI-assisted reality sensor," Alice reminded her. "We aren't sure how advanced Langston's security protocols might be, so be prepared for anything." They'd opted not to tell Sebastian about Leine's earlier infiltration of his company, believing the mission would be better served by broaching the subject afterward, if at all.

"Who's in control of the comms?"

"I'll have operational control," Alice said, "since I'm familiar with the equipment. Just like during the Congruence breach, I'll be able to see what you see and hear what you hear, with the addition of Jana and her team."

"Did Hannah say anything else about the exosuit?" Leine asked. When Hannah mentioned Langston's physical limitations and the prototype exosuit he wore, Leine had asked if she'd seen it in action. Hannah replied that she had, but added that she only witnessed him walk from one end of the room to another.

"Nope. You're on your own with that one."

More unknowns. Wouldn't be the first time.

Leine snugged the gun into her tactical vest and picked up the helmet.

"Let's go."

46

Leine secured the MP5SD submachine gun to the kayak and slid into the seat. One of the HRT guys handed her a paddle. Dressed in full tactical gear, he blended with the environment.

"We're right behind you," he said, and pushed her off from the larger boat. The elite Hostage Rescue Team was well-versed in terrorist scenarios and was a welcome addition to the op. They'd set up on the only road into and out of the peninsula, blocking traffic from entering or leaving the uber rich enclave, and had a RIB ready to deploy from the pontoon boat. Thankfully, it was late enough that there wasn't too much activity on the lake.

The unseasonably balmy temperature and negligible lake traffic lent a strange serenity to the evening. The journey to the beach landing site at the tip of Hunts Point would take fifteen minutes, barring the unexpected. Leine paddled in place, bobbing in the waves while she waited for Remy, Zarko, and Art to join her. A slight breeze brought with it the scent of the lake.

Art sidled up beside her and grinned. His teeth practically glowed in the dim starlight.

"What are you smiling about?" Leine asked, keeping her voice low so it wouldn't carry.

"I always feel more alive on a job." He shrugged. "Just happy to keep my hand in, you know?"

Leine nodded. She could relate. Art was in his late sixties, maybe early seventies. Like all operators who loved their job, he'd talked about how much he'd miss being in the field when it came time to retire. "Just shoot me now. I am not built for a rocking chair," he'd said during one of their conversations. She couldn't imagine him doing anything else—certainly not anything behind a desk.

Remy and Zarko moved into position and the four of them headed for the landing site. The gamer suit had stretchy material built in for ease of use, allowing Leine to move without restriction. The AI-assisted helmet sat between her knees in a Stahlsac waterproof backpack on the floor of the kayak.

Leine kept her eye on her compass, correcting as she paddled. Soon, the lights of Langston's home came into view through a break in the trees. She steered west toward the wooded area where she and Remy would deploy, while Art and Zarko peeled off and moved to their positions. The HRT observer would deploy from the east. The trees and brush would give them cover for the landing.

Leine and Remy slowed as they approached the beach to avoid scraping the bottoms of the kayaks against the gravelly shore. Leine exited her kayak, grabbed the MP5SD, and dragged the lightweight boat up the shore to hide it in the trees. Remy did the same.

Staying low, they moved along the perimeter hedge that ran behind Langston's property. A few minutes later, Langston's home came into view. Leine stopped.

"Let me have the binos."

Remy handed her his night-vision binoculars and she

glassed the rear of the home. There were two security cameras near the roof. She tapped her fingers and turned on the AI assist to see if she was missing anything. Nothing showed in the visor.

"Where do you think he's got motion sensors?" Remy asked.

"One way to find out."

Leine grabbed a rock off the ground and threw it into the yard. It bounced once and rolled a short distance on the gravel walkway that transversed a portion of the landscape. Bright searchlights blinked on, illuminating the entire length of the backyard. The sound of dogs barking erupted from the south side of the building. A moment later, two powerful-looking Rottweilers burst into the yard at a full sprint toward where the rock had landed. Remy reached for his weapon, but Leine placed her hand on his arm and shook her head. The AI-assist was blinking yellow, indicating the dogs weren't real.

"Hologram," she said in a low voice.

Remy stood down.

"Holy cow." Alice's voice crackled over Leine's earpiece. "I would have lost it. Good job, guys."

The holographic dogs arrived at the spot where the rock had landed and milled about, sniffing at the ground, looking for all the world like a couple of actual canines. Tongues hanging out, they both sat near the rock as though waiting for their owner. Leine had to hand it to Langston—most anyone trying to infiltrate his backyard would either have reacted like Remy and fired their weapon to scare the dogs, or would have abandoned the attempt altogether and "lost it" like Alice declared.

The two security cameras whirred as they shifted to point at the dogs. Leine and Remy remained motionless, watching. A few moments later, the dogs disappeared and the outside lights blinked off.

"I'll bet Langston has quite a few false positives with that kind of security," Remy whispered. "Lots of critters around like racoons and deer that could trip the alarm."

Leine scanned the outer perimeter of the backyard. Several large firs and cedars rimmed the property to the north with bushes sprinkled in between, allowing for plenty of cover. "Doesn't look like he's got guards posted. We should be able to skirt the yard behind those trees and come in behind the camera's blind spot."

Staying low and using the hedge for cover, they retraced their steps to the edge of the property and veered right into the wooded area. The breeze off the lake picked up, stirring dried leaves and rustling branches. Still, they moved carefully to avoid stepping on anything that might give away their position.

A short time later they reached the home's northwest corner. There were no cameras and it was dark on that side of the home, likely because there were no windows or other means of ingress into the structure. An enormous brick chimney dominated the outside wall.

Remy stood watch while Leine continued along the rear of the house, skirting beneath the security camera to a set of reproduction 1920s-style French doors. Both the left- and right-side cameras remained pointed at the yard behind her. She pulled out her lock-picks as she scanned the door for an alarm. A security sensor could be seen through one of the glass panes. Leine signaled Remy, who produced a signal jammer from inside his tactical vest and turned it on. Leine bent to work the lock, then eased the door open and slipped inside. As soon as she closed the door behind her, Remy would turn off the jammer and restore the alarm.

She found herself in a sitting room with overstuffed chairs and a sectional facing an enormous television. Leine paused for a moment, listening for activity. Not hearing anything unusual, she moved through the darkened room to a doorway on her right and paused again. A rectangular dining table surrounded by ten chairs took up a majority of the space in the next room. An old clock ticked on top of a fireplace mantel as the wind rustled through the trees outside. There were no other sounds.

Leine made her way around the table and through the kitchen, past another living room, a powder room, and an immense foyer with a generous crystal chandelier and the requisite sweeping staircase. The alarm console on the wall next to the front door glowed green, indicating Remy had done his job. Two security cameras were aimed at the door.

"The entrance to the bunker should be down a hallway to your right, at the rear of the home." Alice's voice crackled through Leine's earpiece. "Hannah mentioned the door to the stairwell is normally unlocked when she's been there, so you should be able to gain access."

"Copy that."

Leine continued along the hallway to the bunker's entrance, listening as she did. When she made the last turn before reaching the door, she stopped. A wooden bookcase stood where the door should have been.

"That's funny," Alice said. "According to Hannah, that should be a steel door."

Leine ran her hand along the outer perimeter of the bookcase, but didn't feel anything unusual. She started selecting books at random, but none seemed to trigger a mechanism. The books on the bottom shelf were a different story. When she pulled on one, the entire row moved.

Leine lifted the row of phony books to discover a set of locking wheels hidden underneath. She unlocked them and pushed. The bookcase rolled aside with minimal effort, revealing the steel door behind it.

The door was unlocked. She eased it open and slipped inside.

A ramp led into inky darkness beyond. A lone wall sconce wasn't enough to illuminate the way forward. The AI assist shifted to night-vision, giving her visibility. Alert for movement, she descended the stairs.

"The bunker—up—careful of—" Alice's voice cut out. Either the surrounding rock walls were messing with the comms, or Langston was deploying some kind of jammer.

Leine instigated a quick reboot of her comms, and Alice's voice resumed.

"Leine, do you read?"

Leine tapped her fingers, acknowledging she had.

"Oh, whew," Alice replied. "Thought we'd lost you. Both audio and video were off for a few seconds."

Using a virtual keyboard, Leine texted a short reply, letting Alice know she would observe radio silence. She then brought up the schematic Sebastian had created of Hannah's bunker description, and continued down the ramp.

As she reached the ground floor, she hesitated. Had she heard a sound? Seen something? She waited, listening.

There was nothing. She started to take a step but then returned her leg to its original position. She switched out of night-vision, allowing the AI free rein. A thin green laser beam near the end of the ramp came into focus.

Leine stepped over the beam and continued through the rock-lined space, hyper-alert for additional security triggers. According to the readout on her helmet console, the ambient temperature had dropped to fifty-five degrees. The gaming suit shifted as it adapted to the change.

A few yards later, an arched wooden doorway came into view. A security camera on the ceiling covered the door and surrounding area.

Alice's voice crackled over comms. "Hannah says Langston controls the door to the bunker from his console, and that it's usually locked. There are three deadbolts that she knows of, which he's able to unlock simultaneously."

Leine tapped her fingers in acknowledgement. She pulled the video jammer from her tac vest and aimed it at the camera.

Soon, Langston would have to figure out why his screen went blank.

47

Remy stood near a huge cedar and scanned the backyard through his NVGs, alert for security. A twig snapped behind him and he turned.

Something slammed against the side of his head. A crack of white lit his brain.

What the fuck—?

He staggered back, shaking off the pain, narrowly avoiding the next blow from his adversary.

The other man wore a balaclava and camo gear, with a rifle on a sling. He went for the sidearm secured in his vest, but before he could raise his weapon, Remy grabbed his rifle and yanked him forward. The other guy's nose met his fist and fractured, evidenced by the pained grunt and blood pouring through the balaclava. Remy unclipped the rifle and shoved Balaclava Boy over his extended foot. The assailant nosedived to the ground and lost his grip on the pistol.

Remy kicked the gun away, then ripped off the other man's facemask, pushing him onto his back.

"What the hell?" He stared down at the bloody face of Detective Sonny Benson. Benson didn't reply. He was too busy pinching his nose, trying to stem the flow of blood from his face. Remy kicked him in the side. "What the fuck are you doing here?"

Sonny started to sit up, but Remy raised the rifle. "Uh-uh. Tell me what you're doing here, Now."

Benson raised a hand, his other still pinching the bridge of his nose. "Calm down, Remy. I'm pulling security for Mr. Langston." His Ms sounded more like Bs due to the broken nose.

"Sure you are, bud." Remy dropped to a crouch and said in a low voice, "Know what? You're fucked. F-U-C-K-E-D." He nodded at the house. "Your employer is, too. But I'll bet you knew you were aiding and abetting a terrorist, right?"

"I don't know what the hell you're talking about. Langston hired me as security. I saw a threat and I tried to neutralize it." He shrugged. "I failed. But at least I know who you are." He gave him a sidelong look. "Why the fuck are *you* here?"

"Where's Carter?" Remy stood, ignoring the question. "I know where there's one dirty cop, the other one can't be far."

"Right behind you, asshole." The man's voice was familiar. "I got an AR aimed at your spine. If you don't want to spend the rest of your life in a wheelchair, you'd best drop that gun. Now."

Kicking himself for letting Bob Carter get the drop on him, Remy placed the rifle on the ground. He sighed and turned to face Carter.

"Raise your hands." Carter wore a tac vest with extra mags, a combat knife, and a suppressed .45 riding a modified holster. The AR-15 in his hands pointed directly at Remy.

Remy raised his hands. Sonny Benson scrambled to his feet and joined Carter. His nose-bleed had slowed to a trickle, although he still had to tip his head back.

Carter gave his partner a look. "You fucking let that animal hit you in the face?"

Sonny didn't reply, his sullen look along with the blood enough of an answer.

Carter turned back to Remy. "I'm only gonna ask you once. What the fuck are you doing here?"

Remy didn't say anything, letting Carter come to his own conclusion. It didn't take long.

Carter cracked a smile. "You're looking into Langston?" He chuckled. "Buddy boy, you're in the wrong business. Private eyes don't make dick. Or didn't they tell you that in PI school? Besides, Langston's way above your pay grade."

"You got me." Remy shrugged. "I was staking out the place, hoping to make a little coin."

Sonny scoffed. "Who hired you?"

"The nightclub owner, Desi."

Carter grew serious. "And just what does your boss at the club know about Langston? Hmmm?"

Sonny muttered, "Told you we shoulda done the ladyboy too."

"Shut the fuck up," Carter barked. He studied Remy. "We got a problem here." His sad smile went way beyond insincere. "Sorry, bud, but I gotta kill you. It just wouldn't do for my employer to figure out you made it this far onto his property without my knowledge. I'm sure you understand."

Something whizzed through the air, followed by a *thwack!* Sonny's eyes rolled back in his head and he dropped where he stood. With Carter's attention temporarily diverted, Remy lunged and grabbed his rifle, wrenching it from Carter's grasp. Carter pulled his suppressed .45 and aimed. At the same time, Remy raised the butt end of the rifle and slammed it against Carter's forehead. The .45 discharged as Carter went down.

White-hot pain seared Remy's side. He grunted and felt where the bullet entered. His hand came away slick with blood.

Dammit. He searched the woods for the sniper. It had to be either Art or Zarko. Remy sank to his knees, gripping his side, trying to stem the flow of blood. He grimaced at the thought that Carter might have finally succeeded in killing him.

I will not let that bastard win. No fucking way.

Breathing heavily to manage the pain, Remy dragged himself to the base of a nearby fir tree for support, taking him out of the house's line-of-sight. Leaning back against the bark, he let out a deep sigh.

He sure as hell hoped Leine was all right.

48

———

Leine stood in the shadows, waiting, the MP5SD at high ready. The locks clanked as they disengaged and the door to the bunker swung open. No one came through.

She remained in position. She must have triggered something, a camera, a laser, something. She tapped out a message to Alice.

Alice didn't reply. Leine checked her comms. No signal. The AI-assist was still active—it just wouldn't be able to send any data to the command center.

She was on her own.

Leine took stock of her situation. The door had opened and Langston didn't appear, which meant he knew she was there. The high-tech suit she wore that made her invisible to infrared and thermal sensors didn't matter now that she'd been discovered. Her helmet would tell her what was real and what wasn't, but that was about it. She had plenty of firepower, but would that be enough, or even necessary? Langston was a glorified hacker. Not a terrorist with a biological to release, or a gun-toting jihadi, both willing to die for their beliefs. Langston was in it for the money, as far as she could tell. His takedown should be a piece of cake.

If he didn't move the data. Would he do that this late in the game? The end of the auction was approaching fast. Moving data seemed a huge risk that might possibly delay the transfer. One didn't play with nation-states with the power and the will to destroy one's life.

She moved to the door. The helmet had sensitive audio sensors, but Leine didn't trust the tech as much as she did her own capabilities. Still, she didn't know what was in that room.

She quieted her internal chatter and pushed out with her mind. The space beyond the door felt devoid of life. In a low crouch, she peered around the corner into the cavernous room. A few yards from the door stood a giant desk with an array of monitors. A motorized chair sat empty nearby. Several servers lined a nearby wall, their indicator lights blinking. There weren't any visible cables. Hannah had mentioned Langston hid them in the floor and the walls because he didn't like how they looked or the vulnerability they posed. The temperature gauge on the helmet marked the room as frigid, ostensibly to keep the servers from overheating. The rest of the room behind the desk remained in deep shadow.

Not seeing anyone, she slipped inside and crossed the floor to access the console on the desk. Sliding the QuanTrace5 from a side pocket, she searched for a port, but hesitated—there were no labels indicating which one to use. With no comms link to Alice, Leine was again on her own. A bead of sweat slid down her temple. The temperature inside the helmet had increased, which contributed to her unease.

Not a great time for the equipment to crash.

Frustrated, she slid off the helmet and gloves, and set them on the desk. She moved the keyboard from the motorized chair to the desk and entered a predetermined command Hannah thought might work to access Langston's console.

It didn't. She was about to try a second command when a voice behind her said, "Hello, Leine."

Leine froze. A chill skittered up her spine. The voice was familiar.

Carlos.

But he was dead.

She turned and scanned the room, but saw no one. Ignoring the raw feelings the voice had evoked, Leine returned to the keyboard and tried the next command.

"It's really me, Leine."

This time, Carlos sounded like he was right in front of her. She snapped up and looked over the monitor.

Her breath caught.

A full-sized Carlos, her first love, stood in front of the desk watching her. He looked devastatingly real. His familiar smile speared her heart, and a sob bubbled in her throat before she shut down her reaction.

He's not real. He's not real. It's a hologram, Leine.

But how had Langston known? The files on Carlos's death had been buried deep within Langley. No one would have access. Except...

Except for a terrorist who had the ability to download intelligence files and search them using AI. Leine's anger spiked. Who the hell did Langston think he was?

He's a terrorist, Leine.

"I've missed you," the Carlos hologram said.

She pushed back her emotions and composed herself. "I see you've done your homework," she said. "It's a good likeness, except he never wore jewelry." She nodded at the ring on his finger. The ring disappeared.

"Well done," Carlos/Langston said. "You made it farther into my home than anyone else who's tried. Brava." The hologram made a moue. "Forgive me for my rudeness, but I expected them to send a strapping young man in black, bristling with weapons and body armor." He gave her a wan smile. "You don't look particularly dangerous. Except for the gun."

"Sorry to disappoint," Leine said. "You don't look like a terrorist."

"Touche. The bodysuit's interesting. Gaming-based?"

"Oh, this little thing?" Leine scanned the room but didn't see anyone real. The voice seemed to originate from everywhere. She moved back to the console. The screen had locked.

"You didn't think I'd allow you to access my network, did you? I'm disappointed, Leine. Your reputation is so...robust."

"Can't blame a girl for trying." Leine reached for the keyboard.

"You won't be able to guess my passcode, so don't even try." Carlos/Langston sighed. "I suppose this was all Hannah's fault. She was the one weakness in my plan. Women are so unpredictable. I should have eliminated her the instant she left Vandenburg after she uploaded the malware. But I wanted her alive as insurance, at least until I was assured control of the satellite. Obviously, an error on my part."

"You didn't have any problem eliminating the others."

"Indeed," Carlos/Langston said. "It's much easier when you don't have to get your own hands dirty. Although, you did give me a sleepless night or two when you and your compatriots proved so resilient."

Leine slid the QuanTrace back into her side pocket. She skirted the desk, calculating the fallout from shooting the servers. Jana had warned her to preserve as much evidence as possible so they could put Langston behind bars for a good long time. But first she needed to verify that he kept the data on those same servers.

"I'm curious," she said. "Why not keep the data offsite, in a non-extradition country? You know, in case things went to shit."

"Why deal with inherently dangerous and untrustworthy people? My other miscalculation was trusting the Russians. Even though the brothers came highly recommended, once they learned what they'd stolen, they had to be put down." Langston sighed. "Besides, I have an enormous amount of leverage. There is no way you or anyone else will compromise the data I now control. You can't cut power to my home—my generators will kick in. You will never be able to locate my internet connection, so you won't be able to stop the data transfer. Everything's automated, so if you or your team of operatives are successful in capturing me, it won't matter—the transfer still happens. All I have to do is keep the forces that be from breaching my defenses for..." Carlos/Langston paused. "Fourteen more minutes, when the auction concludes. At that point it will be too late."

"But you'll be either dead or imprisoned for the rest of your life. Why risk it? You're not that old."

"There's just one tiny problem. You have to find me first."

The door to the bunker slammed shut and each of the deadbolts locked. Dozens of images of Carlos appeared, stacking in formation throughout the room, as if he were an army of one. An excruciatingly painful Hall of Mirrors.

"You're trapped, Leine." Langston/Carlos's voice had amplified as though all the images were talking at once. "This is your final encounter."

A faint buzz began near the dark end of the room and grew louder. Leine stared through hundreds of copies of Carlos toward the sound. A moment later, what looked at first to be a solid airborne object split apart into a dozen mini-drones. They paused as though awaiting instruction, hovering in the air and buzzing like mechanical raptors. Instead of eyes, red indicator lights glowed with apparent malevolent intent.

Leine fired the MP5SD, spraying them with rounds. Several dropped to the floor, but not all. The ones that survived the onslaught surrounded her, the buzz intensifying.

"You can't escape them, Leine. I've fitted them with syringes carrying a particularly lethal form of tetrodotoxin. They're programmed to attack anything that moves once they're unleashed."

Leine grabbed the helmet and dove under the desk, then drew her pistol. The buzzing shifted, signaling the drones were moving. She slid on the helmet and raised the Beretta.

Two drones appeared in front of her. Each had a syringe attached to the underside of their body. Leine shot them both, and they dropped to the floor. Two more took their place, their buzzing louder. One broke formation and divebombed her, hitting the helmet. She swatted it away, then fired. Both fell, but there were two more. She continued shooting until her slide locked open, then reloaded and kept going.

He was getting her to waste ammo. If Langston had wanted the drones to kill her, he could have commanded them all to attack at once. She'd have destroyed several, but likely not all.

What was he playing at?

She demolished two more drones, and the room fell silent. Leine slid out from under the desk and climbed to her feet. The multiple images of Carlos were gone, replaced by six snarling rottweilers near the wall of servers. The AI-assist blinked yellow, indicating they were similar to the holograms she and Remy encountered outside.

Leine aimed the MP5 at the servers and squeezed the trigger. Multiple rounds punched holes in the equipment as pieces of plastic and metal rained down. So much for preserving evidence. The holographic dogs never moved, continuing their snarling, teeth-baring loop.

"Stop. STOP." Langston's voice boomed over the hidden

speakers. "The data's not there. You haven't accomplished ANYTHING."

But Leine heard something in the sound of his voice. She needed to goad him into talking more so she could be sure. "You're done, Langston. You're a two-bit programmer who got lucky when you blackmailed Hannah. Your house is surrounded. They will stop at nothing to take you down. You'll be hunted to the end of your days."

"NO. I WON."

There it was again. An echo? Leine moved toward the rottweilers. The AI-assist glowed red—a warning she'd never seen before. She moved closer to the damaged servers and noticed something odd. Where there should have been evidence of electronic circuits, hard drives and other components, she found only empty shells. Something caught her eye, and she removed the helmet to make sure it wasn't a trick of the light. The submachine gun rounds had punched through the drywall, opening multiple holes at the back of the servers. A faint light glowed through.

Another room?

Leine stepped back, inserted another mag in the submachine gun and fired, rounds pounding the wall, widening the opening, bringing the secret room into view.

"STOP," Langston screamed. "You don't know what you're doing!"

"I think I do." She slid another fresh mag into the receiver and peppered the wall with more rounds, enlarging the hole. A glance at her watch told her to speed things up—only seven minutes remained until the auction concluded.

She grabbed one of the phony servers and ripped its shell from the wall, clearing the way. Breaking off chunks of drywall, she worked until she had large enough access to the space beyond. His eyes closed, Langston lay slumped on the floor against the far wall, blood visible on his neck. He was wearing what Leine assumed to be the exosuit—a black, web-like material that encased his legs and pelvis. It appeared the suit hadn't been built to repel rounds.

Inside, a bank of servers lined the wall behind a table with a similar set-up as the desk in the first room, with the exception of a laptop. Leine climbed through the opening and raced to the table to stop the transfer. She slid the laptop toward her and keyed in the command Hannah and Alice had determined would shut it down.

Something moved in her periphery before she could finish. Instinctively, she reached for her Beretta as she pivoted, although she assumed it was another hologram or some other form of VR trickery Langston had triggered.

But it wasn't a hologram.

It was Langston.

With the exosuit on, he stood a few inches taller than Leine. She raised the pistol, but Langston ducked and came up from underneath, knocking her arm aside as she fired. She kept her grip and spun as he threw a front kick, narrowly avoiding his foot. She wasn't so lucky on his second try, which knocked the gun from her hand.

He swiveled for a roundhouse kick, but Leine twisted to the side before impact and parried with one of her own.

It was like hitting cement.

Shaking off the pain, Leine jumped back as Langston advanced, a cruel smile painting his lips. This time, his expression transmitted his intent, and she was ready for him. She'd sensed a delay in the exosuit's execution on the last kick, which she thought she could use.

As Langston began his next kick, Leine lunged toward him and grabbed a strap on the exosuit, pulling him forward and down. He straightened, and she launched herself up and onto his shoulders, locking her legs around his neck in a modified flying triangle. Then, using her body weight and his lack of balance, she twisted and brought him down, slamming his head to the floor.

Leine released the choke and dove for the Beretta lying on the floor near the wall. Gun in hand, she spun and fired, hitting Langston as he was shaking off the fall. He crumpled to the floor, a blood stain blooming across the right side of his chest.

Leine raced back to the table. The auction populated the screen. A timer was counting down.

Fifteen seconds.

She grabbed the computer and finished typing in the command that would stop the auction.

14...13...12...

Nothing happened.

"Why is it not responding?" Leine demanded.

11...10...9...

Langston grimaced. Sweat poured down his face. His breathing was shallow and rasping, indicating a collapsed lung. "The AI. It's learning. You can't stop it now."

"Dammit." Leine's heart rate skyrocketed. She had to stop the transfer. NOW.

The bundle of exposed cables behind Langston's computer led to the wall of servers, unlike in the main room. Langston hadn't taken the time to harden off the connections.

5...4...3...

Leine lunged for the cables and yanked out every last one she saw.

The servers and peripheral monitors went dark.

She stared at the laptop screen. The timer had stopped at :01.

Too close.

Moments later, the auction's chat box started blowing up with angry comments from spectators, wondering what happened, demanding answers to why the auction stopped. The bidders had disappeared.

Leine glanced at Langston. His complexion had turned a pasty shade of gray, but it was the look on his face that told her.

"It worked." She smiled, relief coursing through her.

Langston closed his eyes.

It was over.

49

———————

Leine was halfway across the floor of Langston's outer room when the helmet lit up, indicating her comms had reconnected. She slid on the helmet and gloves and tapped her fingers to key the mic.

"Alpha, do you read? Come in, over."

Leine smiled at the sound of Alice's voice. "Alpha copy."

"Oh, thank God." Alice sighed. "Where have you been? What happened? Are you okay?" She paused. Her voice low, she said, "We thought we lost you."

"Target neutralized," Leine said. "And before you ask, yes, he's still breathing."

Alice blew out a breath. "That's great news. Looks like the HRT guys are on their way."

"Please tell me I succeeded in stopping the transfer." Even though the spectator's reactions told her she had, she still wanted verification from her side.

"Oh, my God. Yes! We were holding our breath. Well, at least I was. The HRT guys were in position, getting ready to blow shit up."

"Good to know." Why hadn't they gone ahead and breached the home anyway? She wanted to ask Alice, but not with Jana and her team monitoring comms.

Alice lowered her voice even more. "Do you have access to Langston's hard drive?"

"I do, why?"

"The DOD's here. Everybody noticed the satellite program displayed an unusual rate of learning during the auction. The rep from the DOD is super interested in obtaining a copy of Langston's modifications." She added, "You can speak freely. I've isolated our comms so it's just us."

Leine was already on her way back to the secret room. "Copy that, Python."

"I'll give you a heads-up when the team's headed your way."

LEINE RETURNED TO THE MAIN ROOM AS THE HRT BREACHED THE door. Art, Zarko, and a team of HRT operators streamed through the opening, weapons held at high ready. One of them was dressed in civilian clothing, although he sported a high-and-tight and carried himself like a soldier.

Leine nodded at them. "Target secure. He's in the back room. He's going to need a medic."

The team medic separated from the group and double-timed it back to Langston. One of the operators moved to check Leine over.

"I'm fine. Just a couple of bruises."

He nodded and joined the rest of the HRT, leaving Art and Zarko with Leine.

Art gave her a look. 'What the hell happened?" He nodded at the helmet. "The tech?"

Leine shook her head. "Pretty sure Langston deployed some kind of jammer. Once I pulled the plug on his operation the comms came back."

Zarko put his arm around her and gave her a squeeze. "Glad to see you in one piece, ma'am."

"Me, too." She glanced behind them, into the hallway. "Where's Remy?"

"He was shot."

"Oh, shit. How bad?"

"He's got surgery in his future," Art said, "but he'll make it."

"Fantastic." Leine took a deep breath and let it go, helping her body regulate after the adrenaline spike. "How did it happen?"

Zarko answered. "Couple of Langston's security goons got the drop on him. Remy neutralized one of them. The other guy got lucky."

"Zarko took out the second one," Art added, "but the asshole got off a shot before he could bring him down. Says he knew them both. Used to work with them at SPD."

Leine nodded as another piece of the puzzle fell into place. "Glad you had his back."

"It was pure luck on my part," Zarko admitted. "I caught a glimpse of one of them through the trees and figured I'd better get my ass over there and see if either of you needed help."

"Always trust those instincts, right?" Art said.

Leine nodded. "Always." There was no way to program that into a computer. At least, not yet.

The guy in the civvies walked out from the secret room and headed straight for Leine, Langston's laptop tucked under his arm. "The damned laptop is shot to shit, and the servers are toast." He gave Leine a sidelong look. "You have anything to do with that?"

"And you are?" Leine asked.

He smiled. "Call me Carl."

"Well, Carl. Time was short. I thought shooting the shit out of his laptop would be the most expedient choice."

"And then you unplugged the cables?"

Leine shrugged. "I had to do what I had to do, Carl."

Carl raised his chin in acknowledgement. "Well, you did good work today." He nodded at Art and Zarko. "All of you. Carry on."

With that, Carl marched out of the bunker, Langston's wrecked laptop under his arm like he was a quarterback carrying a deflated football off the field.

Alice's voice crackled in her earpiece. "More fun than drilling holes in the hard drive, huh? I might have to give that method a try."

Leine smiled. With Grace and Sebastian's help, Leine had transferred Langston's remote access to the satellite to Alice, who quietly reprogrammed the AI to revert to its original state, overwriting whatever modifications Langston created. Once that was accomplished, Leine had emptied her last mag into his laptop and the real servers to destroy access to the downloaded intelligence data, as well as any copies of the satellite program he might have saved.

Leine followed Art and Zarko outside to the front drive, which was filled with flashing lights, aid cars, and a heavy-duty SWAT-like vehicle with FBI markings. Ambulances waited near the door. Leine walked over to see Remy, who was lying on a gurney waiting to be loaded into the back of one.

He smiled when he saw her. "I knew you'd make it out of there."

Leine took his hand. "Thanks for having my back, Remy." She glanced at his ripped shirt and cocked her head. "Is that—"

Remy raised his head to see what she was looking at. His

cheeks colored. "Yes, it's a fucking camisole. It helps with my PTSD, okay?"

Leine raised her hands in surrender. "Hey, whatever gets you through the night."

Remy leaned his head back and smiled. "It's all right."

Leine returned the smile. "Yes, it is."

50

Alice and Remy went back to Alice's apartment after catching a Kill Bill retrospective at the local movie theater. They'd grabbed take-out from Uwajimaya's. The pain from the gunshot wound Remy sustained when Carter shot him made daily life more difficult, which pissed him off to no end, so Alice had insisted he stay with her and Mr. Tummy while he recuperated.

"Have a seat," Alice said. "I'll get plates." She went to the kitchen as Mr. Tummy circled Remy's ankles, meowing his happiness to have his humans home. Remy set the bags of food on the coffee table and was about to sit down when something in the bookcase caught his eye. He went over to the shelves to have a closer look.

"Hey, babe?" he called, eyeing the object in question.

"Hmm?"

"When did you get the Han Solo?"

"Oh, that." She emerged from the kitchen with the plates and set them on the table. She shrugged. "I can't remember, exactly. Pretty dope, right?"

Her smile could light up any room, as far as Remy was

concerned. He grinned, happy to have things back to normal. "Yeah, babe. It's dope."

LEINE DROPPED HER SATCHEL ON THE FLOOR AND CLOSED THE door behind her. A wonderful aroma emanated from the kitchen.

"Honey, I'm home," she called. She kicked off her shoes with a relieved sigh, and followed the amazing smell of onions, oregano, and thyme to find Santa at the stove, cooking what appeared to be his family recipe of Cochinita Pibil. "Yum. My favorite." She nuzzled his neck. He smelled of citrus and cedar. "Mmm, I've missed you."

Santa turned and wrapped her in a bear hug. "Not more than I missed you."

They shared a long, languorous kiss. Santa broke first and handed her a glass of chilled white wine.

"Dinner's in about an hour. How about you go freshen up and I'll meet you in the living room. Then we can talk about how you saved the world."

Leine smiled. "That sounds heavenly." She took her wine into the master bath and turned on the shower.

A woman's voice came from somewhere behind her. Leine spun, hands up in a defensive position.

"Leine Basso shower temperature one hundred- and two-degrees Fahrenheit. Estimated time to reach maximum temperature: twenty-seven seconds."

Startled, Leine searched for the device that was somehow connected to the damn shower. The small, glowing piece of tech was sitting next to a box of tissues. Leine resisted the impulse to smash it on the floor, and instead located the battery compartment and removed the batteries.

With a relieved sigh, she started to undress. Santa peeked in, a big grin across his face.

"I wanted to see your reaction to—" his gaze drifted to the box with the batteries removed. "—our new AI-powered shower regulator." He frowned. "I take it you aren't impressed."

Leine placed her hand on his cheek. "Darling, if I ever have to deal with another AI device in my lifetime, it will be too damn soon."

Santa slapped his forehead. "Oh, shit. Yeah, sorry about that." He went over to the device and scooped it up. "Forget you even saw it."

After her shower, Leine joined Santa in the living room. He poured her another glass of wine and they settled back while dinner cooked.

"So, whatever happened between Grace and Sebastian? Did they ever reconcile?" he asked.

Leine nodded. "Sebastian invited her to become his partner in Convergence. She said yes on one condition—that she be in charge of product safety and security, and that she have equal say who they license their work to."

"And he agreed?"

"Yep."

"What's happening with Hannah and Langston?"

"Langston's toast. Hannah tied him to the malware, hijacking the satellite, having people killed to keep his operation secret, the works. Her attorney is negotiating for a more lenient sentence."

"Did the FBI ever find out who was backing him? Or was he going solo?"

"There's talk that the CCP had their hands in the cookie jar."

Santa whistled. "The Chinese government? Yow."

"No shit. If we hadn't captured him, I predict Langston would have wound up dead or disappeared."

"What about the sex tape involving the mayor and the minor?"

Leine shook her head. "The damage I did to Langston's hard drive and his servers took care of that, unfortunately. Unless the girl Hannah ID'd in the video comes forward, or the footage is in the cloud and somehow surfaces, he gets to skate."

He studied Leine. "I know that look. You're going to try to find her, aren't you?"

"If she's still alive, yeah. But there's not much to go on. I could always look more deeply into Winters. He used a minor at least once that we know of. Experience tells me he'll continue."

"Let me know how I can help."

Leine smiled. "I will."

"Your friend Desi is happy?"

"He is. He seemed relieved when I told him Langston was behind the deaths and had used Remy's old cop buddies to do his dirty work."

Santa shook his head. "Man, that whole thing hits too close to home. I don't know what I'd do if I found out any of the guys I work with were dirty." He took a sip of wine. "It's tough when you can't trust your team."

Leine heartily agreed. Betrayal sucked. "Carter confessed to planting drugs in Remy's car. The SPD has officially apologized and offered him his choice of reinstatement or taking his pension."

"Let me guess. He took the pension."

She smiled. "You must be psychic."

"You know, I only have a few months to go before I start collecting mine."

"Any ideas where you want to go?" Scivoloso didn't work out well, and Leine was afraid the same thing might happen again. But Santa had been working on her and she could feel herself softening. LA wasn't exactly where she wanted to spend her golden years. Although, she wasn't positive she was finished working yet. What the hell would she do? Like Art Kowalski, she doubted she'd do retirement well.

"I've been thinking...what about Costa Rica? It's warm, the people are friendly, they got great health care..."

Leine smiled. "Let's talk about this tomorrow. Right now, I just want to be here with you and not think about anything life-changing."

Santa returned her smile and held up his glass. "Here's to no life-changing decisions."

They clinked glasses.

A woman's voice emanated from the vicinity of Santa's pants. "Interesting places to visit in Costa Rica include the Monteverde Cloud Forest, Manuel Antonio Beach, and the Osa Peninsula..."

"What the hell, Santa?" Leine asked, her annoyance obvious. Was nowhere safe?

Santa gave her a sheepish look as he slid out his phone and turned off the AI assistant. "Sorry."

Leine leaned her head back and closed her eyes. Artificial intelligence was here to stay, whether she liked it or not. With a deep sigh, she pushed its real-life implications from her mind, content in the moment. It was enough.

For now.

ACKNOWLEDGMENTS

Special thanks to everyone who helped make this book possible: Mark Lindstrom, husband extraordinaire and always my first reader; long time alpha readers Jennifer Conner, Ali Mosa, Michelle Van Berkom, Brian Yelland, and the inimitable Ruth Ross; eagle-eyed editor Stephen England; FBI consultant Mary Rook (Ret.) who managed to find time for my questions in between teaching gigs; Les Flynn, Systems Engineer (Ret.) for coming along at the exact right moment and sparking the satellite-heist idea, as well as for information regarding satellites and NRO; long suffering cyber security consultant Luke Denney – ITIL, PCNSA, A+, Net+, Sec+, CySA+, Project+, PenTest+, who went above and beyond to help make my ideas somewhat plausible; my amazingly dedicated Advance Reader Team (ART); and last but definitely not least, weapons and tactical consultant TSODA134 (Dewey Rumsey, Special Forces, Ret.)—my books are so much better because of you. Who knew making an ass out of myself in a Zumba class would lead to so many years of working together?

Any mistakes are absolutely my own. It's entirely possible I took a few minor liberties with the facts if it worked better for the story, but almost all the tech mentioned is either readily available or coming soon to a government near you.

Writing is never a solitary endeavor.

ABOUT THE AUTHOR

DV Berkom is the USA Today bestselling author of riveting action-adventure and crime thrillers. Known for creating resilient, kick-ass female characters and page-turning plots, her love of the genre stems from a lifelong addiction to reading spy novels, thrillers, and action/adventure stories.

A restless soul and adventurer at heart, she spent years moving around the US and traveling to exotic locations before she wrote her first novel and was hooked. More than twenty books later, she now makes her home in the Pacific Northwest with her husband, Mark, and several imaginary characters who like to tell her what to do.

Her most recent books include Claire Whitcomb Westerns *Legend, Gunslinger,* and *Retribution,* and the Leine Basso thrillers *Final Encounter, Terminal Threat, Fatal Objective, A Plague of Traitors,* and *Shadow of the Jaguar.* DV's currently hard at work on her next book.

For more information, visit her website at www.dvberkom.com. To be the first to hear about new releases and subscriber-only offers, go to: bit.ly/DVB_RL

Retribution

Gunslinger

Legend